Wild Cat Books presents

by

BARRY REESE

Illustrations by William Carney

THE ROOK
A Wild Cat Books Publication

The Rook© copyright 2008 Barry Reese

Cover art by Storn A. Cook
Interior artwork© copyright 2008 William Carney
Production and Design by William Carney

ISBN 978-1-4357-1209-6:

Ron Hanna, Editor and Publisher
Published by Wild Cat Books © copyright 2008
www.lulu/wildcatbooks.com

A Wild Cat Books Publication

Volume One   Spring 2008

THE ROOK

Contents

Dedicated to my son,

Julian

INTRODUCTION

This collection of stories compiles the adventures of Max Davies, *aka* the Rook, who starred in the novellas *"Lucifer's Cage"* and *"Kingdom of Blood"*. He's a modernized version of the classic pulp heroes whom I grew up reading about – a tragic figure whose tortured beginnings led him to dedicate his life to protecting the innocent. Like all pulp heroes, he's sometimes torn by self-doubt but in the end, he always finds a way to prevail, frequently after battling outlandish villains hell-bent on world domination.

"Lucifer's Cage" was my second novel to be published and marked a tremendous shift in my writing. Before this, I mainly focused on writing pastiches (deliberately mimicking the styles of other authors) but with *"Lucifer's Cage"* I began to let more of my personal style on to the page. To this day, I'm as proud of this first Rook story as anything I've written. It has action, some nice characterization and really starts the whole series off with a bang. I really grew to like the character of Evelyn and the relationship that develops between her and Max helps set the series apart from many other pulp tales, which usually feature a rotating cast of romantic interests.

"Kingdom of Blood" came not long after. I had promised myself I would take a break from the Rook after the first story but within a month I had an idea that just wouldn't take no for an answer. In some ways *Kingdom* suffers from "sequel-itis" in that some of the best things in the story are really just progressions from a prior tale. Nevertheless, the story proved popular with fans and introduced McKenzie to the series as well as "Mr. Benson," who is a thinly veiled homage to a famous pulp character. If you recognize him, take a bow! If not, just know that he's one of my favorites and I just loved working him in somehow.

When I first started writing *"The Gasping Death"*, the plans were for it to be the third novel in the series. As it progressed, I realized that it worked better as a short story. Since I had other ideas that also seemed better suited to the shorter style, the decision to do an entire collection was easy enough.

"The Gasping Death" features a team-up between the Rook and one of my favorite pulp heroes, the Moon Man.

The Moon Man appeared in a series of well-written adventures courtesy of Frederick C. Davis, who created a modern Robin Hood with one of the coolest visual designs of the era. I'd hoped to create something that felt true to both the Rook and the Moon Man – for those of you who have read the original stories, I hope you'll find that I did the Moon Man justice. All in all, I feel that *"The Gasping Death"* is actually the weakest entry in the Rook canon, but it certainly has its merits (I hope!).

"Abominations" gave me an opportunity to return the series to Atlanta (after the trips to Great City and abroad in the first two tales in this collection) and pit the Rook against one of the greatest villains of the pulp era. Of course, Sax Rohmer's creation is still a copyrighted figure so I've had to change the name of our villain but I'm sure the more pulp-minded of you can figure out who he is. I was really pleased with how this one turned out and feel it's the strongest tale in this collection and possibly my favorite Rook tale, period.

"The Black Mass" features an idea that I came up with several years ago: a magical barrier surrounding the world that restores the old magic to the modern world. If you'd like to see more stories about the Rook of 2009, feel free to start the clamoring now.

Throughout the series, you'll also find references to the Grace family. Eobard Grace starred in *"The Conquerors of Shadow"* (my first novel) and one of his sons, Leopold, has been mentioned more than once in the Rook tales. *"The Black Mass"* introduces a descendant by the name of Fiona Grace, while another member of the extended family, Charlotte Grace, marries Felix in "The Great Work" story that appeared in the Thrilling Adventures published by 86th Floor Productions.

Will there be future Rook stories? Only time will tell, I suppose. In the meantime, sit down in a comfy chair and grab your favorite beverage. The pulp adventure is about to begin!

Barry Reese

LUCIFER'S CAGE

Chapter I
The Temple

Tibet – April 1933

The snow was blistering, whipping past the exposed portion of his face. He had no idea how far below freezing the temperature was, nor did he truly care. The horrors of the expedition lay far behind him now… ahead lay the summit of his dreams, the culmination of years of study and research.

Inch by inch, he ascended the side of the mountain. His muscles ached from the exertion and there was a pounding in his ears that threatened to overwhelm him. "Just a little bit more," he whispered to himself. Those words had been a mantra for him, repeated over and over again over the last few days. They were the only words he'd spoken since the last of his expedition party had died screaming in the frozen wastes, torn apart by—

He pushed those thoughts away from his mind. There was no point in dwelling on those who had lost their way along the path; after all, he'd known it would come to this in the end.

Of all those who had undertaken the search for Lucifer's Cage, none had shared his dedication. This was far more than a mere archaeological quest; this was the end of a spiritual journey that had begun in his freshman year at the university. He'd found one particular professor who'd opened his eyes to the glories of the past, to the forgotten lore of the world. There was a secret history at play, one that was kept in the shadows by men who embraced science over spiritualism. Jacob Trench had found this secret world beguiling. He had devoured every text his professor could put before him and had then abandoned the university altogether, realizing that the kind of knowledge he sought would never be learned in a classroom setting. To the ends of the world he'd traveled, selling everything he'd ever owned, betraying his parents' good faith until they could no longer trust him with money.

And it had all led him here, to the snowy mountaintops of Tibet.

Jacob pulled himself over the edge of the mountain with a grunt, his hands feeling like two huge blocks of ice within their gloves. Rope was slung over one shoulder, a mountain axe held tightly in the fingers of his right hand. He felt naked as he rose to stand before the temple, as if he'd come unprepared to an important meeting. "Just a little bit more," he whispered, a smile making his frozen lips crack open.

Staggering, he pushed past the wooden door, not even noticing that it was open already, as if someone had been expecting him. Jacob felt heat radiate from within, warming the blood in his veins. The temple consisted of only one large room, with a series of mats along the outer sides of the room. These were for the monks whose task it was to guard the sacred relic housed here… but there were no monks to be seen today. Jacob felt this was a good sign.

In the center of the room lay a single pallet, upon which rested a small wooden pedestal. Atop the pedestal was a crystalline object, about the size of a milk bottle. A fiery red glow emanated from the interior of the object and Jacob felt himself growing stiff in his trousers, his penis responding to some horrible lust for the thing before him. He could feel the touch of women all over him, could smell their sex and their perfume. A laugh rang through the room, like the beckoning call of a whore, summoning him into her bed.

Jacob fell to his knees, his legs unable to bear his weight any longer. His shaking hand reached out for the object, his dry tongue snaking out to lick at his cracked lips. An awful yearning made him whimper like a starving child, desperate for sustenance.

Just before his fingertips made contact with the crystal, a wooden staff came down hard on his hand, shattering his knuckles. Jacob howled in surprise and pain, twisting around to look at the source of the attack. There was a man there, dressed in black robes. The man's bald head was speckled with liver spots and his long white beard trailed down past his waist, curling at the end.

Jacob pushed himself backwards awkwardly, unable to stand. He fumbled in his clothing for the pistol he knew was there but he couldn't seem to find it and the old monk was fast approaching, staff raised high. His broken hand throbbed painfully and his other hand no longer seemed capable of functioning.

"Please," Jacob pleaded, his eyes fastened on the end of the staff. He could easily imagine it splitting his head open like a watermelon. "I've come so far…."

The old man paused, his lips parting in a leer. Rotten teeth were exposed to Jacob's eyes and a scent like spoiled meat seemed to pour forth from the man's mouth. "You think you have suffered?" he asked, his English thickly accented.

Jacob blinked in relief. If the man spoke English, he could be reasoned with. "I've come looking for Lucifer's Cage. I want it," he explained, knowing how foolish he must sound.

The old man nodded slowly, the staff still raised. "You are the first to make it so far in centuries. All those who have come before you since my master built this temple have died, either on the mountainside or just outside the temple. Many I have slain myself. Others have died by Yeti."

Jacob nodded, the fingers of his non-broken hand finally finding hold on the gun. He didn't draw it out, but he felt confident he could do so before the man struck again. "I saw them. They attacked us."

"But you fled, leaving your fellows to be eaten." It was not a question and Jacob didn't answer, though his eyes widened. The old man began to lower the staff. "You bankrupted your parents to fund your research, murdered your professor in cold blood so you could take his papers and now you have betrayed the fools who came with you in search of the great prize. Is all this true?"

"Yes, it is. How did you know?"

The old man laughed and it sounded like the cracking of dry leaves. "Because I have waited for you. You are the one." He gestured towards Jacob's wounded hand. "You have not yet begun to suffer. But in time, you will gain the favor of our master and you will free him from his prison. He slumbers, waiting for your voice to awaken him."

Jacob turned back to the crystal. Its glow once more reached into his soul and stirred him. "I'll do anything."

"Such passion," the old man chuckled. "It will serve you well in the days and weeks to come. Rise, Jacob Trench. I am K'ntu and I will prepare you.

Chapter II
A Man of Means

A tlanta, Georgia – June 1936

"This heat is simply unbearable." Max Davies swept his fan back and forth in quick little motions, doing little to generate a cooling wind on his sweat-covered face. He wore a white suit, one that was quickly growing stained by sweat and dust, and an expensive hat that served to keep the sun from his eyes. He was a handsome man, with a slightly olive complexion and dark green eyes. He was trim, with a swimmer's athletic build, and seemed exceptionally poised and collected, though the hot Georgia summer was testing his famous resolve.

Sitting next to him on the porch of the grand house that Max had recently purchased was his personal banker and close friend, Samuel Kincaid. Samuel was a large-framed man with a belly that was slowly crossing the line from pudginess to fat. "You're the one who moved down here, Max. It's not too late to sell this property and move back to Boston, you know." He cast an appraising eye over the land, watching as the numerous farmhands tilled the soil and took care of the livestock. The house had once been part of the largest plantation in Georgia, but much of it had been sold off after the Civil War. Now it consisted of a lovely house that whispered of the antebellum days and enough land to make Max Davies a prominent member of the local community but nothing more.

"It's like going back in time. Up north it seems like the War Between the States was forever and a day ago. Down here… Hell, you'd almost think it never ended. The Negroes are still treated like slaves, aren't they?"

"Hmm," Max said in careful thought. He raised a glass of iced tea to his lips and sipped it slowly. "There's still many who don't think of them as equal to whites, that's true enough. But it's better than it was… and the ones who live here with me are paid just as handsomely as any white worker."

Sam glanced at his own glass of tea, which sat untouched on a small table situated between his chair and Max's. "Why the hell do they ruin a perfectly good batch of tea by putting ice in it?"

"Because it's hotter than the devil's backside down here?" Max offered. Both men laughed at the ribald comment but their serious natures returned in seconds. "Why are you really here, Sam? You could have telephoned if all you really wanted to do was check on my health and state of mind."

Sam leaned forward in his seat, a large sweat stain becoming visible on the back of his own shirt. His jacket had long since been discarded and his sleeves rolled up soon after, but it had done little to stem the effects of the heat.
"Commissioner Croft says you've been cleared of all suspicion. There's no reason for you not to come back." Sam took a deep breath before adding "There hasn't even been one trace of the Rook in the last six months. He's gone. Kaput."

Max twirled the dwindling pieces of ice in his glass of tea. "And what happens if I return… and the Rook starts up his vigilante activities again? The cloud of suspicion would be much worse this time. No, Sam, I think I'll stay here. A fresh start."

Sam hesitated. "Croft also told me that there'd been a murder down here, took place a couple of weeks ago. You know anything about it?"

"Are you an amateur detective now, Sam? A modern Mr. Holmes?"

"I'm being serious. What if that nutcase followed you here?"

Max sighed, setting his glass down on the table. He rose, somehow managing to look good even covered in sweat and grime. Sam envied him and always had. Max was the sort of man who could enter a room and steal the heart of your best, most faithful girl, without even trying. Not that Max would have encouraged such things. In all the time Sam had known him, he'd never seen Max take a fancy to any woman.

"Sam… I'm not afraid of this Rook fellow. He kills some men who have escaped the law through duplicity and graft. He leaves behind a business card with the image of a bird upon it." Max shrugged. "He's never struck out at anyone like me. I made my money legitimately."

"The last three men he killed were at that gala you threw on New Year's Eve, Max! He was in your penthouse, for God's sake! And when you went skiing, he was there to knock off Boss Zucko, who just happened to be staying at the same resort. Is it any wonder Croft thought you might actually be the guy? If I didn't know you myself, *I* might have wondered…."

Max turned and smiled."Maybe Croft was right.They say you never truly know what lurks in the heart of another man. For all you know, I might dress up in black, skulk about in the shadows and kill criminals.All in my spare time, of course."

Sam snorted, leaning back. "Right. I'd say the Rook is a man of passion and anger.You're neither.You're a businessman at heart, my friend.You look at the final balance and make your decisions based on the ledger sheet."

"Perhaps the Rook does, as well. He tallies up the positives and negatives in a man's life and decides whether or not his continued presence adds or subtracts from the good of society."

"So what are you saying, then? That you *are* the Rook?"

"No.That's not what I'm saying, Sam." Max pushed his hands in his pockets and laughed."I'm just being difficult."

"Ah.The same as usual, then? You're more hardheaded than my wife."

"How long are you staying?" Max asked, not allowing the playful insults to degenerate any further.

"I'm leaving in the morning.You think I'm going to condemn myself to any more time in this heat than necessary? I came because I was worried about you… and I want you to come home."

"I'm touched. I really am. But this is my home now. Go back and monitor my investments for me and maybe I'll be up for a bit of skiing when winter comes."

Sam rose, dusting himself off."That man who was shot a few weeks back," Sam whispered, keeping his voice low, lest a servant might overhear."Croft says he heard there was a card left behind. The Rook's signature. Now, I don't believe you're a killer, but it might mean that this guy has a thing for you. An obsession. Could be he's followed you down South."

"I'll be careful, Sam.You have my word."

Chapter III
Visions of Evil

Max ran the cold washcloth over his naked chest, examining the extensive network of scars that ran across his flesh.There was a story behind each and every one of them, most involving gunfire, whips and fists. Moving here to Atlanta had been Max's way of saying enough was enough and that he was now ready to put the life of pain and death behind him.

That decision lasted approximately three weeks. It was that long before he'd discovered that a man named Felix Darkholme had begun a series of vile experiments on the local poor. Max had found himself falling into the old roles all too easily, donning the skintight black jumpsuit of his own devising.The material of the suit was made of a light-absorbing material that was resistant to small arms fire, without restricting his movement in the least. The fabric had been one of Max's first discoveries, created during his time in the Orient. Max had traveled the world shortly after turning eighteen, spending time with a Sensei in Kyoto and studying under many of the world's great scientists and philosophers. All of it had been part of his ongoing mission to better himself, so that the entire world might benefit from his experiences. He had become the Rook to ferret out the evils of society, to find those who slipped through the cracks like hungry snakes, seeking out the innocent to prey upon.

Darkholme. Memories of the man came rushing back to him, turning his thoughts away from those concerning his distant past. Max set aside the washcloth and dried himself off, feeling refreshed but knowing that the sweltering heat would find him drenched in sweat again soon enough. Still, the sense of being clean would last at least long enough for Max to make it to the party being thrown by his nearest neighbor, a local banker by the name of Beauregard Ellis.

Donning a clean shirt, Max picked up the unfinished letter that lay upon his nightstand. It was addressed to the Nova Alliance, a group of men and women based in Boston who shared his passions. Leopold Grace was the current president of the Alliance and one of Max's oldest and dearest friends. They had met in Paris back in '27, when the Red Lord had tried to seize power in the Parisian underworld. Heady days, those were.

Max plucked up a pen and sat down, the sheet of paper still gripped in his fingers. He ordered his thoughts before resuming the narrative he'd begun before Sam's arrival.

> Leopold, you should have seen the horrors that Darkholme had foisted upon the poor fools he'd trapped in his lair. It brought to mind some of the stories you've told me about your family's own adventures in the realms of shadow and nightmare. The madman had turned his storm cellar into a torturer's delight, with chains that hung from the ceiling and beds wired with electricity. But worst of all were the noxious smelling chemicals that he fed his prisoners, forcing their bodies to alter in ways that God never intended. He'd taken the core components of the chemicals from several lakes and streams located near Tunguska, the site of that horrible explosion from '08. Apparently, the source of said explosion was a meteorite that fell to Earth and detonated in mid-air. The meteorite contained creatures, Leopold! Tiny, almost microscopic creatures! They floated in these solutions of Darkholme's, looking like brine shrimp... only with such malevolence to their appearance that it chilled the blood in my veins! Darkholme was feeding these things to the poor souls he captured... and the beasts wrought horrible effects upon them, devouring parts of their brain and making them susceptible to Darkholme's suggestions.
>
> Luckily, Darkholme's pets proved to be no match for my revolver, though it pained me to end their lives. I kept hoping that there would be some cure to be found for them... alas, their murderous intent made it impossible for me to snare one for study. Darkholme himself nearly escaped into the countryside but I managed to catch his trail before the

moon's light faded behind the clouds. I shot him dead, ridding the world of a great evil, and then set fire to the house itself, to ensure that no one else would ever duplicate his experiments. The only thing I kept from the awful place was a silver dagger inscribed with mystic runes. Eventually, I'll send the weapon on to you for study, but in the meantime I've been carrying it with me.

I left behind one of my calling cards, though I knew it would be wiser not to. There's something that compels me to take responsibility for my actions, Leopold. Perhaps it assuages my guilt somehow, for the taking of human lives. Or perhaps it is vanity....

Regardless, my actions have brought renewed scrutiny upon myself. Had things gone differently, I never would have chosen the life of secrecy in which I now hide. I would have made my deeds public, like our friend Clark did. I hear that the authorities welcome him and his friends these days. Of course, his preferred means of dealing with criminals is lancing into their brains and removing the parts of the mind that compel them to commit evil deeds. More humane than putting a bullet into their skulls, I suppose.

I will endeavor to stay out of the limelight for the time being, old friend. Give my regards to Clark, Lamont and the rest.

Max finished the missive by artfully drawing in the shape of a blackened bird. He sat back in his chair, closing his eyes for a moment as pain began to throb behind his forehead. These horrible headaches had plagued him since his youth, when he'd seen his father gunned down... they'd appeared with regularity ever since, usually carrying with them visions of dark portent. Leopold had claimed they were bursts of precognition, helping guide Max along his path. But to Max, they were as much a curse as a blessing. They had led him to Darkholme and others like him. They made it impossible for him to set aside the Rook identity and live a life of peace.

Max gritted his teeth, trying in vain to avoid crying out in pain. He saw a crystalline object, glowing with an inner fire. A man held it in one hand, a look of almost orgasmic pleasure flitting across his features. There was a name attached to the man and Max whispered it aloud as the pen slipped from his fingers, clattering to the floor. "Trench," Max said, before the image shimmered to reveal the face of a bald man with a long white beard. From the shape of his eyes, Max thought him to be Chinese... and very, very old. "K'ntu," Max said, the pounding in his skull increasing until spittle flew from his lips and he jerked out of his chair. He heard his servants' footsteps, hurrying to his bedroom door. They'd heard him cry out and were concerned.

"Can't be found like this," Max whispered, forcing the images from him. As he did so, the pain became a dull ache in the background of his consciousness.

Sorry, Sam. I really did mean to stay out of trouble... but it looks like the Rook's going to be needed again.

Chapter IV
Evelyn

The home of Beauregard Ellis was not what it had once been, but it was still one of the few plantations that had managed to survive the burning of Atlanta. Much of the surrounding property had been sold off since the War Between the States, helping to keep the family's manner of living intact, but Max could tell that the Ellis clan was heading for hard times. There was no more land to sell, save for the house itself, and the way Ellis decorated the place, the remaining fortune would be gone in one or two generations.

As Max stepped into the grand foyer, Beauregard and his wife, a somewhat heavyset woman named Gladys, greeted him. Both of them wore old-fashioned attire, with Mrs. Ellis' considerable bulk squeezed into a corset. Beauregard himself was dressed in a long coat and tails, his hair swept back by an overuse of hair cream.

"Mr. Davies!" Beauregard exclaimed, moving forward to shake hands. "I am so pleased that you decided to attend. How have you enjoyed the Southern hospitality so far?"

"Aside from the heat, I've quite enjoyed myself," Max replied honestly.

"You Yankees just don't know what a real summer's like, is all," Gladys said. She offered her hand daintily and Max played along with the game, bringing it to his lips. On the three occasions he'd met her so far, Gladys had never missed an opportunity to lament the many faults that Yankees possessed... but she always seemed somewhat attracted to him, as well.

"I'm sure there are hotter days to come," Max agreed. "It looks like an excellent turnout."

"Social event of the season," Beauregard laughed. "Go on into the study. The men folk are gathered there, having some smokes. We'll meet up with the ladies later on, for food and dancing."

"Do you dance, Mr. Davies?"

Max paused at the question, recognizing the woman who had teasingly asked him. He turned to see Evelyn Gould moving up the stairs and into the foyer, looking breathtakingly beautiful. She wore a soft yellow dress that left her shoulders bare. Auburn hair was pulled back on her head, leaving small ringlets to dangle invitingly down her neck.

"Only with women such as yourself," Max answered.

"And what kind of woman is that?" Evelyn inquired, coming to a halt just before him, close enough that her perfume reached his nostrils.

"One who is far too lovely for words." Max reached out for her hand, not having to feign a desire to lift it to his lips, as he had with Mrs. Ellis.

"Flatterer," Evelyn said with a small but pleased smile. She had arrived from Boston just a month or so before Max had moved to Atlanta, working as an actress. There was a small but increasingly vital arts community in the area and Evelyn had hopes of contributing to it. Her talent, from what Max had heard, wasn't enough to get her onto Broadway or into the higher class of film, but she seemed content with what she had: which was more than enough to appease the typical theatergoer or matinee aficionado. "Did you come alone?"

"I'm afraid so. And you?"

"Yes. Shall we remain close to one another in hopes that no one will notice?"

"I was going to suggest the very same thing."

"Great minds think alike," Evelyn teased. She glanced around, noticing that several people were casting annoyed looks at them. "Seems we're blocking the entrance. Are you going into the study to smoke those foul cigars and drink liquor?"

"Well, when you put it that way, it does lose some of its charm." Max gently took her by the arm and led her towards the parlor room where the ladies were gathered. Laughter spilled out as various gossips were spread and fashions were compared. "Are you anxious to spend time with the old biddies of Atlanta?"

Evelyn's eyes flew open and she emitted an unladylike snort of laughter. "You better hush before someone overhears you! We'll be branded as uncouth Yankees and will never be invited back!"

Max grinned, marveling at how alive she made him feel. He'd long ago put aside notions of romance, for fear of how his nocturnal activities might impact such things. But whenever Evelyn was about, he found himself flirting like a schoolboy. "I suppose we should conform to local notions of propriety. Shall I find you once the males and females are brought back together?"

"Yes, please." Evelyn squeezed his hand before moving into the parlor, leaving behind a most enticing scent. Max indulged in it for a moment before heading to take care of his own social duties.

"**D**arkholme was a bastard and I'm glad he's gone!"

This heated pronouncement from a man named Gilbert Smith was met with a general murmur of approval. The topic of the recent unpleasantness had not been long in coming, for the party's host himself had broached the subject within moments of the men-folk's retiring to the study. "What does everyone think about this Rook fellow?" he'd asked, sipping a brandy and looking altogether too impressed with himself. "If the rumors I've heard are even half true, I'd say a bit of Southern justice would have dispatched Darkholme as well as this Yankee vigilante did."

Max had smiled at those words, but Gilbert had spoken up before he could have voiced any kind of reply. He could see that Beauregard was watching him closely, however, as if waiting for a response.

"What sort of rumors have you heard, Beauregard?" Max asked, honestly curious.

"Only that Darkholme was conducting perverse experiments on negroes and gypsies. Fiendish stuff." Beauregard took another sip of his drink and added "But you were up North during the Rook's previous killings, weren't you? Do you think he's followed you here?"

The look in Beauregard's eyes made Max a bit uncomfortable. *He's heard the stories, Max realized. I knew I was getting sloppy… that's why I tried to stop this madness before it landed me in jail.*

Forcing a look of nonchalance, Max shrugged and replied "I was there. The cad even made a few of his crime busting efforts on my private property. Gave me a bit of notoriety, I have to admit. Can't say I'm glad to see him in these parts, though I think we'd all be in agreement with Gilbert that some of these people need to be taken care of."

"True enough," Beauregard confirmed. "Perhaps he's someone you know, though? Did you bring any servants with you?"

"No. I traveled alone." Max averted his gaze, as if losing interest in the discussion and was saved from any further defense of my honor by the arrival of a new gentleman, one whose late arrival caused everyone to look in his direction.

The figure's appearance caused a profound effect on Max, who recognized him immediately. The man was slightly older than him, but in good shape and with a dark intelligence evident in his eyes. He wore the most fashionable of modern suits and a fedora was held tightly in one hand, which was slightly bent, as if it had survived great trauma. It was the figure from Max's vision, the one named Trench.

"Jacob! Welcome," Beauregard said, moving forward to shake Trench's good hand. "I'm so glad you could make it. You'll notice a few new faces in the crowd, so I'll introduce you."

Beauregard took to his task with great relish, introducing Trench as a collector of curiosities and the owner of a downtown Atlanta establishment called Jacob's Ladder. Max noticed that many of the men who already knew Trench seemed to regard him coolly, so he made his way towards Gilbert, who had moved to stand near the window.

"You know Mr. Trench, I presume?" Max asked.

"Hmm? Oh, yes. Interesting fellow," Gilbert replied, in a voice that definitely implied that he found Trench anything but interesting.

"He looks familiar to me, though I can't quite place him."

"Some of the newspapers ran stories on him a few years back. Feared lost on an expedition, turned up hale and hearty, only survivor, heroic case of human will overcoming nature. All that sort of thing."

"Sounds like it, doesn't it? And he never lets you forget that it is." Gilbert surprised Max by reaching and touching his arm. "He's a dangerous man, Mr. Davies. Be wary of him."

Max nodded, feeling a bit unnerved by the fear that he'd seen in Gilbert's eyes. Before he could question the man further, he heard Beauregard clear his throat from behind him. Turning, Max came face-to-face with the man who had haunted his mind earlier today.

"Mr. Davies, may I introduce you to...."

Beauregard's words were lost in a sudden scream that made everyone in the room jump. Max shoved his way past Trench and his host, running full speed towards the door. He recognized the woman who had emitted the sound, which had been full of agonizing terror.

It was Evelyn.

Chapter V
Bodies in the Mist

Max burst into the parlor room, barely able to stop himself from retrieving the pistol he wore strapped under his coat. He found the women staring outside the windows, into the thickest fog Max had ever seen outside of London. It tumbled about like small clouds of mist, borne along by mystic winds.

Evelyn stood closest to the window, a hand raised over her open mouth. The poor woman looked as pale as a ghost and she jumped when Max touched her shoulder.

"What's happened?" Max asked, feeling the way she shivered beneath his hand.

"Out there... Can't you see them?"

Max followed her gaze, aware that the other men had entered the room and were asking their own wives and girlfriends for information. Outside, in the mist, were men... shambling mockeries of men, stooped over and somewhat misshapen. "Stay here," he whispered. He turned and found himself face-to-face with Trench.

"Going somewhere, Mr. Davies?"

"There are people out there. I'm fairly certain that Beauregard didn't invite them."

"I'll come with you, if I may."

Max hesitated, remembering the dark terror of his earlier visions. Despite them, there was no way he could avoid the offered help without seeming rude to the other guests. "If you'd like. Just stay behind me." Max reached under his coat and drew out his pistol, careful to keep it hidden from the women.

"Do you always come so well prepared to parties?" Trench asked.

"Only ones where unnatural mists spring up out of nowhere." Max hurried out the front door, stumbling a bit as he reached the stairs. The fog was so thick that he could not see more than a few feet in front of him. He thought he saw two of the mysterious figures ahead of him, but he could not be sure. "You there!" he yelled. "Identify yourself!"

Trench's voice came from just over his left shoulder. "Look to your right."

Max did so and felt the blood in his veins chilling at the sight before him. A man with bluish-tinted skin had come into view, his clothing soiled by dirt and blood. His eyes were rolled up in his head, leaving only white showing. There was an awful nature to his gait that made Max feel sick and confused. "God in heaven," he whispered.

"I don't think God had anything to do with these things," Trench whispered.

The undead creature shifted at the sound of Trench's voice, seeming to zero in on the two men. It picked up speed, raising its arms and forming the hands into fists.

Max shot it twice in the chest, but the bullets only seemed to stagger the creature. It continued on, closing the gap quickly. Just as its fingers began to close around Max's collar, he unloaded a bullet directly between its eyes. Blood sprayed backwards, along with white fragments of bone and gray matter.

The monster fell to the ground, twitching. A noxious odor rose from it and Max recognized it from the numerous scenes of horror he'd witnessed. It was the smell of death and decay.

"More," Trench hissed.

Max whirled about as two more of the things ambled towards him from the other side of the porch. He leaped towards them, aware that his ammunition was limited. The first of the things was met with a hard chop to the throat. It didn't harm the undead monster the way it would have a normal man but it gave the thing pause, allowing Max to fire his pistol at point-blank range into its temple. As before, damage to the cadaver's brain seemed to bring its rampage to a halt.

Armed with knowledge of how to stop the things, Max made quick work of the thing's companion and stared out into the mist, wondering how many more might be waiting.

Trench appeared again at his side, staring down at the twitching monsters. "Fascinating. Reminds me of the zombies I've heard about in Haiti."

Max fought the urge to put the last of his bullets into Trench's head. The visions had seemed to make it clear that he was a villain of the worst sort... but something stayed Max's hand. He had never killed anyone who hadn't forced the action and he held on to that last vestige of morality like a crutch.

"The fog is lifting," Max said, noticing that the mist was beginning to part as quickly as it had arrived.

"And the bodies are going away," Trench remarked. "Look."

The two zombies at Max's feet faded into nothingness, becoming as immaterial as the mist itself.

"What do you think could do such a thing?" Trench wondered aloud. "And why?"

"They were a distraction."

"I don't understand."

Max frowned, wondering if that was true. It was certainly possible that whatever threat Trench posed was unrelated to his plague of undead… but Max had a feeling that Trench was anything but innocent here. "The men didn't do anything other than wander around, attracting our attention."

"They did attack you…."

"Yes, but rather ineffectually. There's something more at work here." Max looked over as Beauregard and several of the men hurried over, some of them brandishing their own gentlemen's pistols. "Mr. Ellis, might I recommend that you have the servants search the house and make sure that nothing is missing?"

"You think some of those men the ladies saw might have gotten inside?" Beauregard asked, looking alarmed.

"It's possible."

"Where are they now?" Gilbert wondered. "I don't see a damned thing."

"They fled," Trench replied, drawing a glance from Max. The two men seemed to share an understanding that discussions of walking undead would not go over well with men who hadn't seen them firsthand.

Max spotted Evelyn slipping quietly out of the house and he excused himself quickly, moving to catch up to her. "Evelyn! Are you alright?"

She turned to face him with fear in her eyes. "No! Those men… they weren't right! I saw one of them! He… It was awful!"

Max brought her into his arms, comforting her. "I believe you. I saw them myself."

Evelyn drew back quickly. "You did? Thank heavens! I thought I had gone mad!"

"No, you mustn't think that. There are things in this world that are beyond the rational. The sooner you accept that, the better. Can I take you home? I have a feeling you aren't going to want to stay for tea and dancing."

"Please. I would very much like the company," she said, looking profoundly grateful.

Poor girl, Max mused. *She's not used to such terrors. I almost envy her.*

Walking towards his parked car, Max cast another glance back at the house. Trench was there, talking quietly with Beauregard. He looked up and gave Max a perfunctory nod. *I think I'll pay Mr. Ellis a visit tonight and find out what went missing. Because something most certainly did… and it's looking more and more like a case for the Rook.*

Chapter VI.
Questions at Midnight

The Rook arrived at the Ellis home just before twelve, a full moon giving him ample light to work by. He was cloaked in his dark garb, allowing him to blend in to every shadow. On his face was a small domino mask affixed with a birdlike beak over the nose. It was a bit of melodrama, he'd always reasoned, but it helped hide his identity amongst those frightened few who saw him and lived.

Though he was definitely in business mode, he couldn't help but think about Evelyn. The young woman had recovered from her fright quickly, which had impressed him greatly, but it was clear that she didn't want to be alone. She'd asked him to stay for a while longer and the implications of her offer were all too clear, but Max had been forced to excuse himself as politely as possible. There had been neither more visions nor their accompanying headaches, but he knew they were coming. Best to deal with the mystery head on rather than wait for him to be drawn into it against his will. Besides, he reasoned, whoever had done all of this had upset Evelyn… and the very notion of her being hurt roused in him a sense of chivalrous honor. He would find out who had done these things, be it Trench or someone else… and he would make them pay.

Max crept through the quiet house, not making a sound. A light in the study was on and the fireplace was burning brightly as Beauregard sat in a large chair, smoking a cigar and staring into the dancing flames.

"Mr. Ellis?" Max hissed, making sure to keep his voice low and deep.

Beauregard glanced around in mounting terror, his eyes wide. "Who's there? God knows you've taken everything you could have wanted! Why come back again?"

"I'm not the one who ruined your party, Mr. Ellis." Max stepped partially into view, staying to the far side of the room so that Beauregard only saw what Max wanted him to see: a dark-clad figure with bird-like features, wielding a pistol. "But I want to know about them. What did they take from you?"

Beauregard hesitated, swallowing hard before speaking. "You're the Rook, aren't you?"

"What did they take from you?"

"A book…."

"All that over a collection of writings, Mr. Ellis? Seems unlikely. What kind of book was it?"

"A 17th century copy of *Axiomata*," Beauregard said, looking back into the flames. He looked like a broken man, with none of the confidence he'd shown earlier in the evening. "Are you familiar with it?"

"No. Tell me."

Beauregard sighed. "It was an important work in the collection of the Fraternity of the Rosy Cross."

"The Rosicrucians," Max whispered, remembering the name from his studies into the occult. He didn't know much about them, but was sure that the Nova Alliance would know more. "Are you involved in witchcraft, Mr. Ellis?"

"No! I acquired it by accident, I assure you, knowing nothing of its origins. I was hoping to sell it to Trench but he claimed the price was far too high. And now it's gone forever… and my hopes of getting my family out of debt is gone as well."

"Why is it so important?"

Beauregard shifted in his seat, looking more forlorn by the minute. "The Fraternity was founded by a man named Christian Rosenkreuz. He was born in 1378 and lived until the age of 106. He was buried in a seven-sided vault and it's said that he would return 120 years after his death."

"Did he?"

"I don't know!" Beauregard wailed. "But the *Axiomata* is said to contain references to where the vault can be found. The tomb is reputed to contain all the order's books, plus magical mirrors, lanterns and more." Beauregard sat forward in his seat, warming to the subject. Max thought he looked a bit mad, recounting these strange legends. "I've heard rumors that the Germans are looking for the true location of the tomb. Hitler's a fanatic when it comes to occultism. Do you think the Nazis might have done this?"

"I think the thief might be a bit closer to home than that," Max replied.

"What do you mean?"

"Nothing you need concern yourself with." Max began to turn away but Beauregard rose from his chair, sounding desperate.

"Wait!"

Max glanced over his shoulder, noting the way Beauregard's hands shook with impotent rage. "Yes, Mr. Ellis?"

"I don't care if you are a madman, like the papers say. I want you to find the men who did this unspeakable thing, who violated my home and my honor. I want you to kill them!"

Astonishing how quickly a man becomes murderous when it's his own property being threatened, Max thought. "I'll be in touch, Mr. Ellis. In the meantime, I wouldn't throw any more parties."

Beauregard remained where he was, scarcely believing his eyes. It seemed that the Rook vanished into thin air, melding into the very shadows that blanketed the room. "Kill them," he whispered again. "If what the ladies said about those men is true, they are abominations…."

Chapter VII.
Jacob's Ladder

"So, tell me again why you've brought me to this dreadful place?" Evelyn looked out of place, in her cosmopolitan fur-lined coat and small hat. Atlanta was fast returning to its glory of the pre-War days, but it still retained a lot of its country heritage. Evelyn, on the hand, reeked of 20th century sophistication. It was a dichotomy that attracted Max to her, for she certainly stood out amongst the women of the South. Someday that would change, he knew, and Atlanta would take its place amongst the leading cities of America… but that day was not today.

Max was standing in the dimly lit shop of curiosities, staring intently at an authentic sarcophagus. Trench's place of business was full of interesting odds and ends, many of which were no more than elaborate forgeries. But several of them were the real deal and Max wondered why Trench didn't ply his wares in New York or London, where the prices for such items could be much higher. "I thought you might appreciate a shopping excursion," Max said to Evelyn. "To take your mind off the events of last evening."

"A charming notion, but when you suggested it, I was picturing… I don't know, some place that didn't include mummies or haunted mirrors."

Max turned to face her, trying not lose himself in her deep green eyes. "The best shops in the city, I promise. But I want to see Mr. Trench first."

"I didn't realize the two of you were so close."

"We aren't. But he was with me last night… he saw the same things you and I did."

Evelyn's features shifted at the mention of the walking dead. "I dreamed about them, you know. I barely slept a wink."

Max reached out and touched her cheek, a move that surprised them both. Though they'd engaged in harmless flirtations before and there had been the hint of physical pleasures in her invitation to stay last night, there had not been overt touching between them. "I won't let them harm you," he said.

Evelyn looked both amused and touched by his sincerity. "You're a rare man, Mr. Davies. There are times I look at you and think you're a modern day knight, springing right out of those old storybooks of my childhood. But sometimes when I look in your eyes…."

"Yes?" he asked, moving closer to her.

"I'm not sure I know who you really are. I mean…."

"Ahem."

Max and Evelyn abruptly moved apart, startled by the sudden presence of Jacob Trench. He stood in a doorway leading to an off-limits storage area, his eyes taking in the scene before him. Max noted that there was a hint of blush to Evelyn's cheeks.

"Mr. Trench," Max said, moving to greet him. "Fascinating place you have here."

"Thank you, Mr. Davies," Trench responded, not accepting the offered hand. "I'm surprised to see you here, however. I didn't realize you had an interest in antiquities."

"I've traveled the world many times," Max answered, holding the other man's gaze. He saw questions aplenty in Trench's eyes and Max felt relieved. If Trench had heard any of the stories about the Rook, he had apparently paid them no heed… or at the very least, was not worried. "In fact, some of your items are clever forgeries. But I'm sure you know that."

A corner of Trench's mouth turned upwards. "Of course. But for some of my customers, these forgeries are the closest they will ever come to being to afford the items they dream of. I have authentic versions of everything on display here… I merely choose to leave some of them in safer places."

"Evelyn and I were just discussing the things we saw last night. Have you given them any thought?"

Jacob sighed, finally nodding in Evelyn's direction. It was apparent that he'd been involved in something of interest when Max had entered the store and was now resigning himself to the fact that he would be delayed from returning to it.

"A bit… but I'm sure you'll understand if I say that it's not something I'd like to dwell upon."

"You handled yourself far better than most men would have," Max offered. "I daresay that poor Beauregard would have been beside himself when faced with the undead."

Trench glanced past Max, watching as Evelyn occupied herself with a small brass scarab. "Are you a spiritual man, Mr. Davies? Do you believe that someone might have the power to raise the dead and send them forth to ruin someone's party?"

"You mentioned that you'd seen zombies before," Max answered.

"Yes. Explaining why I'd be so receptive to the notion of the undead. But as for you… just as you thought that most men would have run screaming from the things we saw last evening, I'd expect most men to come up with every excuse possible… other than the obvious: that what we saw was real."   Trench turned his eyes away from Evelyn's trim form, taking the time to examine Max more closely. "But you seemed quite at ease amongst them. You've seen such things before."

Max merely shrugged as Evelyn finished her browsing and came up to join them.

Jacob inclined his head in her direction. "Miss Gould. So wonderful to see you again. Have you found anything in my shop that catches your fancy?"

"Actually, I think the beetle is quite nice."

"The scarab was taken from a Pharaoh's tomb and is said to be quite cursed."

"Do you really believe in such things?" Evelyn asked, her skepticism tinged by the remembrance of what she'd seen the night before.

"I never put limits on what the world might bring, Miss Gould." Trench returned his attention to Max. "So… to answer your earlier question, no, I have not thought much about the events of last night. Was there anything else?"

"Only one thing… I'm interested in acquiring a manuscript. A copy of the *Axiomata*. Do you think you might have something like that on hand?"

"Recent copies only," Trench replied, looking like he was ready to bring the game to an end. "And they are far from accurate, or so I've heard. Are you a member of the Fraternity, Mr. Davies?"

"No, just interested in helping a friend. Beauregard's copy has gone missing."

"How tragic."

"Isn't it?" Max took Evelyn's arm in his, ignoring the look of confusion on her face. It was obvious that she was curious as to the real reason behind their visit to the store, but Max knew she was smart enough to hold her questions for later. "See you around, Jacob. Let me know if you happen to stumble across a copy of the *Axiomata*, won't you?"

Trench watched in silence as Max and Evelyn left the store, though he crossed over to a window and peeked beneath the blinds, following them with his eyes until they turned the corner and were out of sight.

"You should have dealt with him before now," a heavily accented voice said from behind.

Trench glanced back at the aged form of K'ntu, noting that the old man looked the same today as he had during their first meeting in Tibet. In all that time, Trench had never seen him eat a thing, nor found him sleeping. He came and went like a wraith in the night. "Even if the stories are true, he's nothing more than a maniac with a gun. He can't stop me."

"You shouldn't ignore them. Even a small pebble can lead to a great man's demise."

Trench sighed. He'd barely begun to study the *Axiomata*, but so far everything pointed to his eventual success. With the information contained in the tome, he would be able to find the last items he needed to open Lucifer's Cage…. But perhaps K'ntu was right: Jacob might need to grind the bothersome pebbles of the world – staring with Max Davies – into the ground first, before moving on to the next stage of his plan.

Smiling, Trench said, "Old master, I'll take care of him. Trust me."

The man who had tormented Jacob Trench mentally and physically did not return the expression. He regarded Trench as a tool, one that was necessary for the revival of the ultimate master they both served, but nothing more. If Trench died, K'ntu would shed no tears, but he would be forced to return to his lonely vigil in Tibet and the Cage would not be opened for many a year. That simply could not be allowed to happen. "Take no chances," K'ntu warned. "This man must die or he will ruin everything."

Chapter VIII
The Devil's Night

Max sat in the damp grass, staring up at the moon. It was well past eleven at night, but he couldn't sleep. It was too hot and he was restless. The dreams had come again, two since dinner. In the first, he'd been running down a dusty corridor, something nipping at his heels. In the second, he'd seen Evelyn, her pale arms bare in a thin gown of some kind. An ornate headdress adorned her head and she was bound to a large bloodstained altar. A snake had coiled itself around her left foot.

The nature of the dreams disturbed him greatly. Not just because it seemed that Evelyn was in danger, but because none of his visions had been quite so… vague… before. Normally, he saw the face of those he needed to kill, perhaps augmented by scenes of their crimes. But he didn't recognize the cobwebbed lair that he had found himself in during his dreams tonight, nor did he see signs of Trench or anyone else. Was it supposed to be the tomb of Christian Rosenkreuz? If so, that meant that Trench was closer to his goal than Max would have ever dreamed.

"Mr. Davies?" a tremulous voice asked.

Max looked up to see Nettie, his chief maid, standing not far away, clutching at her robe. She was an elderly black woman with fiery, intelligent eyes and skin so thin that you could see it stretched taut over her bones. In the short time that he'd known her, Max had come to recognize several endearing qualities about her. Most notable amongst them was her deep and abiding faith in God, which had allowed her to endure a lifetime of racism and blocked opportunities. "Yes, Nettie? What is it?"

"Gonna catch your death of cold out here," she warned.

Max couldn't resist smiling. He had been burning up in the house, but the locals considered this weather to be abnormally cool for a summertime night. "I'll come inside in a little while. Did you need something?"

"There's a call from you. From New York City." These last words were spoken with great solemnity, as if Nettie had just told him something that simply could not be believed.

"Thank you." Max rose and dusted off his bottom. Nettie followed him as they headed back to the house, her eyes turned this way and that. "Something wrong?" Max asked her, noticing her nervousness.

"It's a devil's night."

"I don't follow you...."

"That's what my mamma called it when the moon was all pink like it is tonight. A blood moon."

Max didn't say anything to that, though the old woman's words chilled him on some primeval level. He'd heard similar things in his own youth and had found them true often enough.

Stepping into his study, Max picked up the phone. To his delight, the voice on the other end was Leopold Grace, the current head of the Nova Alliance and one of Max's dearest friends. "Leopold! You got my message, I see."

"Yes... and I take it that your retirement didn't last very long?"

Max grinned. Leopold knew about his activities as the Rook and had shared his own nocturnal activities with Max in turn. Leopold possessed a book which allowed him to travel between worlds, a gift from his father, Eobard. "Let's say I'm keeping busy. Do you have anything for me?"

"There are a number of other copies of the *Axiomta* floating about, but the earliest I've been able to put my hands on is only from the late 19th century. It is allegedly a good copy, though, with many details not found in other translations."

"How soon could you get it to me?"

"Through normal means? A few days. Via some of our more... esoteric methods... how does tomorrow sound?"

"Fantastic. When you're in Atlanta in the fall, I'll take you to the Fox Theatre. You'd enjoy it."

"I thought it was bankrupt," Leopold answered.

"That was back in '32. The city took it over for a few years but it was sold to some gentlemen named Lucas and Jenkins last year. They're using it as a movie house these days... a very opulent one."

"I'll take you up on that," Leopold answered with a laugh.

Max was about to ask Leopold how some of their mutual friends were getting on when the line went abruptly silent. He checked the connection several times, a frown settling on to his face. Without even looking, he knew that there was someone outside the open window, perched low at the side of the house. Those sorts of feelings had saved Max's life again and again over the years and he'd long ago lost any inhibitions he'd had about following his hunches.

Setting the receiver back in its cradle, Max knelt down and reached under his left pants leg, retrieving his pistol. He hated that whomever was out there had chosen his home as the battleground... Nettie and the other servants were innocents in the affairs of the Rook. *My two worlds keep getting meshed together,* he mused. *If I don't find some way to make peace with this, someone I love is going to die eventually.*

The Rook crept towards the window, allowing his mind to shift gears from Max Davies to his nocturnal alter ego. The shift was not a dramatic one, for there were far fewer differences between personalities than Max sometimes liked to think. Ultimately, Max affected the attitude that the Rook was another part of him to assuage his own guilt over his actions.

A rustling sound made him pause. Whomever was crouching on the other side of the wall was rising, perhaps to peer inside the window. Max readied his pistol.

A face came into view, one that was so awful that it sent goose bumps racing up and down the Rook's arms. It was another of the undead, though one that was obviously possessed of a dark and sinister intelligence. This one looked about the room, his tattered lips parting in a sneer. The thing's skin was pockmarked with sores that oozed a yellowish pus and Max was taken with the sudden notion that this man was recently deceased. He still smelled of voided bodily fluids and moved with a motion not that dissimilar from a living creature.

The Rook leveled his gun, taking careful aim. Just before he fired, the thing glanced down and took sight of him. With astonishing speed, it threw itself backwards, even as the Rook pulled the trigger. The shot just missed him, echoing loudly in the still house.

Max was on his feet, springing through the open window. He would have enough difficulty explaining all this without Nettie or one of the others coming upon the shambling corpse outside. The Rook landed on his feet, stunned by the speed of his attacker. The corpse was on him quickly, wrapping its hands about his throat. Max grunted as the thing began exerting tremendous pressure against him, choking the life straight out of him.

At this range, however, there was no chance of the Rook missing with his pistol. He placed the barrel against the undead's temple and pulled the trigger. White chips of bone, intermingled with blood and gray matter, splattered against the side of the house. For a moment, he feared that even this would not be enough to stop his foe, for the pressure did not lessen on his throat. But finally, the thing's fingers grew lax and the body collapsed to the ground before shifting into mist. Within seconds, all traces of the monster were gone.

"Master Davies! Are you okay?"

Max glanced over at Josh, the farmhand who did most of the heavy chores around the property. The handsome black man was dressed only in a pair of thin breeches and looked like he'd been awakened from a sound slumber. Inside the house, Nettie's screams of alarm could be heard. "I'm fine, Josh... I just startled a prowler, that's all."

"Where is he now?"

"Took off... but not before I unloaded a couple of shots at him. I'll call the police in the morning."

"Want me to stay up and watch the place in case he comes back?"

Max smiled, but it was an odd one... unlike any other that Josh had seen from his employer. It was the smile of a killer and it chilled Josh to the core. "No thank you. Go back to sleep. I'll handle this."

Chapter IX
The Reich

Trench compulsively tapped his finger on the cafe tabletop, staring at the newspaper spread out before him. *Attack on local businessman, assailant on the loose* was splashed across the front page in bold letters. There was no mention of the assailant being a member of the shambling undead, of course, but Trench knew that Davies would be back soon enough, continuing his investigation.

"One creature," K'ntu had said with a shake of his head earlier in the morning. "You send one lone creature to deal with this man. Perhaps I was wrong about you. Perhaps you are not worthy of the Master's grace."

Trench had stood there, not answering the taunts. They burned away at him, but he knew that K'ntu was right. He had underestimated Mr. Davies, it seemed.

"Mr. Trench. I hope I have not kept you waiting."

Trench looked up to see a handsome blond man, dressed in a dapper black suit. The man's ice blue eyes, clear complexion and soft German accent made it all too clear where his heritage lay. "Not at all, Mr. Schmidt. Please take a seat."

The German did so, glancing around the crowded café. They were in the very heart of Atlanta, which still retained much of its Southern charm. A black minstrel sang a song outside, a small hat lying in front of him. A few whites tossed coins in to it, but not many. Across the street, an old man in a tattered Civil War regiment coat ambled by, muttering to himself.

"Interesting taste in meeting places, Mr. Trench. I had hoped for something a bit more… discrete."

"The best hiding place is always the one in plain sight." Trench leaned back in his chair, studying the man before him. Schmidt was a high-ranking member of the Nazi occult department. It was men like him who fed the Fuhrer a steady diet of prophecy and folklore, all proclaiming the eventual success of the German regime. "What did you think of my offer?"

"An intriguing one. As you know, our researchers have been working on the same problem. The location of the tomb is something that we covet very much."

"I made a breakthrough last evening," Trench replied, his words quickening. He was being honest in this, for a vital piece of the translation code had finally slid into place for him. "I think I know exactly where the tomb is located… but I'll need supplies and men, both of which you have in abundance. Fund my expedition and I'll turn over all mystic artifacts… save one. A silver key engraved with a single word, written in Sumerian. That prize is mine."

"Agreed." Schmidt pursed his lips together, making him look a bit prissy. "Of course, you realize that our coffers are not endless. If you fail to deliver on this… we will exact payment in return."

Trench grunted. "I'd expect nothing less." He raised his glass of water, clinking it against the German's. "To a successful partnership."

Chapter X
Secrets Revealed

The Rook crouched low atop a building facing the front of Jacob's Ladder. He wore a long trench coat and low-brimmed hat, both of which hid much his features from sight. His mask was in place, along with the bird-like beak that accompanied it, but Max had no doubt that Trench would recognize him if given the opportunity.

It was another warm night in Atlanta and Max could hear the sounds of bluegrass drifting by on the breeze. A local night club was filled to the brim and every now and again a drunk redneck would stumble by on the street below. Aside from that and the occasional motorized vehicle, there was no motion in front of the curio shop… which suited the Rook just fine. He allowed himself to enter a meditative state, running through all that he had seen earlier in the day. After the attack on his home last evening, he'd stayed awake, dreading the coming of more visions. None had come, but around noon a driver had arrived, bearing a tightly bound package.

Inside had been a tattered copy of the *Axiomata*. True to Leopold's word, it appeared to be an excellent translation, with handwritten notes in the margin, scrawled there by some previous researcher. These notes discussed at length the differences between this edition and earlier ones, which aided Max greatly. He had a feeling that Trench was on the verge of a breakthrough and Max badly wanted to keep pace with the man.

A little voice in his head whispered to him *Just kill him and it'll all be done. Why play the game? Why let him try to lure you into his death traps? You know how it'll end up… you standing over his body, a smoking pistol in your hand. Just do it!*

Max frowned at the persistent suggestion, trying to still his mind. He was a vigilante but not a murderer. If Trench died, it would be because he had forced the Rook's hand… that's the only way Max could justify his own actions.

A black sedan pulled up in front of the shop and the Rook leaned down a bit to remain hidden from sight. Trench emerged from the vehicle and moved towards the door, while another man that Max recognized from his visions pulled the car around back: it was K'ntu, the aged Chinese.

Once Trench had moved inside and the car's driver was out of view, the Rook was on the move. He descended the side of the building using a grappling hook and wire, landing silently in the dark alleyway. A quick scan of the area revealed that no one was watching and he sped across the street, coming to a stop on the same side of the building that the car had turned down. A small garage lay in the back and Max silently watched as the bearded old man exited the vehicle and entered the store through a rear door.

Something about the old man made Max uneasy, as if he were in the presence of a shark or some other kind of predator. The man was dressed simply enough, with a warm fur coat and a dark suit, but there was certainly an aura about him that suggested barely restrained violence.

The Rook crept around back after the man entered the building, checking to confirm that the door was locked. To his surprise, it opened at the twist of the knob, allowing Max an easy entranced. Holding his pistol tightly, the Rook moved inside. He was in a darkened kitchen area but there was light around the corner and Trench's voice could be heard easily enough.

"The tickets are supposed to be waiting for us at the airport," Trench was saying.

A thickly accented voice replied "And you mean to leave Atlanta… with this Davies person still breathing?" Max could hear the disdain in the man's voice.

"Davies will have problems that go far beyond any attempts on his life. I'm going to destroy him without firing another shot."

"Overconfident fool," the other man replied. "You will waste the only opportunity the Master will ever have!"

"I am the chosen one, K'ntu… you've said it yourself. Now trust in me."

Max felt the throbbing in his head and he bit down hard on his lower lip. The urge to kill, to slay evil, was almost overwhelming… what stopped him? Why not end it now? *Do it,* the voice inside him urged. *Kill them.*

"What is this place we are going to?" K'ntu asked, giving Max something to focus in on. As long as he could concentrate on the conversation in the other room, he could fight off the voices inside him.

"Kassel. It's in west-central Germany, along the Fulda River. The Brothers Grimm lived there and it was there that they wrote most of their fairy tales."

"Childish stories, but ones inspired by the dark deeds of truth," K'ntu answered. "And the tomb is in this place?"

"Yes… and more importantly, the key that's housed in the tomb. I suspect there are several such keys in the world, but this is the only one we know of… and so it's the one we have to gain." Max heard Trench putting ice into a glass. Soon afterwards, the sound of something being poured over the ice. "The Germans will provide us with all the papers we'll need… and the manpower, as well. I've been careful not to give them any more details than are necessary. The last thing we need is for them to decide they no longer need us around."

"The Druselturm. An odd name. Wasn't it built long after Rosenkreuz's death?"

"It was built in 1415… used to be a prison. But now it's a historic ruin." Trench sipped his drink. "But, yes… it was built after Rosenkreuz was dead. It was built on top of the tomb."

A triumphant chuckle came from the old man. It sounded like sand paper rubbing together and made the pain in Max's head even worse. "A prison built atop a prison, eh? Clever. And from there we shall gain the means to free *our* master from his own prison."

Max felt his vision blur as Trench joined the old man in laughter. Images passed through his mind's eye… of the dank temple with an elaborate altar, upon which lay the screaming form of Evelyn. A man with sunken flesh and empty eye sockets was clawing at Evelyn's dress and skin, leaving long streaks of red on her pale body. Her screams were piercingly loud, the shrieks of terror that one produced when death was pressing its clammy hand directly upon your breast.

"Did you hear that?" Trench asked.

Max froze in place, the images fading. He heard the men approaching and hurried towards the door, hands shaking. *Turn and fight them now!* a voice urged, but he knew that he was too weak after the vision.

A shout, followed by a burst of gunfire, put fire to Max's heels. He sped outside, a small warmth on his left shoulder telling him that the bullet fired by either Trench or K'ntu had grazed him, finding one of the few places on him not protected by his costume.

Again and again he heard Evelyn's screams of horror echo in his head and they propelled him forward. The squeal of tires rang out through the night as a passing car swerved to avoid hitting him.

Back in the shadows across the way, the Rook fell to his knees. The pain in his head was awful and he retrieved a series of small capsules from his coat pocket, eagerly tossing them on to his tongue. They were a potent series of pain killers, mixed together in his own combination, that helped fight off the migraines that often accompanied his visions.

They're going to keep getting worse. Just like way you hear me a lot louder now than you used to. The walls between the living and the dead are very thin… and growing ever more so as the day of Lucifer's return draws near.

Max sighed, closing his eyes. The voice… it had always urged him in one direction or another… but it had never held a conversation with him….

"Who are you?" Max asked, knowing that he should keep moving but unable to force his legs to work.

Open your eyes… and see.

Max hesitated, but finally did so.

There, before him in the same suit he'd worn the day he'd died, was Max's father.

Chapter XI
Shades of the Past

The Rook was standing in a field of blinding white snow that whirled all about him. For a moment he could see no further than the hand in front of his face and the howling of the wind made it impossible to hear even the screaming of his own voice.

He staggered forward, sensing warmth up ahead. Through the maelstrom he made out a small temple of some kind, hidden in the massive mountains he could now make out all around him.

And his father – Warren Davies – stood before the temple, watching him with a mixture of exasperation and obvious pride. Max's father had never been an emotional man and had always held himself at arm's length, both figuratively and physically. But there had been a bond between the two that had always remained firm in Max's memory.

The Rook came to a stop before this man who could not exist and whispered through cracked lips, "This isn't real. The bullet was drugged... wasn't it?"

"Considering all that you've seen... is it really so hard to believe that you might actually be speaking to me?"

"I'm sure as hell not in... wherever this is. I'm in Atlanta."

"You're in a dreamscape, Max. A mental projection. You've always been gifted... even when you were a little boy. That's the reason I was able to guide you over the years. Make myself heard. But with the walls between the living and the dead becoming so weak these days..." Max's father opened his arms. "Well, you can see that I'm capable of a lot more now."

"You're telling me that the voice in my head... the source of my visions and the headaches... is my own dead father?" Max's voice was dripping with disbelief. "This is a trick."

"No. It's not."

Max paused, letting the implications sink in. "Why would you do this to me? Make me a vigilante?"

"I didn't *make* you do anything. I merely offered certain paths to you and you chose to take them."

"Or else suffer those headaches of yours! Not a fair choice, from where I'm standing!"

"You sound like a little boy, Max. Stop. Listen."

Max seethed inside, still finding it hard to fathom. Could it be true? Could his father have been haunting him all these years? And if so… did that mean that someday Max would be free of his compulsions? Would his father leave him alone?

"Pay attention!" his father snapped.

"What do you want to say?"

"What's happening to the world is not just the work of Trench and his manservant. They are chess pieces, being maneuvered about by the source of all evil in this world. These men seek to unleash the father of demons from his cage." Warren Davies moved towards his son, locking gazes with him. "The forces of sin know their day is coming closer and they've begun weakening the barriers between worlds. That's why you're able to see me now… that and your own telepathic powers are becoming stronger."

"Now I'm a telepath, too?"

"You've always been good at sensing deceit in others… but it's a gift you may not have the luxury of mastering. You have to stop Trench or the entire world will suffer."

"Why have you haunted me? Why did you make me into… what I am?"

"The costuming bit was your own creation, Max. A bit too theatrical for my tastes. I was killed because I was in the wrong place at the wrong time… a victim of senseless violence. There are too many people in this world who escape the clutches of man's law… my anger, my sense of vengeance, kept me on this plane… and I knew you could become my weapon against the kinds of men who killed me!"

"You used me… just like this demon is using Trench."

Warren shook his head. "I gave you a purpose. Do you know how many men would give anything to have a real *purpose*? But you're growing careless… and soft. Don't wait for the visions to force you into action. You know what needs doing."

"I'm not a murderer."

"You've killed dozens of men, Max."

The Rook turned away from his father, confusion making his thoughts difficult. He honestly wasn't sure how he should feel at this moment. "You brought me here for what? To tell me that Trench is dangerous? I know that."

"You need someone you can trust. With Leopold and your friends so far away, you'll need an aide. Someone who knows your secrets… and to whom you can confide all your troubles."

"I don't need a sidekick."

Warren Davies smiled sadly. "I knew you would say that… so I took the liberty of taking a few precautions."

Max whirled on his father, anger making his face splotchy and red. Despite the cold air all around him, he felt like he was burning up. "Damn you! I *loved* you. I've tried to *honor* you. And this is what you do to me? Treat me a damned puppet?! Go back to Hell!"

The snow began to blow harder than ever, blotting out all visions of his father. Max felt himself falling backwards, tumbling head over foot… and he wondered again: was this real? Or just some awful nightmare?

He hoped for the latter.

Chapter XII
The Rook's Nest

Max sat up with a start, recognizing his surroundings at once. He was in the storm cellar of his home, which he always kept locked up tight. It contained his equipment and papers, everything that would link him to the Rook….

"You startled me," someone said from the shadows and it only took a second for Max to place the pleasing feminine voice.

"Evelyn?" he asked, all too aware that his mask was still in place and that his pistol remained tightly clutched in one hand. He looked down at it as Evelyn, lovely in a black dress and coat, moved into view.

She followed his gaze, shrugging. "You wouldn't let it go," she said by way of explanation. "And I learned a long time ago not to argue with an armed man." Evelyn followed with a small laugh that was a bit too shrill. She was nervous… and so was Max.

He rose from the cot upon which he lay, reaching up to remove his mask. There was no point in hiding the truth now… and Max felt certain that his father, if he truly existed, was responsible for this. "How did we end up here? The last thing I remember was being downtown."

"I was out with friends – a producer and his wife – when I thought I heard you calling my name. It was strange, really… we were all alone on the street and they said they heard nothing but…" Evelyn chewed her lower lip, her gaze locked on some faraway place. Max thought she looked beautiful. "I excused myself from them and went looking for you. A couple of blocks away, I found you. You were lying in an alleyway, bleeding from your shoulder."

Max glanced over at his wound, which had been patched up rather clumsily. He peeled away the bandage and saw that there was a small bloody furrow where the bullet had grazed him.

Evelyn moved to stand beside him, still looking uncertain. "You told me to bring you here… even walked me through how to fix your arm. But you never woke up. It was like you were… sleepwalking." Evelyn reached out and took the Rook mask from Max. "Is this what you do at night?"

"You must have heard the rumors about me…."

"Of course. But who would really believe them? How many men dress up like a bird and shoot people?" Evelyn gazed into his face, seeking some sign of the cultured, funny man she'd been so attracted to. "Why do you do this?"

Max contemplated coming up with a lie… but in the end, he decided to tell her the truth. Perhaps his father had been right, because relieving himself of the whole story seemed very cathartic. He told her everything, beginning with the death of his father, all the way up to his odd vision that preceded his awakening. During the whole affair, Evelyn remained at his side, even taking his hands in her own.

When all was said and done, she whistled softly and said, "And I thought I had daddy issues…."

Max laughed a bit too loudly but Evelyn joined in easily enough. "You must think I'm a candidate for a sanitarium."

"Not really. We all have our vices and oddities."

Max raised her hands to his lips and kissed them softly. The move surprised them both, but it felt natural, as well. "What are your vices, Evelyn?"

A wicked smile touched her full lips. "Perhaps I'll tell you about them, Mr. Davies. But now is not the time."

"Why not?"

"Because, in your little fever dream, you told me to call the airport and have them clear us for flying."

That brought Max clear of any fantasies he might have been developing. "I did?"

"Yep. We're supposed to be flying to Kassel, Germany. Wherever that is." Evelyn shook her head, sending her lovely curls flying. "Do you really have a plane that can fly that far?"

"Yes. A special one. It's the fastest plane in the world and capable of making several round-the-globe trips without refueling."

"That's amazing! Did you invent it?"

"Well, parts of it. A friend of mine named Clark aided with other aspects." Max smiled at the look of amazement she wore, reaching out to touch her cheek. "But you're not coming with me. Remember the visions I had about you being in danger? The only way I can see to avoid that is for you to stay here."

"Absolutely not." Evelyn's eyes flashed. "This is the most exciting thing that's ever happened to me, Max. And I'm not about to let you cut me out of it."

"But what if those visions were real?"

"Then I'll take the experience of being mauled by a mummy and put it into my next performance."

"You're the crazy one," Max laughed.

Evelyn jumped as the phone rang upstairs. Max held a finger to his lips and then moved over to another phone, gently lifting the receiver from its cradle. He heard Nettie's voice immediately.

"Mr. Davies isn't in, Sheriff. But I'll sure enough tell him you called."

"Make sure you do. Mr. Beauregard Ellis was found shot to death this evening… and next to his body was a small note pad with your employer's name on it. That makes him a suspect, Nettie… so if you see him, you best let me know… or you're an accessory."

Max set the phone back down, not bothering to hear Nettie's answer. "We have to go. Trench has set me up." He looked around the storm cellar – his "nest." Should he burn its contents? Once they found out he was missing, the police would surely search the house.

A spiteful thought came to him. *If you're listening, dad... I'll leave it to you that no one disturbs this place. If they do, my usefulness to you is over....*

Evelyn was brushing back her hair, looking flushed and excited. "So now we're fugitives, are we?"

"You seem to like that."

Evelyn shrugged, but the smile never left her face. "I need a fancy name like yours. Maybe Swan? Goes well with Rook, I think."

Max put his mask back into place, wondering just where all this would go in the end. Evelyn seemed to enjoy the danger just a tad too much... but she would certainly keep things interesting, he suspected.

Chapter XIII
Winged Devils

"This plane is amazing."

The Rook sat at the controls of his proudest creation, allowing himself the briefest of smiles. During his solitary crusade against evil, Max had missed out on the pleasures of sharing his creations with others. "I call her Nite-Wing. She's the fastest plane in the world... if I open up the engines all the way we can reach speeds of 340 mph."

Evelyn's eyes flew open. She sat at Max's side, dressed in a pair of khaki slacks and a safari-style button-up shirt. A leather flight jacket completed the outfit and gave her the look of an adventuress.

Max, meanwhile, was dressed in full Rook regalia, including mask.

"You get more interesting all the time, Max" she purred, watching in admiration as his fingers danced along the controls. Out the main window, she could see ocean waters through the fog.

The Rook found himself telling her more than she probably wanted to know, in an effort to impress her. *I'm acting like a school boy,* he thought wryly. "The Nite-Wing has an 18-cylinder engine and 15-foot propellers. It's also got a triple-fin tail to aid in flying."

"How did you pay for it? It must have cost you a mint."

"My parents left me a large nest egg... and some of my inventions have been put to private use by the government, providing me with even more income."

"Does anyone in the government know you're the Rook?"

"One or two friends, yes. They help keep a few of the prying eyes out of my business. But there's only so much they can do without arousing suspicion on their end. And I've gotten sloppy lately. Attracted too much attention on the local level. That's why I left my home and came to Atlanta." He paused, swallowing hard. "I wonder sometimes if I'm not trying to get caught."

"Your father's the reason you can't give it up, though. It's not like you're crazy." One corner of Evelyn's lips turned upwards in a smile. "Is it?"

"You believe me about my father being a ghost?"

"Why not? You dress like a bird and shoot people. We're flying in your super-secret airplane. I can certainly believe in ghosts when all that other stuff is around."

Max nodded, understanding her point. His life was full of oddities and once you began to accept them, everything else fell into place. He glanced over at Evelyn and grinned. "When all this is said and done, how about you and I go someplace? Away from Atlanta, I mean."

"What exactly are you proposing?" she asked, arching an eyebrow.

"A vacation. That is, if you're not busy with a new play."

"Nothing that starts in the next few weeks." She reached out and squeezed his hand. "I'd like that."

Before Max could respond, the entire plane began to rattle loudly. Checking his instruments, the Rook noticed that the fog had increased tenfold, leaving him flying blind. "We can't be far from Germany," he said, shouting over the rising din. "We're in the North Sea now."

"Turbulence?" Evelyn asked, checking to make sure her seatbelt was buckled.

Just then, the fog parted a bit in front of them and Max saw something through the haze… a figure of pure impossibility. "I don't think we're that lucky," he whispered.

"What do you—oh my god!" Evelyn's voice became strained as she, too, saw the thing ahead of them. It bore the body of a woman, bare-breasted, but the lower extremities transformed into feathery bird legs complete with claws. The thing's face was a mockery of humanity, its mouth parting to reveal razor-sharp teeth. Gigantic wings spread out from its back, flapping as it remained airborne. "What is that thing?"

"A harpy," Max answered, banking the plane away from the creature. From the back of the vessel came a terrible ripping of metal, following by a steep decline in altitude. "And she's not alone from the sounds of things."

"What should we do?" Evelyn asked, her hair beginning to whip about wildly. The cabin was beginning to depressurize and Max knew that there was no saving his plane.

"Unbuckle," he shouted, doing the same. Grabbing Evelyn's wrist, he pulled her towards the back of the plane. "We haven't got long. Have you ever parachuted before?"

"What?" she asked with alarm. "Of course not!"

"What about that movie you made? *Perils of Gwendolyn*?"

"That was three years ago!"

"Evelyn…."

"That was a movie, Max! I didn't actually jump from a plane!"

The Rook plucked up a parachute in one hand and began slipping the straps over Evelyn's shoulders. "Count to three and pull this cord."

"You're not serious!"

Another sudden impact knocked both of them off their feet. Max was up first, drawing his pistol. "Something just entered the rear of the plane," he said.

"A harpy?" Evelyn asked, pulling herself up by holding on to the side of the plane.

Max didn't respond – the answer was clear enough when one of the horrible creatures, hissing and snapping at the air, moved into the cabin. The harpy looked from Evelyn to Max, obviously trying to decide which would make the better meal. The Rook decided to make the choice a simple one by unloading his pistol in the thing's direction. The bullets struck home, driving through the harpy's body and sending a stream of bluish-tinged blood to the floor.

The plane's nose took another steep turn downwards and Max felt the wind buffeting him. "You have to jump, Evelyn!"

"What about you?"

The Rook pulled her towards the door, which he opened with a grunt. He peered out enough to see that they were no more than a few hundred feet up… and dropping rapidly. Two more of the harpies were outside, circling the falling plane. "I'm coming… but I'll be distracting them away from you."

"Max," she screamed as he pushed her towards the door. "I love you."

The Rook paused for a second. She couldn't actually mean those words, for they barely knew each other… at least in the intimate way that led to such things. The power of the moment was at work, he mused… but the look in her eyes….

Throwing caution to the wind, he kissed her hard on the mouth before whispering "I love you, too." Before she could reply, Max hurled her out of the plane. She fell, screaming, to the rapidly approaching ground.

The Rook grabbed hold of a spare parachute and leaped from the plane, targeting one of the harpies with his pistol. His first shot went wide left, but the second shot caught the thing in its wing. While Evelyn opened her parachute, Max drew a bead on the remaining creature. It saw him and lunged, clawed hands outstretched.

Max waited until the thing was so close he thought he could smell its fetid breath. Then he fired a bullet straight between her eyes.

With a quick yank of his own chord, the Rook felt salvation at hand. He tried to angle his landing towards Evelyn, who had come down in a heap of parachute and limbs in a tangle of trees. Behind him, the plane came crashing down with a thunderous roar. The heat of the flames burned at Max's back as he reached the ground. He rolled with the impact, stopping at Evelyn's side. She was lying on her back, eyes closed, and for a moment Max felt an overwhelming rush of fear. Had she damaged something in her landing? Had one of his stray bullets struck her?

And then she began laughing, her eyes opening to find his.

"What's so funny?" he asked, unable to keep from laughing himself.

"I can't believe you saw *Perils of Gwendolyn*. That film was awful."

"It was," he admitted. "But you looked very nice in it."

Evelyn reached behind his head and pulled him to her. They kissed briefly but a second explosion from the plane sent fiery debris high into the air and made them both scramble to their feet.

The Rook stumbled further into the countryside, holding Evelyn's hand in his own. "From the looks of the land, we're in northern Germany. We need to head south. Kassel is close to the center of the country."

"How are we going to get there without your plane? And where in the world did those… things… come from?"

Max grinned, stopping where he was and stripping off his Rook attire. "Trench is getting stronger. He's near his goal… I wouldn't be surprised if he had a few more tricks up his sleeve." Max shoved his clothes into a small knapsack he'd brought along and strapped it to his back. Now he looked like a wealthy American on vacation, though there were fewer and fewer of those in Germany these days. War was in the air, despite the fact that many liked to believe otherwise. "Trust me," was all he said in reply to her question.

Evelyn sighed, but she knew that was enough. If there was one thing she'd learned about Max thus far, it was that he was never at a loss for a plan.

Chapter XIV
Ghostly Visitations

Nettie looked past the sheriff's burly form, holding Josh's gaze. "Mr. Davies isn't here. Can't you come back later?"

The sheriff sighed, pushing his hat back so that it perched atop his balding head at an awkward angle. There were large patches of sweat visible under his arms and around his midsection, soaking right through the shirt he wore. His belly hung over the front of his pants, giving him the look of a pregnant walrus. "Now you know I can't do that. If your master ain't home, then I'll just give myself a look around and wait."

"You can't be doin' that," Josh warned. He stepped up next to the sheriff, who regarded him coolly. "This is Mr. Davies' property."

"I'm an agent of the law, boy," the sheriff warned and the look in his eyes was one that Josh and Nettie recognized all too well. It was the look they got from men and women who regarded them as something less than human… like the same property of which Josh had spoken. "Now if you don't want your behind thrown in jail, you're gonna back away from me."

Josh did as the sheriff said but there was no fear evident on his face as he did so. He was twice as tall as the lawman and could break him in half easily enough… but Josh also knew how Southern justice would view such a thing. "Mr. Davies ain't gonna be happy if you mess with his things," was all Josh said.

"Yeah, well that'll be too damned bad, 'cause I don't work for Mr. Davies." The sheriff ambled down the hallway, looking into various rooms in the house, his thumbs hooked through the belt loops of his overloaded pants.

"Hello, Sheriff," someone said from the doorway to the last room. "Something I can assist you with?"

The sheriff came up short, looking into the face of a man who resembled Max Davies in more than a few ways... but who was obviously not the same man. He wore a tweed coat and a smart suit, his features those of the cultured elite. "Who are you?" the sheriff asked, intimidated by the upper class air that the man carried with him.

Behind the sheriff, both Nettie and Josh exchanged confused looks. From their vantage point, it looked like the sheriff was talking to thin air.

"My name is Warren Davies. I'm Max's father."

"Oh. Well, I have a few questions for your son. Do you know where I can find him?"

The elder Mr. Davies smiled in a slightly condescending manner. It brought a flush to the sheriff's face and he slipped into the natural way that he handled all rich people – by completely and totally caving in. "He's away on business, Sheriff. Is there something I can help you with?"

"Well... there are questions about a murder...."

"Surely you don't suspect my son of being implicated....?"

"Oh, no! But I have to ask...."

"I've never understood why you have to waste your time with such nonsense. You should be able to focus on truly important matters... like finding the true killer behind Mr. Beauregard's death."

"How did you know–?"

The elder Mr. Davies leaned in close to him and the sheriff found himself unable to look away from the man's eyes. They seemed to hold such power... such knowledge... as if their owner had been to Hell and back, returning with truths that the sheriff could never comprehend. "There is nothing to be learned here. You will return to your car, speaking politely to Josh and Nettie as you go... and then you will refuse to follow up any more leads related to my son. Do you understand?"

"Sheriff?"

The sheriff jumped, whirling about to see Josh and Nettie watching him with fearful expressions. The sheriff looked around for Max's father but there was no sign of him. Hitching up his belt and trying to calm the pounding of his heart, the lawman answered "Just getting' ready to head back to the station. Tell Mr. Davies and his father that I'm sorry for the trouble."

Josh watched the man's back as he hurried out the door, a dumbfounded look upon his face. "Mr. Davies... and his father? What the heck was that about?"

"Don't ask me," Nettie answered. "Mr. Davies' daddy died a long, long time ago."

"Maybe it was a ghost."

"Don't you be startin' on about ghosts," Nettie warned. "Plenty of strangeness in this world without bringin' in ghosts. They need to stay where they be and let the livin' do the livin'."

Chapter XV
Tomb of Horrors

Jacob Trench wiped the sweat from his brow. He had grown used to pain and discomfort over the past few years, but even he felt the stifling air settling into his lungs, making him long for fresh air. The German workers he'd been given were laboring hard, most of them having dispatched their shirts to keep cool.

When he'd first entered the area beneath the Druselturm, Trench had enjoyed the cool air and the moist smell of earth... but as soon as the work began, the setting became more and more oppressive. The only thing that gave him any solace was the knowledge that Max Davies was probably suffering through even worse times. Even if he managed to evade the police back in Atlanta, there were creatures given the singular task of preventing him from reaching Germany.

"How goes it, Mr. Trench?"

Jacob turned to see his agent in the Reich, Schmidt, approaching. Much to Jacob's chagrin, Schmidt looked fresh as a daisy. "They've moved away a lot of earth with their shovels and revealed a sealed doorway of some kind. One of them is lining the area with dynamite now. As soon as it's blown open, we're inside."

Schmidt smiled, showing perfectly straight teeth. "You make it sound so easy. That is something I have noticed about you Americans – no matter how incredible the task, it is always something that can be overcame by your... ingenuity."

"Our work ethic is second to none," Trench replied, all too aware that he was standing to the side, sweating, while the Germans did the backbreaking labor. "I'm sure you'll get a medal for your role in this. Hitler loves anything related to the occult, doesn't he?"

"He does not view this as some sort of hobby, Mr. Trench. He values things that might help him and the German people."

"Right." Trench relaxed a bit as one of the foremen stepped up to him. Trench had forgotten the man's name but he had been in charge of setting the explosives. "Are we ready?"

The other man nodded, answering in fractured English. "Ready to go boom. Back away."

Trench did so, aware of Schmidt at his side. K'ntu had disappeared, which wasn't unusual. The Asian had a tendency to vanish for weeks at a time, reappearing just when it was most inconvenient for Jacob.

Kneeling in the dirt, Trench heard the men counting slowly in German. He glanced up at the ceiling, hoping they knew their explosives as well as they thought they did. The last thing he wanted was to join Rosenkreuz in a tomb beneath the Druselturm.

The explosion made his ears ring and sent dust flying. Jacob coughed, burying his face in his hands until the cloud began to fade. He moved forward, even before he could see the gaping hole the dynamite had left behind. A new odor was drifting into the room, one that carried the weight of ages.

He paused in the newly-revealed doorway, staring into a complicated series of passageways, all adorned with runes that carried tremendous occult power. "We've found it," he whispered.

"Yes. You have."

The voice came from the depths of the tomb and made the workers at Jacob's back jump in alarm. How could there be someone inside there? Someone alive? It was impossible!

Trench stumbled away from the door, hearing footsteps within. They were coming closer....

"Trench!" Schmidt shouted. "What is going on here?"

"I don't... I don't know."

Suddenly several creatures burst forth from within the tomb. They looked like desiccated corpses, but they moved with astonishing swiftness. Each was naked, with sunken cheeks and flesh that outlined the bones underneath. One or two had been female in life, but most were obviously male. They attacked the workers with glee, making sounds that reminded Trench of dogs at play. Amidst the yips of the attackers and the cries of the dying, Trench realized that he alone was untouched.

Trench turned towards Schmidt, seeing that one of the female monsters had the German gripped about the head. Her hands were pulling his face towards her open moth, as if to give him a gory sort of kiss. When he was within range, the female leaned forward and bit down hard, tearing away at Schmidt's handsome face.

"She is ravenous," a voice said from behind Trench. It was the same man who had spoken before and Trench turned slowly to face him, wondering what he would see.

The figure looked old, like a dried-up husk... but he retained much more vitality than the monsters did. He had long dark hair that hung in a braid down his back and his clothing was that of an ancient Egyptian priest. A ceremonial dagger hung on one sunken hip. A cobra wrapped itself around lovingly around one of the man's ankles.

"They... belong to you?" Trench asked when he'd found his voice.

"They are my spiritual children. Men and women who chose the life eternal...."

Trench felt the urge to retch as the man reached out and touched his shoulder. The odor of him was like that of spoiled fish. "Are you....?" He started, but found his throat seizing up, rendering him unable to finish the question.

The man nodded sagely. "I am Christian Rosenkreuz. And I possess the key to Lucifer's Cage."

Trench's eyes flew open wide. He felt like he had years ago, when he'd finally found the temple in Tibet. "Give to me," he hissed, startling himself with the forcefulness of his desire.

Rosenkreuz laughed softly. "Patience. Since gaining the Secret Knowledge of the East, I have found that a man must always exercise patience as his highest virtue. There is something I expect from you before I share the key."

"What?"

Rosenkreuz's lips parted in a leer. "A bride."

Chapter XVI
Arrival of the Rook

Evelyn fidgeted a bit, trying to ignore the smell of the pigs that grunted all around her. "This was your plan?" she asked, for seemingly the thousandth time. "Max Davies, I will never trust you again!"

Max smiled, jostled a bit by the bumpy road. The two of them were in the back of a truck, one loaded with pigs and slop. The latter was thankfully sturdily contained, but the former were too plentiful to ignore. "It's gotten us here, hasn't it?"

"Not very quickly, I'm afraid! Trench is likely to have opened the tomb and taken off by now." Evelyn tried to ignore the stains that dotted her trousers. Whatever that was, she bet it would never come out in the wash.

"I don't think so," Max answered, reaching over to remove a small twig from the curls of her hair. "I haven't had a single vision since we arrived in Germany and I'm positive that if Trench had opened the cage, I'd know."

"Isn't it a silly thing to even try?"

"What?"

"Opening this Lucifer's Cage thing. If it is the embodiment of evil inside there, what makes Trench think that the thing won't just betray him? I mean, it *is* evil."

"That's a good question… and it's one that's plagued me many times, in similar circumstances. There's something inside some people that make them susceptible to foolish risks, I believe."

The truck came rumbling to a stop, just a mile or two away from the Druselturm. Max had paid the driver handsomely to take them there as quickly as possible and the poor farmer had readily agreed, particularly after seeing that Max was offering American money.

"We're here," Max said, jumping off the truck and offering a hand to help Evelyn down. Despite the smudges on her cheeks and the slight disarray to her hair, she looked lovely in the moonlight and Max told her so.

Evelyn gave him a secret sort of smile, her eyes shining. "If you think I look good now, wait until later. I clean up much better, I promise."

"I can't wait," Max answered, giving her hand a quick squeeze before walking around to the driver's side door. He thanked the man in German, slipping him an extra five dollars if the driver would disavow any knowledge of them.

When the truck had continued on its way, Max turned back to Evelyn, his expression grown cold and serious. "I still wish you would wait for me."

"Don't worry... whatever strange vision you had about me isn't necessarily going to come true. You said that yourself."

"It's a lot less likely to come true if you're not in the tomb with me," Max countered. "Please."

Evelyn avoided his gaze, instead reaching into her ample cleavage and retrieving a small strip of black cloth. To Max's astonishment, she tied it about her head, fitting two small eyeholes over the appropriate areas. "There. To protect my identity."

"You're being quite silly," Max whispered, though he couldn't help but be amused. He realized that this was the first time he could ever recall being on a mission and feeling so jovial at the same time. *Maybe you were right, father,* he mused. *Maybe I let my crusade be a solitary one for far too long.*

"Shouldn't you don your own mask?" Evelyn asked. She had produced a small pistol from somewhere and was checking to make sure the gun was fully loaded.

Max stepped off the road, into the growing shadow. He changed quickly, old habits stepping to the fore. If Evelyn were serious about this, he would stop trying to dissuade her. "That gun won't do much damage to a full grown man... and even less to a monster from beyond."

"You have a spare I could borrow, then?"

Max considered it, but finally shook his head no. He had two pistols on him but he would most likely need both. "Just be aware of its limitations. Use it to threaten an attacker, but don't have faith it'll save your skin in a pinch."

"You fill me with confidence," she responded dryly.

The Rook didn't bother responding. Instead, he began moving through the shadows at a steady clip. He heard Evelyn keeping pace behind him but he didn't allow his own speed to slacken. If they were going to make it out of this alive, he would have to –

Max stumbled to the ground, pain suddenly rendering him unable to move. In his mind's eye he could see Trench, standing alongside another man... one dressed like an Egyptian priest. They were moving through the oddly shaped tomb of Christian Rosenkreuz, a tomb that was filled with objects of dark power. "He's alive," Max said aloud, realization flooding through him. "Rosenkreuz is alive...."

"Max?" Evelyn asked, reaching out a shaking hand to grasp at his shoulder.

The Rook shook his head to clear it of the dark images, but one lingered beyond the rest. Rosenkreuz had been showing something to Jacob... a golden key. Turning his attention back to Evelyn, the Rook answered, "I saw him. Trench has opened the tomb. Rosenkreuz is with him. He's going to give him the key!"

"But... how could he still be alive? Is he one of those zombie things?"

"No. He seemed different from those that we saw in Atlanta." The Rook rose to his feet again, his jaw firmly set. "I think he's something else entirely."

Evelyn started to ask something further, but her words were lost in the sudden roar of flames. A wall of fire rose up between her and Max, one that would have swallowed her whole had the Rook not shoved her back at the last moment. Beyond the flames, which extended now in a full square around the Rook, Evelyn could see nothing… but she heard voices.

Alongside Max's, there was another.

Chapter XVII
K'ntu

The Rook coughed as the smoke filled his lungs, but he been in many fires during his adventuring career. Flame did not frighten him… nor did the Asian man who had materialized before him.

It was K'ntu, the aged advisor to Jacob Trench.

"Is your boy Jacob with you?" the Rook asked, drawing both his pistols and brandishing them before him.

K'ntu stood with the flames dancing behind him. A self-satisfied smile lay upon his face and his eyes, which seemed so ancient and wise, were full of mirth. His robes whipped about in the wind, which had appeared to fan the flames. "He is busy at work. Our master will soon be unleashed from his prison."

"Shouldn't you be there with him? Celebrate the occasion?"

"I thought it best that I come to you, Mr. Davies. Jacob does not realize the threat you pose."

"But you do, I take it."

"Most certainly. You have a gift, one both potent and terrible. Your mind is attuned to the Other Side. That is what allows your father to keep his tether to this world. You are the portal through which he exists."

Max frowned. How did K'ntu know….?

"I know many things," the old man answered, as if reading the Rook's thoughts. "For I have lived a very long time… and my eyes can see past the veils of reality."

"Then I guess you knew these were coming, didn't you?" Max raised both pistols and fired, unleashing a torrent of bullets. To his amazement, however, K'ntu dodged them all. He was a blur of movement, his actions too fast for the human eye to follow.

"You think I am human, do you?" K'ntu taunted. "You think that I have stayed alive all these centuries because of some spell or potion? I still live because my kind are far older than you and yours!"

Beyond the flames, the Rook heard Evelyn calling his name. He didn't respond, hoping to keep K'tnu's attention fully on him. "Then what are you? A demon?"

"There was life on this sphere before mankind's ascendance, Mr. Davies. My kind once ruled over land and sea… until the false God of the Christians chose to hand over power to the short-lived hairless apes that he loved so much!"

The Rook jumped back as K'ntu rushed at him, the man's aged fingers elongating into claws. They raked at the air, just missing Max's face and neck. The Rook answered with another flurry of bullets, emptying his chambers. He began to reload, noticing that this time there were bloody smears appearing beneath the Asian's clothing. He had hit his foe, but it was not enough. He hurriedly reloaded, this time using the special rounds he himself had invented. These could take down an elephant….

K'ntu whirled about, his face changing in color. Beneath his skin, scales began to appear, gradually becoming larger until they swelled out and over the human mask he wore. These scales spread out over his entire body and Max watched in mounting horror as something began to press against the backside of the old man's pants. It burst through a moment later, swinging from side to side. A reptilian tale.

"Do you see me now?" K'tnu hissed. "Mankind's primal fear of reptiles dates back to the wars our kind waged, long ago. But once the master is free, he will reward his faithful followers… and humanity will serve as our cattle!"

K'ntu jumped into the air and the Rook fired again, this time using his more powerful rounds. They tore into the lizard man's belly, spilling blood that sizzled upon the ground. But they did not prevent K'ntu from landing hard atop the Rook, sending him tumbling down. Claws and teeth raked across Max's torso, drawing bloody lines across his flesh.

Max twisted beneath his powerful flow, disgusted by the way K'ntu's skin felt against his own. It was like rolling about with a python, one whose stamina was far greater than any human's.

The Rook managed to swing his feet up, latching them around K'ntu's head. He rolled then, knocking his foe from atop him. K'ntu landed close enough to the flames that his tail brushed against them and made him jerk away.

Ignoring the pain he felt, the Rook struggled to his knees and reached into his cloak. He drew out a dagger, the one that he'd found in Darkholme's lair. The blade was inscribed with mystic runes of a sort that Max did not recognize… but given the fact that his bullets were having too little effect, Max hoped they might carry some power he could use against K'ntu.

The lizard man was stalking his prey once more, blood dripping from a dozen or more bullet holes. "You are brave for a human, Mr. Davies. But surely you realize that there are cycles to all things… mankind and its God have ruled in ascendancy for far too long. It is only natural for things to reverse upon occasion. Put down your weapons and beg for mercy… perhaps I shall grant it to you. Perhaps you will be allowed to serve in our master's army!"

"Go back to Hell," Max answered. He dove forward, pushing the blade in front of him. It met with resistance when it struck the lizard man's stomach and for a moment Max feared he lacked the strength to pierce his opponent's scaly hide. But then the runes began to glow and an awful ear-splitting wail filled the air. Then the blade was on the move, slicing through the lizard man's skin like it was a warm knife passing through butter.

K'ntu howled in pain, a scream of torment that only worsened as Max began digging the blade in deeper, twisting it from side to side until a deep rift had appeared in the scaly flesh. Intestines, warm and slimy, gushed out upon Max's hands and the repugnant smell made him retch. He finally shoved K'ntu away from him, holding firmly onto the still-glowing blade.

The lizard man landed hard on the ground, gasping for air. He wheezed like an old man who had run too far, too fast.

The walls of flame began to burn down to nothingness, revealing the worried visage of Evelyn. She started to run to Max, but the Rook held her back with a shake of his head.

Stumbling over to the prone form of K'ntu, the Rook knelt down and nudged the lizard man's arm. The elder being turned to stare at him with glassy eyes. "The Master will remember my sacrifice, Mr. Davies." K'ntu coughed, sending a spray of bloody droplets into the air. "And he will remember you and yours forever. I curse you and your bloodline. I curse you to…"

The Rook raised the dagger and brought it down into his foe's chest. He repeated this action twice more, stopping only when he was sure that K'ntu was dead.

"Max…."

The Rook turned to face his beloved, reaching up to wipe blood from his chin. The action only spread more of the gore across his face. "I'm fine. My wounds are superficial ones. Were you hurt?"

"Of course not," Evelyn laughed nervously. "You were the one fighting… whatever the hell that was."

The Rook sighed, feeling tired. "That… was what awaits the world if we don't stop Trench."

Chapter XVIII
A Match Made in Hell

"A bride?" Trench found himself unable to quite grasp what he'd been told. His eyes kept drifting back to the golden key that rested under a glass seal. Rosenkreuz had taken Trench to the key, but had warned that he would not be allowed to take it until their awful bargain had been completed.

"Yes," the ancient being replied. Rosenkreuz was pacing about the chamber, oblivious to the dust and cobwebs that surrounded him. In his eyes, this was still a palace of wonders, a place where he and his followers could live out their days in splendor. "I once intended to take a mate, a woman who would bear me holy children. I have conducted many experiments upon myself, Mr. Trench. That is why

I am so long lived… and so powerful. But my bloodline cannot continue unless I have a woman who can bear such unholy seed."

"Bear it?"

"Most die at its touch. It burns them up alive, from the inside out."

Trench swallowed hard, trying to ignore the images that came to mind. "I don't understand why you think that I could…"

"Have you ever seen a woman like this?" Rosenkreuz held out an open palm. An image began to form in the air above his hand, slowly shaping a familiar visage. "Long ago, I coveted this girl… but she was denied me, through her own willful arrogance. But my second sight has told me that in this time, in this place, she lives again. Give her to me."

Trench licked his lips before speaking. "I do know her. Her name is Evelyn Gould. She's a rather poor excuse for an actress."

"She is beautiful," Rosenkreuz responded, his eyes flashing hotly.

"My apologies. I didn't mean to insult her." Trench ran a hand through his hair, unsure how to continue. The girl was in America… and Trench didn't have time or patience to journey back there just to retrieve her. Could he somehow steal the key?

And then he felt it… a subtle shift in his reality. He felt bile rise up in his throat and he turned away from Rosenkreuz, vomiting up the contents of his stomach. He smelled burning reptilian flesh… and heard the dying screams of his mentor.

"What is wrong?" Rosenkreuz asked. The ancient being had approached Trench but avoided touching him. Instead, he gazed at the sick features of the other man with distaste.

"K'ntu is dead. The man who tutored me in the dark arts… who prepared me for the opening of the Cage. He's dead."

"How do you know this?"

"I think he sent me a message… right as he was dying." Trench straightened, wiping at his mouth with the back of a sleeve. "You have weapons?" he asked.

"Of course."

"Good. Because my mentor's killer is on the way here… and best of all, he's not alone."

Rosenkreuz narrowed his eyes. "And this is a good thing?"

"You bet it is. You ready to meet your bride-to-be? Because she's with him."

Chapter XIX
Into the Tomb

"This place stinks."

The Rook grunted in agreement. He and Evelyn had crept down the stairs of the Druselturm, able to see very little in the pitch black darkness. Here and there they saw shattered lamps and snuffed-out candles, alongside digging equipment. But all was silent down in the basement area, which only put Max further on edge. The scent of the place was one of earth and age, but there was something else, as well.

Death.

Max stepped into the basement and immediately felt his foot come into contact with something. He knelt and examined it with one hand, identifying it. "Evelyn. Stop where you are."

The girl did so, gripping her pistol and remaining poised for a fight. She was truthfully scared to death but she didn't plan on letting Max know that.

The Rook reached into his pocket and retrieved a flare. He lit it, illuminating the entire basement area. Evelyn gasped behind him as the bodies and gore came into view: a small army of Germans, slaughtered and torn apart. It looked like a pack of wolves had been set upon them.

But far more intriguing was the shattered hole in one of the walls. Max could see a passageway on the other side, one that led directly into the tomb from his visions.

"Do you think there are more harpies here?" Evelyn asked. She had tended to his wounds as best she could on the way here, but Max had been a bit cold to her. He felt like he'd reached the end of this particular adventure – or at least close enough that there could be no more hesitation.

"No, I don't think so."

Something scuttled above them, making both Max and Evelyn glance up. What they saw confirmed Max's suspicions. These were no harpies perched from the rafters, dangling upside down. These were thin, emaciated looking humans, with glowing cat-like eyes and mouths which dripped warm saliva. One of them, a woman, held on to the rafters with her thighs and one hand. In the other hand she held a human ear which she gnawed upon like a dog.

"Max… I don't think we're in a good place right now." Evelyn moved up so close to the Rook that she bumped against his arm. "Have any suggestions?"

"Yes. Start shooting."

Evelyn didn't need a second word of encouragement. She singled out the ear-gnawing woman and fired. The bullet hit home, burying itself in the woman's upper left arm. The gunshot sent the entire room into a flurry of activity. All of the monsters from above began dropping from their perches, including the wounded one, who snarled and jumped at Evelyn.

The Rook tried to put all thoughts about his lover's safety to the back of his mind. Tossing his flare to the ground, he drew his pistols and waited.

The first of the creatures jumped up in Max's face, punching and kicking. Max was able to block most of the blows, using fighting techniques he'd learned in the Far East. A well-placed kick to the thing's solar plexus sent it sprawling in the dirt and the Rook spun about to meet another foe. This one he dispatched with a well-placed bullet to the skull. A third wrapped its arms about the Rook's torso and bit down hard on his shoulder. Max felt a warmth begin to spread from the wound but he refused to give in to the pain. Instead he threw himself backwards against one of the stone walls. He heard the thing grunt from behind him and Max repeated the maneuver again and again, until he was free of his opponent. The Rook then turned and finished off his foe with another bullet.

The Rook then drew out the dagger that had saved him from K'ntu. He would definitely have to send it to Leopold for study at some point, but for now it had much more immediate uses. Max saw that the first of his foes was back on its feet and he lunged for the creature, eager to finish him before the thing could regroup. His first swipe with the blade dug deep into the creature's belly and elicited a squeal of torment. The second sliced through the thing's neck and ended its vile existence.

Panting, the Rook stood amongst the dead. His heart was hammering in his chest and he felt the blood rushing in his ears. It was the way it always was in combat, when the world seemed to move in white-hot flashes. The flare was flickering out now, leaving only brief spurts of light intermingled with darkness.

"Evelyn?" Max asked, looking about but seeing no trace of her. He moved through the dark towards the spot where he'd seen her last. Kneeling, he found the dead body of her foe, the woman-thing who had been snacking on the ear. She had been shot neatly between the eyes, which caused an involuntary smile to form on Max's lips. Apparently her little pistol *was* capable of killing, at least at close enough range.

The smile died when he realized that Evelyn wasn't answering him. He tensed, straining his ears for any sound, any sign of her breathing. Dimly, he heard something… but it was moving away from him, down the corridor he'd seen earlier.

Still not moving, Max focused on the sounds, identifying them. The muffled cries of a woman, the shuffling sounds of her feet being dragged across dirt-covered floors.

The visions he'd seen earlier… of Evelyn bound to an altar… sprang fully to mind. He began to run towards the corridor's entrance but a sudden sharp blow to the back of his skull sent him tumbling to the ground. The cracking sound seemed louder than was possible inside Max's head and he felt his consciousness begin to fade. "No... Evelyn...." he whispered.

Someone crouched at his side, prodding him with a steel bar of some sort. The voice that answered him belonged to Jacob Trench. "She's gone to her rightful place, hero. While you... you're going to Hell."

Another blow landed squarely atop Max's skull.

Chapter XX
The Altar of Blood

The world returned in a swimming haze.

Max found that he was on his knees, hands tied painfully tight behind his back. The throbbing in his head was painfully harsh and made him feel like vomiting, but he managed to focus on his surroundings and that distracted him a bit.

He was in a large circular chamber of some kind, one with a very high ceiling. In the center of the ceiling was an intricate carving that resembled a rose, one whose stem was covered with sharp thorns. Just in front of Max was an altar, one stained with dried blood. Atop that altar, dressed in the flimsiest of attire, was Evelyn. Her long legs were bare and covered with goosebumps and her breathing was shallow and rapid. All of that was deemed a good sign by Max, for it meant she was still alive. A serpent was coiled about her left ankle, slowly making its way up her leg. Its tongue darted out now and again, tasting the air.

"Welcome back, Mr. Davies. I had begun to wonder if my ally had accidentally killed you."

The Rook craned his neck to see a tall figure approaching. It was Rosenkreuz, still looking like a dried-up mockery of an ancient Egyptian priest. His long hair-braid danced along his back as he moved.

Max forced a bit of confidence into his voice, though he felt very little of it in truth. "You look very good for your age. Clean living?"

"If only it were that easy. No, Mr. Davies... my long existence is due to personal sacrifice and an overwhelming desire for knowledge. The sorts of knowledge that many rational men fear to know."

"I understand why you've got me here. I mean to stop Trench from succeeding. But why Evelyn? She's nothing to you. Let her go."

"Nothing to me?" Rosenkreuz stopped next to the altar, gazing lovingly down at Evelyn. He reached out a thin hand and stroked his leathery flesh against her cheek. "You have no idea how wrong you are. When I was a young man, I turned away from feminine pleasures. I thought I was above such physical concerns. But I was wrong, and I knew it from the moment I first laid eyes upon her, all those years ago."

Max frowned in confusion. How could Rosenkreuz know anything about Evelyn? "You've seen her before?"

Rosenkreuz glanced up and nodded. "Oh, yes. Your... Evelyn, is it? She's the reincarnation of a woman I treasured above all others. But she spurned me. She chose to die rather than accept eternity at my side. The pain was so intense... but I knew she'd return to me eventually. I merely had to wait."

"She's not your old girlfriend. Her name is Evelyn Gould and she's an actress." Max drew himself up as much as was possible. "And she's spoken for."

At that, Evelyn opened her eyes and smiled. She quickly resumed her act, however, after giving Max a quick wink.

Clever girl, the Rook thought. Max just hoped she could hold her cool with the serpent slowly making its way up her thighs.

Thankfully, Rosenkreuz seemed oblivious to the ruse. Instead, he was looking at Max with an almost pitying expression on his sunken features. "I wonder if you would recognize the face of the woman you loved, even over the course of centuries. I do. This is her, given new form."

The Rook tested the tenacity of his bonds but found that they surpassed what little strength he had left. His struggles increased when he saw Rosenkreuz produce a dagger from the interior of his robes. It was the golden blade that Max himself had used to rid the world of K'ntu. "If you love her, why do you want a knife?" he asked aloud, hoping to distract Rosenkreuz from whatever his plans were... at least long enough for Max to figure out what to do next.

"My mistake last time was in trusting that she would recognize the love I held for her... and return it freely. In the years since, I have studied many ways of binding one soul to another... and that is what I shall do now. I shall make her love me. In all ways. For all time." Rosenkreuz held up the dagger, studying it. "An intriguing weapon, Mr. Davies. It will do most nicely."

Max barely contained himself. He wanted to scream out, warn Evelyn to move, but he dared not. What if it caused the madman to strike sooner?

Evelyn continued to lay where she was as Rosenkreuz raised the dagger, holding it above her slowly rising and falling chest. His lips moved, producing words that chilled Max to the bone. They were old, from a time when man was far more primitive. They were words of calling, of beseeching, to elder powers that still lurked in the gray mists of mortal souls.

A dark cloud began to form over Evelyn's prone form, slowly beginning to develop arms and a skeletal face. Max struggled to his feet, unable to balance well because of the way his hands were bound. If need be, he would throw himself into the fray and do what he could...

"Give her to me," Rosenkreuz whispered. "Make her mine forever!"

The cloud shape reached out for Evelyn, its hands grasping at the air. A dark voice rumbled "Pierce her heart! Let me invade her veins and then I will bind her to you...."

Rosenkreuz leered, baring his gums and teeth. "Forever," he whispered once more.

Before Max could move to stop him, Evelyn jammed an elbow into Rosenkreuz's groin, sending him staggering away. She kicked the snake away from her and it landed at Max's feet. He stomped at it mercilessly, but never let his eyes slip away from the scene before him.

Evelyn slipped from the altar, dropping all pretenses of maintaining her modesty in the skimpy garment. Her bare flesh was in clear view as she delivered a powerful roundhouse kick to Rosenkreuz's head. "Sick bastard," she hissed. Before the ancient being could rise, she punched him once more in the jaw, sending him to the floor.

Evelyn whirled about, casting a brief glance at the cloud creature, who was beginning to fade without Rosenkreuz empowering it. Making an expression of disgust, she moved around the thing and knelt beside Max, untying his bonds. "Where's Trench?" she asked.

"I don't know… I'd imagine Rosenkreuz gave him the key and he's gone to open the cage."

"Then let's go!"

Max admired her dedication to the mission but he was more concerned with the fact that Rosenkreuz was recovering quickly. "My weapons! Do you know where they put them?"

"In the next room… where they stripped me. Oh, Max… it was awful! The way he and Trench kept pawing at me and…."

"Get my guns!" Max yelled, pushing her behind him. He wasn't as gentle as he should have been, but the look on Rosenkreuz's face chilled him. He looked like a man who had suffered his last indignity.

"You stupid little cow!" Rosenkreuz bellowed. "Again you mistreat me! After I have waited for so very long for you!"

"You don't sound very enlightened to me, friend." Max moved forward, decking Rosenkreuz with a left hook. "The lady's not interested in you."

"You think she loves you?" Rosenkreuz asked. "She is a deceitful witch… all women are!"

"I guess you weren't close to your mother," Max jibed, dancing back as Rosenkreuz swung out at him.

Rosenkreuz shot beams of eldritch energy from his eyes, narrowly missing Max. They tore chunks of rock from the wall and made Max wonder again just what magicks Rosenkreuz possessed.

"Max! Catch!"

The Rook glanced over to see Evelyn, still clad in her beguiling attire. She held out his pistols and then tossed them high into the air. Max realized they weren't going to make the distance between them and so he lunged for them, even as Rosenkreuz targeted him once more. Twin beams of energy came sizzling through the air as Max caught one of the pistols. In a single breathtaking motion, he gripped the gun and twisted in mid-air, firing at his attacker. Max landed hard, for the beams of force had struck a glancing blow on his leg. His bullets, however, flew true.

Christian Rosenkreuz, who had survived centuries, was felled by a bullet to the brain. He landed atop his own altar, his eyes staring up into nothingness.

"Max! How badly are you hurt?" Evelyn stood over him, watching as the Rook examined his wounded leg.

"It hurts like hell but I can walk on it. Help me up."

Evelyn pulled him to his feet, struggling with the task. "Do you really think I'm his old girlfriend?"

Max looked over at Rosenkreuz's dead body. He limped over to him, taking the golden dagger and slipping it into his own belt. "I've heard stranger things. I can't fault him for his taste in women but he doesn't seem to learn from his mistakes, does he?"

Evelyn wrapped her arms around Max's waist, shivering for the first time since she's sprung into action. Now that the adrenaline rush was gone, she looked confused and frightened. "How will we find Trench?"

"It won't be that hard," someone said from behind them.

The Rook turned slowly, his heart thudding. It was his father, looking far more solid than he had in Max's vision. "I thought you'd be busy with the police back in Atlanta."

"Already taken care of. But you need to head to the Lindner Hotel. That's where you'll find Trench… and he's preparing to open the Cage."

"Max? Who are you talking to?"

The Rook looked down into Evelyn's eyes, realizing that she didn't see anyone besides him and Rosenkreuz in the room. "No one important. Ready to go?"

"Depends… do I have time to change?"

"Probably not."

"Cad. You just like me in this tawdry thing."

Max grinned, glancing over to see that, once again, his father had disappeared. "Let's go… partner."

Chapter XXI
The Devil Within

Jacob Trench stared into the crystal, seeing the shapes and colors within. For so much of his adult life, this moment had been his reason for existence. He had killed dozens, defiled sacred places and damned his own soul to a thousand hells. But it would all be worth it… when the dark beast was free of his prison, he would reward the one who had freed him. That much was well known. Ultimate power would be Jacob's… and he had dreamed nightly of the things he would do with it.

First there would be any old enemies that he had made over the years… they would kneel before him and lick his boots before he ended their lives. And the women…! Oh, yes, there would be many women who would serve him.

Licking his lips, Trench withdrew the key from his pocket. A small clasp at the bottom of the cage accepted it easily enough. The key settled into place with a soft clink, making Jacob think of the poem by T.S. Eliot, the one that ended with "This is the way the world ends, Not with a bang but a whimper."

Trench took a deep breath before turning the key. "Dark Lord," he whispered. "Be free."

The tumblers slipped into place and the latch on the Cage opened, allowing painfully bright light to suddenly sweeping out into the room. The temperature also changed, seeming to rise twenty degrees in the space of seconds. Trench found himself groaning from the sudden shift in the environment and he took a step back as the spilling light began to coalesce into something dark and frightful. He brought a hand up to cover his eyes, his nose wrinkling in disgust. A smell that he found difficult to place was permeating the room now... but then he found himself recognizing it in some deep, dank recess of his mind.

Brimstone.

"Jacob Trench," a voice said and its power made the room tremble.

Trench lowered his hands, feeling the force of the entity before him making it hard for him to stand. He was staring up into the face of a being far older than recorded history... at times alternately beautiful and horrifying. It was not human but it bore the same general shape, though its eyes were pools of inky blackness and its skin was the color of dried blood. The beast was naked and possessed of prodigious genitalia, though it was oddly shaped, ending in a pronged tip. He was taller than any normal human, having to stand with stooped back brushing the ceiling.

"My Lord," Trench whispered. "You're beautiful."

The dark creature laughed softly and it sounded like rolling thunder. "To be free again after so very long... you have earned your triumph, Jacob Trench. You have earned the power you have so long sought."

Trench stepped forward impulsively, holding his arms out to the creature, as if expecting to be swept up into an embrace. "I will bring glory to thy name," he whispered. His expression had become one of rapt admiration... he was a zealot, one blessed to be in the presence of his God.

The devil reached out an oversized hand, one whose fingers were tipped with razor-sharp claws. "This world is not meant for the likes of me. My form can exist here only so long... if I wish to bring my dark majesty to the entire world I shall have need of a vehicle."

"Tell me what you need and I will provide."

"I know you will, my pet. What I require is a suit of living human flesh, one that can contain my glory while I walked amongst men."

Trench felt the first tremulous rush of apprehension. "I don't understand. You require a sacrifice?"

"Do not fear. What I need coincides with what you desire. You wish for power and you shall have it. You wish for other mortals to fear you and you shall have it. But I need a body to cloak my spirit within... and I shall have that."

Before Trench could even begin to fathom the meaning of those words, the dark lord had wrapped one of his hands around Trench's neck. Jacob was pulled off his feet, yanked towards the burning eyes of his master. "No, please," Trench begged, trying in vain to weaken the grip he was held in. "I have served you so well...."

"That you have," the entity agreed, reaching out with his other hand to restrain Trench from struggling. "And what I offer you is an honor given to only a very few."

Trench screamed as he felt his soul being forced downwards, into a long dark tunnel. He could no longer see or hear but he felt very cold and alone. It was as if he had been locked in a basement, one where he could beat on the walls until his hands bled but no one would ever hear.

The physical body of Jacob Trench was far from abandoned, however. The demon now looked at the world through mortal eyes and he inhaled noisily, like a drowning man who had been pulled to shore.

"You did very well, Jacob." The demon spoke with Trench's voice and smiled with Trench's mouth. He strode over to the window, looking out into the slowly approaching dawn. A new day was upon the world… and the sleepy residents of Kassel had no idea about what awaited them. "I shall start by seeking out this Hitler," the demon mused, having sorted through Jacob's memory in a matter of seconds. Human minds, he had found, were exceedingly simple things. "His capacity for war impresses me."

Two figures running through the night made the demon pause, however. He recognized them from Trench's memory. The so-called Rook… and his female companion. He resisted the urge to sigh, but found it impossible to stop. Why was it always so? That foolish mortals should throw themselves into the fire, acting out some noble but stupid desire to destroy themselves?

Of course, he *had* been trapped by a mortal, long ago.

It wouldn't do for him to simply ignore such threats, no matter how trivial they might seem. He would have to destroy them quickly before their threat could grow.

Chapter XXII
Dance with the Devil

The Rook found it difficult to get into the hotel. A number of frightened Germans were pushing their way out of the building, many of them screaming things about demons and death. Max knew where they were coming from, for he could feel it, too. It was like someone had left the back door to the house standing wide open… and something dark and scary had scrambled into the kitchen.

"Max. I'm not sure we're up for this."

The Rook had managed to get both himself and Evelyn to the foot of the stairs, the ones that led up to the second floor. It was there that Trench would be… Max could sense it. He was holding Evelyn's hand, a pistol in the other. "What do you mean?"

"You're hurt. I'm half naked. And we're about to fight the devil. Doesn't that sound wrong to you?"

"I don't see any alternative. If Trench and this monster get free of this place, we might never get close enough to strike again!"

"But shouldn't we call for help? Those friends of yours you mentioned… or even the damned Vatican! This isn't the kind of thing you, me and some pistols are going to solve!"

Max leaned in close and kissed her, letting the moment linger as long as possible. When they parted, both of them had quickened their breathing. "I won't ask you do come with me," he whispered. "But I can't stand back and let them leave this place. I think this demon is only going to grow stronger the longer he's here."

Evelyn smiled softly, shaking her head. "A few days ago, my biggest concern was whether or not I was ever going to become a star. Now I'm seriously discussing heading off to face Lucifer himself. You certainly make a girl feel special."

"Stay here."

"No."

"But…."

Evelyn put a finger over his lips. "We die together or we live together. End of discussion."

The Rook nodded quickly. "Alright."

Together they ascended the stairs, the oppressive nature of their surroundings growing stronger with every step. Evelyn couldn't stop herself from trembling as they approached the last room on the second floor. The door was made of strong black wood but it was bending outwards as if a great weight were pressing against it.

"Is your father still here?" she asked, for he had told her of the ghost's recent visit.

Max glanced at her as he reloaded his gun. "No. Why?"

"Just wondering if I'd get to see him real soon. You know… as in, we'll all be dead."

"I didn't know you were such a pessimist."

"I'm full of surprises."

The Rook shook his head, impressed that she kept her sense of humor at times like this. He kicked in the door and it splintered into a thousand pieces. Flame shot out from the interior of the room, driving both Max and Evelyn away from the entry way.

Jacob Trench – or rather, something wearing his skin – stepped into view. Max could tell that he was no longer the same man, for his eyes now seemed illuminated from within. "The Rook. That's what you call yourself, isn't it?"

Max leveled his pistol at Trench's chest. "You did it, didn't you? You released that thing."

"That… thing… is now me. Trench and I are one." He looked at Evelyn, who stood just behind the Rook. "Run, little girl. I can sense you want to."

Evelyn swallowed hard, raised her own gun… and fired. The bullet struck Trench in the shoulder, but he looked no more bothered than if he had been buzzed by a gnat.

"Is that the best you can do?" the devil asked. "Because I've suffered a lot more pain than that. Let me show you." He raised a hand, clenching it into a fist.

Immediately, Evelyn screamed. It felt like her heart was being squeezed into a bloody pulp. She clutched at her chest, falling to the floor in spasms of agony.

The Rook threw himself at Trench, knocking him back into the burning room. The smoke was growing thick here but Max took note that nothing in the room seemed to be catching fire... rather, the flames danced merrily atop the bed and floor. "Stop hurting her," Max hissed, slamming a fist down into Trench's face. A cracking sound was followed by blood pouring from a broken nose.

"Would you rather feel the pain yourself?" the devil taunted. He gripped Max by the ears, channeling more of the strange flame in a direct line against the Rook's skull. "Feel my Hellfire."

Max lost track of the world for a moment. All was red and black, as the horror of the situation overwhelmed him. He thought he smelled his flesh sizzling, cracking and popping like bacon. *It's not real,* he tried to tell himself. *The flames don't really burn. They don't really burn. They don't really burn!*

And then the fire was gone, replaced by the coolness of snow, falling heavily upon his shoulders.

Max looked around, finding that he was once more outside the strange temple. His father was there, looking as stern as ever. "Am I dead?" Max asked.

"No. You're still locked in battle with the thing inside Trench. But you're going to lose... unless you open yourself to your full potential."

Max rose quickly, rushing over to grab his father by his arms. "Send me back! Evelyn needs me!"

"You're not listening to me, son."

Max shoved his father away from him. "Fine. Tell me what to do."

"You're able to tap into parts of your mind that normal people can't. That's why you can see and hear me so well... even before the rise in magic that's been going on since Trench started working on opening the Cage. It also allows you to channel energy, from the world of the dead to the world of the living. And vice versa."

"What the hell does that mean?"

"Find Jacob. Use him."

"I don't understand what...."

Max found himself being thrown away from the devil inside Trench. He landed amongst the dancing fires of Hell, barely able to focus as his opponent rose up over him.

"How did you do that?" the devil asked, in a tone that spoke of confusion, anger... and perhaps a bit of fear, as well.

The Rook groaned, trying to shake off the pain that was overwhelming him. His injured leg was throbbing and he felt a grinding motion in his side every time he took an inward breath. Broken ribs. Two, maybe three. "Do what?"

"Your soul... disappeared. For a moment, I held lifeless flesh in my hands."

Another moment of that and I might have really been lifeless flesh, Max mused. He reached for the glowing dagger and drew it forth but the devil swatted out a fist and knocked it aside. The knife skidded across the floor into the midst of the inferno.

"No," the thing inside Trench hissed. "None of that. It's time we ended this."

"Get away from him, you bastard!"

Max looked up as Evelyn jumped on Trench's back, raking at his face with her nails. Long trails of red followed the action and Evelyn capped off the attack by digging her fingers into the man's eyes.

Trench howled, reaching behind himself and grabbing hold of Evelyn's dangling hair. He ripped a small patch of it from her skull and she lost her hold on him, landing hard on her rump.

Max took this as his cue. He still didn't understand his father's words, but he was weaponless and that meant he had no choice but to come to blows with this thing. He wrapped his arms about Trench's chest, hissing out the words "Where are you, Jacob? I need you."

Somewhere within the devil wearing human flesh, there was a stirring. Jacob was locked inside his tiny little cell… but he heard a faint knocking of sorts. He called out an answer….

And Max heard it.

Even as the devil began thrashing about to get free, Max's eyes were rolling back in his head. He felt like he was falling from some great height, tumbling head over heels.

"How did you get here?" Jacob asked. He was staring open-mouthed at the Rook, who had appeared from nowhere in this dark prison.

Max looked around, understanding dawning on him. "You're trapped, aren't you?"

"He took my body."

"Are you okay with that? Is that what you really want? To exist inside his head, while he takes the power you wanted for yourself?"

"I knew the risks," Jacob answered sullenly. "You don't bargain with the devil without knowing he's the Prince of Lies."

"Then why do it at all?"

"You wouldn't understand, would you? Born into money, adored by your parents, I bet. But my family saw me as an aberration. Something different from the rest of their children. It wasn't until I discovered the legend of Lucifer's Cage that I found a purpose. I lied, betrayed and murdered to get to this point… for power. For prestige."

"I don't fully understand… and I suspect I don't want to. But I'll ask you again: is this how you want the story to end? With you locked away inside here until he's done with your body?"

"I have no choice."

"Yes. You do." Max offered a hand to Jacob, who stared at it in confusion. "Help me."

Evelyn was on her knees, the magic fire in the room beginning to sear her lungs. Though its touch did not harm her, the smoke and heat from it seemed real enough.

She glanced up at the devil, which had managed to knock Max off of it. The Rook lay on the ground like a broken doll, barely breathing.

Before Evelyn could contemplate her next move, the Rook sat upright and began crawling towards the fallen dagger. The devil moved to intercept him, but stopped in mid-movement. Evelyn could see anger and dismay on the devil's face and he began to speak nonsense:

"Stop that! This is my flesh now! You have gotten your prize! Now begone!"

The devil doubled over, growling. He looked upright, staring into Evelyn's eyes… and for a moment, she was positive that the being staring back at her was truly Jacob Trench. He smiled wickedly at her.

The Rook rose up over the devil, raising the dagger high. It was brought down with awful force, stabbing straight through Trench's neck and protruding through on the other side.

Evelyn gasped and looked away as droplets of blood fell on her like rain.

Chapter XXIII
Endings and Beginnings

Evelyn slipped out of the tub, checking her reflection in the mirror. She looked none the worse for the harrowing adventure in Germany, though the first few days back had left her feeling sore in places she didn't even know she had. As she wrapped a fresh towel about herself, she wondered which dress she should wear for the evening: the black one was her favorite but she'd noticed that Max favored the red.

Red it would be, then.

After dressing and applying her makeup, Evelyn cast a glance over an open script next to her bed. It was a good one and it promised a return to the silver screen, both of which appealed to her. Working on the stage in Atlanta was fun but there was always a tiny part of her that wanted more.

She stepped out of the room and went downstairs, where Max was waiting for her. He'd arrived early for their date, which was par for the course. In the month or so since they'd returned from Germany, they'd gone out practically every evening and he'd made it a standard practice to show up an hour or so early each time. It had annoyed her at first but she'd come to recognize it as a compliment of sorts. He wanted to see her as soon as possible.

She found him in the den, standing next to the radio. His expression was grim, but it didn't detract from his handsome features. In fact, it only added to them. "Something wrong?"

Max turned to face her, his eyes drifting over her curves. In some men, such a look would be worthy of a slap… but for some reason, Evelyn didn't exactly mind that Max found her body pleasing enough for the occasional leer. "You look wonderful," he said.

"Thank you. But you didn't answer the question."

"It's nothing. Are you ready to go? The movie starts at six-thirty."

"Don't give me that, Mr. Davies. There's something whirring away in that mind of yours, so spill."

"There was a news report, that's all. The police have found another body. That's the third one in the last week."

"Another child?"

"Yes. A boy of about nine."

"Awful business." Evelyn studied his face. "Have you had any visions?"

Max stiffened and Evelyn wondered if she'd gone too far. Since their return, he had said nothing about visions or ghosts. She didn't think he was hiding them from her… she truly believed they hadn't plagued him. After they had disposed of the now harmless Cage by turning it over to some of Max's friends, it had seemed like a door had closed on that portion of his life and she could sense his newfound peace of existence.

"I did see something, yes," he admitted at last.

"What was it?"

"I saw a woman, working with a hack saw. She was… slicing up a little girl."

"A woman's doing this? I can't believe it…."

"Women are just as capable of violence as men. I've learned that often enough." Max ran a hand through his hair. "I'd hoped this was all behind me. That my father had left me be."

"Maybe he has. Maybe you're tapping into your own powers now, without his help."

"I just want to be your boyfriend, Evelyn. Not the Rook."

Evelyn felt her eyes grow moist and she reached out to take his hand. "Why not have it all?"

"Evelyn…."

"Let me tell you a little secret, Max. The Rook *is* my boyfriend. And you're the Rook. You're not two different people. And I hope you don't think you're going to keep me from stopping the murders of little children."

Max sighed. "You mean to come with me, then?"

"Of course I do. I've even designed myself a mask."

"You didn't."

"You'll like it! And I found the perfect fabric for the leotard."

"I have fabric you can use. Bulletproof."

"All the better." Evelyn tossed her pocketbook down on the couch. "We'll catch the movie tomorrow."

"You're an amazing woman, Miss Gould."

"Then we're a perfect match, Mr. Davies."

They kissed once, quickly, and then moved to the waiting car outside.

Somewhere, a killer lurked.

THE END

THE KINGDOM OF BLOOD

Chapter I
The Quiet Place

Manhattan – August, 1936

A small, flickering light danced on the cobblestone walls, illuminating the man's passage through the tunneled walkway. He was dressed in a crisp black suit that was dotted here and there with dirt and grime, an oil lamp held firmly in one liver spotted hand. In his late forties, Reed Barrows was still as trim as he'd been in his youth but in all other regards age was weighing heavily upon him. It showed in the sickly pallor of his skin and the creaking of his knees. He paused beside a gold-and-crystal casket, the dim glow from the lamp illuminating the figure within. It was a mummy, one wrapped in linens that had begun to rot from exposure to damp air in the years before Reed had bought it. He'd brought it here, to his quiet place, where it now rested in an airless case. With luck, it would last far beyond the few years left to its owner.

Reed stared into the lifeless eyes for several moments, soaking in the ambience of the dead female before him. What had she been like in life? How had she traveled through history, ending up here, beneath one of the oldest buildings in Manhattan?

Putting such frivolous wonderings aside, Reed turned away from the mummy and continued his descent into the quiet place. All along the narrow tunnel were small glass cases containing oddities that he'd collected: a "Fiji mermaid," which was actually nothing more than the top half of a monkey sewed on to the body of a fish; a crystal skull from South America; a battered, somewhat mistranslated copy of one of the *Tomes of Blood*. He loved these things, far more than he loved his wife or children.

The passageway narrowed a bit towards the end, finally opening onto a small chamber in which a wooden coffin rested atop several large stones. Reed stood there for a moment, breathing in the dank smell of earth. The sounds of the world above were a faint, distant memory.

Setting the lamp on the ground, he reached into his coat and withdrew a slender knife. The shadows cast by the lamp made his body appear elongated and inhuman, but Reed took no notice of it. He grunted with the exertion of shoving the heavy lid from the coffin, letting it fall to the floor with a thump.

The strong scent of death wafted up from within and Reed coughed a bit, wrinkling his nose. The woman inside was long dead, wrapped in a long black gown that, in its day, would have barely contained the lovely female curves of its owner. Wispy strands of black hair still lay about the corpse's shoulders and her hands were neatly folded over her bosom. A stout piece of wood protruded from that same bosom, driven deep by the actions of a strong man, many years before.

Reed licked his lips, aching to reach out and caress the body of his mistress. There had been many nights when he'd snuck from the bedroom he shared with the horrible shrew he'd married… snuck down here, to pour out his heart to the only woman he truly felt comfortable with.

"It's time," he whispered. He fought the urge to bend down and press his lips to hers. It seemed fitting to wake her with a kiss, like in an old fairy tale. But this was no nursery rhyme, to impart wisdom or morals to a child. This was something far worse: a mockery of all that was holy. Reed was about to awaken the dead.

He raised his hand over the corpse's face, driving the knife roughly into the skin of his wrist. The cut was a ragged one, for he had never handled a knife for anything more than cutting his food at dinner. He gasped as the pain spread through his arm, but he kept cutting until thick red droplets fell from the wound, landing one after the other against the mouth of his beloved.

When he was satisfied that enough of his blood was seeping down her throat, he tossed aside the knife and grasped the wooden stake with both hands. He immediately regretted the order of his actions, for his wrist ached so horribly that he was almost unable to pull upon the stake. But he fought through the agony, desperate for what was to come.

Slowly the stake moved. It felt like it was wedged in concrete, but Reed groaned aloud as he yanked with all his might. The point of the stake eventually came free and Reed fell backwards, landing on his bottom. He panted, his eyes tightly closed as the hammering in his chest slowed to a steady thump.

When he looked up, he realized that he had missed a stunning transformation. The woman in the coffin was now sitting up, her skin a lovely, healthy shade of pink. Her wispy hair was now lustrous and deep black in color, perfectly suited to the obsidian orbs that were her eyes. Her lips were stained red with blood, with small droplets running down her chin and neck. The hole where the stake had been was now filled in with warm flesh, her ample bosom rising and falling as she enjoyed the renewed sensation of breathing. Reed found that last part amusing and he smiled.

"What is so humorous, my savior?" she asked, her voice sounding both grateful and mocking in equal amounts. She spoke in husky tones, with a slight Eastern European accent.

"You're breathing. I didn't know you could do that."

"It is only a semblance of breathing… all the better to blend in with humanity." She rose from the coffin, extending her long legs over the side and hopping down almost delicately. "Where am I? And what shall I call you?"

"My name is Reed Barrow. And you're in New York. Beneath my home." He stood up, suddenly self-conscious in her presence. She was a creature of unearthly beauty, while he… he felt so *old*. "I love you," he suddenly stammered, blushing like a schoolboy as he said it.

She laughed softly, reassuringly. "Thank you, Reed. You may call me Camilla."

Reed sighed, letting his lips and tongue practice saying the name. He liked it.

"How did I come to… this *New York*, Reed? And why have you awakened me?"

"I bought you," he whispered, hoping the explanation didn't offend her. "I… collect unusual things. When I saw you and learned you were supposed to be a vampire… I became obsessed with you."

"You wish to be my lover?"

Her frankness made his blush deepen. "I… I have a wife."

Camilla reached out and touched his face. Her fingers felt electric as they slid over his skin. "Shall I kill her for you?"

"Oh, yes. Please."

Chapter II
Death Takes a Holiday

London – July, 1937

Max Davies was a good-looking man. He knew this in the same abstract way that a gifted athlete knew they could accomplish things that others simply could not. Their physical prowess was so much a part of them that they barely noticed it. Max's good looks were a bit like that. He stole the heart of virtually every woman who met him, while their husbands or boyfriends looked on in jealous fury… but he was never arrogant about it, for he rarely gave consideration to his appearance beyond simple courtesy.

Max had a slightly olive complexion to his skin and wavy black hair, the sort that made women want to run their fingers through it. He favored well-tailored suits and wide-brimmed hats, but was going decidedly casual today, wearing a pair of pressed slacks and a sweater vest over a tan-colored shirt. "Our dinner reservations are for seven thirty," he reminded his wife.

Evelyn Davies fixed him with a critical eye. She was a second-tier actress on stage and screen in the United States, but here in London not a second glance was given her…at least, not because of her fame. She was a striking woman to look at, however, no matter what country she was in. She wore her auburn hair pulled back today and a white safari-style shirt with brown slacks. "That's the third time you've mentioned that to me. In the last hour."

"I just don't want us to be late."

"I never knew you were the worrying type," she replied with a shake of her head. The two of them were standing near the Halls of Parliament, along with a group of some twenty or so tourists who had booked the same walking tour they had. Max had tried to argue that he knew London well enough to show her the city without the need of a tour guide, but Evelyn had won out on the basis that she was on her honeymoon and it would simply have to be done correctly. They would stay at the finest hotels, eat at the finest restaurants and take the best tours… because she didn't plan on doing a second honeymoon at any point in her life. "We'll be there in plenty of time," she continued. "Now hush so I can what our guide's saying."

Max grimaced but inwardly he was pleased that she was enjoying herself. His life had rarely featured moments where he could bring pleasure to others… in fact, most of his existence seemed predicated on the exact opposite.

When he'd been a young boy, Max had seen his father killed in front of him, in an act of senseless violence. Though he had not known it then, his latent telepathy had opened his mind to the world that lay beyond this one, allowing the ghost of his father to invisibly haunt him. His father's rage over his own death had led him to induce painful visions of crimes directly into Max's head, propelling him along the path of vigilantism. He had become a master of criminal science and gained degrees in Engineering, Chemistry and Psychology, all before his mid-twenties. And there were his many travels throughout the world, where he'd learned fighting skills from the best the planet had to offer. In the end, he'd become something more than mere man. He'd become the Rook, the shadowy nocturnal avenger who dispatched criminals with efficient ease… always leaving behind a single calling card adorned with the image of a bird in flight.

That calling card had nearly led to Max's capture by the police on more than one occasion, leading him to flee Boston for the relatively safer confines of Atlanta, Georgia. There he'd become embroiled in the schemes of Jacob Trench… and there he'd fallen in love with Evelyn Gould. Now she shared his secret, even going so far as to join him on occasion. It was a match made in heaven.

Max withdrew a cigarette and lit it, cupping one hand about the match so it didn't blow out in the wind .He'd always detested smoking but had picked up the habit in the last few months. For some reason, it seemed to keep his headaches at bay… or at least that's what he told himself. Since ending Trench's life the summer before, he'd only experienced four visions, far fewer than in the past. Each had compelled him to seek out murderers and rapists… and kill them. He had not made contact with his father during this time and was uncertain if he still being haunted… though he suspected he was.

"That smells horrid," Evelyn hissed. She disapproved of his vice but had never pressed the issue beyond verbal reproach.

Max ignored her, exhaling a long plume of smoke and clapping lightly as the tour guide wrapped up his spiel. Dark clouds loomed on the horizon, a sure sign that it was going to be another wet and chilly night in London.

"Well, it's all done. We can get dinner now. In plenty of time, I might add." Evelyn took his hand and began crossing the street with him. "Have you had fun?"

"With you? Always."

"So have I. I still can't believe you proposed to me… and that we're married. It all feels like a dream." She gazed up at him shyly. "You really don't mind that I keep Gould as my stage name, do you?"

"I told you I didn't. I understand how important it is for producers to remember your name."

"Good. I love being Evelyn Davies in private, though. It's…."

Max failed to hear the rest of her words. He stumbled a bit, nearly falling to his knees in the street. A rushing sound filled his ears and a terrible pain started behind his eyes, quickly spreading to encompass his entire skull. Images, fuzzy and indistinct, ran through his mind, showing a succession of horrors: a stunningly beautiful woman wearing a clinging black gown, her lips and chin stained crimson with blood; a man… her thrall… standing outside a grand old house in Atlanta, watching nervously as a pine box was lowered from a moving truck; the screaming death of a police officer, the woman's teeth tearing into his neck. And the words 'Kingdom of Blood,' hanging like a shroud over his mind….

"Max!"

Max gasped for air, sounding like a drowning man at sea. He came to his surroundings, seeing that he was leaning against a wall while a small crowd gathered about, curious to see what had set him off so. "I'm… I'm okay."

Evelyn looked about at the confused faces. "Epilepsy," she shrugged, feigning a smile. One by one, the gawkers moved away, though many still glanced over their shoulders at Max. "What did you see?" she whispered, turning her attentions back to her husband. "It was a vision, wasn't it?"

"Yes. It was a very powerful one, too."

"Well?" she pressed.

"We need to get back to Atlanta. She's there."

"Who's there?"

Max hesitated, thinking it would sound absurd. But then he remembered that this woman had stood at his side as he fought demons, harpies and resurrected magicians. "A vampire."

"Like that Bela Legosi character? Dracula?"

"More shapely than that."

"Cad."

"Sorry, can't be helped. She's beautiful."

"And dangerous, I take it."

"Very."

"Well, the honeymoon lasted longer than I thought it would."

Max sighed. "You could stay here without me, I suppose."

Evelyn placed her hands on her hips and regarded him coolly. "Very funny. Besides, do you really think I'd send you back to Atlanta to face some shapely vampire without me?"

Chapter III
The Snowy Mountain

The Rook ascended the snowy cliff, the feel of biting cold nipping at his cheeks. He wore the long trench coat and domino-style mask that had become infamous amongst the criminal element, but his clothing did little to warm him from the elements. He ignored the discomfort, however, telling himself again and again that this was not real, that this was a figment of his imagination.

But that was not quite true.

This mountaintop existed on another realm entirely, one composed of pure mental energy. The Astral Plane his father had called it, during one of their chats during the Lucifer's Cage affair. It was here that Max had come when he'd been shot, it was here that he'd learned the truth about his father and the visions that had plagued him.

"Father?" Max yelled over the howling wind. The same Tibetan prayer temple lay up ahead, looking abandoned. "Come to me!"

Abruptly, the wind ceased blowing, startling Max. He froze in place, the air still bone chilling but no longer as harsh as before.

"I'm here, son."

Max whirled around, seeing that his father was approaching, still wearing the same blood-stained clothing that he'd had on the night he'd died. "Do you have to look like that?" Max asked, the fury rising in him again. He hated the fact that his father had turned him into a killing machine, had used him to further his own need for vengeance.

"I can appear however I want to, Max... but I think you need to see me like this."

"I remember the way you looked."

"Hmm. Why did you come here, son? I thought you wanted nothing more to do with me."

Max paused, staring into the gray-white haze that surrounded this place. "Evelyn and I are on a plane, returning to the States. I... had a vision. Of a woman who drank blood. A vampire."

"And you want me to guide you, is that it? Give you some important piece of information that might help you with the dangers to come?"

Max fidgeted. "Well... yes."

His father adopted the same stern expression that he'd used to adopt when Max would behave foolishly. "You denied me, Max. You said you wished I had never done these things to you… and now when you have need of me, you expect me to counsel you?"

Max felt stung by the rebuke. "Well…yes."

For a long moment, neither man spoke a word and then Max's father let out a long, weary sigh. "Why not? You'll just go and get yourself killed if I don't help you. And then what good would you be?"

Max didn't answer, though he couldn't help but marvel at how his father could discuss his son's death in such a matter-of-fact manner.

"The vampire's name is Camilla, that much I've been able to see through the ether," Warren Davies said. "Her companion… his name is unclear to me. They've traveled to Atlanta to pillage the remains of Jacob Trench's collection."

"But his curiosity shop, Jacob's Ladder, burned down shortly after his death," Max replied.

"True enough… but there were levels below the ones accessible to the public. They seek something that was once in his possession… something of dark power."

"Can you tell me what it is?"

Max's father lowered his voice, allowing it to take on a dreamlike quality. He appeared to be staring past Max, into the furthest reaches of the outer realms. "Cursed the ground where dead thoughts live new and oddly bodied, and evil the mind that is held by no head."

Max blinked. "What in hell does that mean?"

His father's face darkened. "Words of warning. You'll hear them again soon enough." He turned, as if to leave.

"Wait!" Max shouted. When his father paused but did not turn around, he said, "I married her."

"I know. I was there."

"Is it always going to be this way between us? You and I? You lurking about like some awful specter and me resenting you?"

"That's up to you, isn't it, Max?"

Max sighed, watching as the mists rose up to envelope his father's form. "I'll come back," Max promised

"**M**ax?"

Max opened his eyes, hearing the soft roar of the plane still surrounding him. He looked over at Evelyn, who was watching him with a peculiar sort of smile. "Yes?"

"You were talking in your sleep."

"What did I say?"

"Mostly just mumbles, but you said something about coming back to see me?"

"Sorry. A dream." He noticed she had a few sections of the Atlanta paper spread out on her lap. "What's that?"

"Before we left I packed away some of the society pages. There's a review of my latest film in it, *Queen of Atlantis*."

"Did they like it?"

"They said I looked quite fetching in my coconut shell bikini."

"Good for you," Max yawned. Truth be told, he'd also thought she'd looked quite good in the coconut shell bikini.

"Didn't you say that this woman and her companion were new in the area?"

"Yes. Why?"

"Well, there's a small mention here that might interest you. Says Reed and Camilla Barrows have recently moved to the Empire City of the South, taking up residence in the old Matthews Plantation. Mr. and Mrs. Barrows come from old money and are sure to add spice to Atlanta's upper crust."

"That's them. My father told me her name was Camilla." Max leaned over and kissed his wife on the cheek. "You're a godsend, Evelyn."

Blushing, Evelyn sat back and smiled.

Chapter IV
Blood Work

Camilla ran her tongue along the curve of the policeman's neck, savoring the racing pulse she could sense beneath his skin. "Shh," she purred into his ear, making him squirm. "The pain will only last for a few seconds… and then you'll experience nothing but ecstasy."

Reed tried to ignore them, but it was difficult. She looked lovely in the moonlight, all pale and luminous. Her thin dress wrapped around every curve of her body, especially as she pressed herself against her victim. He was a police officer, one who'd had the misfortune to stumble upon them as they sifted through the remains of Jacob Trench's store. It had been laughably easy for Camilla to entice him into a dark alley, though it made Reed jealous to see her teasing another man.

As if sensing his thoughts, the vampire turned to face her companion, a wicked smile on her red lips. "Go on and look for the hidden room, beloved. I'll only feed for a bit, I promise."

Reed swallowed hard, nodding. He turned away and resumed his digging. According to their sources, Jacob Trench's storehouse of curiosities was not truly housed in plain view at all – the real treasures lay beneath the ground, locked away in a hidden vault. Despite his jealousy, Reed felt a sense of keen excitement building within him. Even before meeting Camilla, he'd delighted in the unusual or

strange. Those things lifted him up from the drudgery of his life, transformed him into the owner of something powerful and pure.

A small wooden door set into the floor suddenly caught his gaze and Reed grinned delightedly. He started to yell for Camilla but he heard her lustful moans, intermingled with those of her victim, and refrained from doing so. Instead, he poured his jealousy into strength, gripping the steel ringlet that was set into the door. Reed was surprised by the barrier's weight and he grunted with effort. He felt sweat beading up on his back, dripping down his spine. A pounding in his head made the world sway before him and a whispering voice seemed to fill his ears, speaking in a tongue that predated humanity. It spoke of dark, loathsome things that made Reed shiver from fear… he tried not to listen, for the speech promised nothing but madness, but he was unable to tear his focus from the words. He felt himself sinking into a deep, dark pit of nothingness….

"Wake up."

Reed blinked several times, the feeling of Camilla's hands on his arms pulling him back to reality. "What happened to me?" he asked, only able to stand upright because of Camilla's help.

"You opened the door… and then I felt… something." Camilla's dark eyes bore into Reed's.

Reed nodded suddenly, vitality returning. "Yes! It wasn't just in my head, was it? It was real… You heard them!"

"No, my love. But I have met others who have heard such things… and I have seen the same look in their eyes. What you heard were the children of the Old Ones. They lurk in places of dark power." Camilla turned away from him, her pink tongue darting out to lick at a remainder of blood lurking in the corner of her mouth. Reed couldn't help looking back at the man she'd fed upon: he lay on his back, looking like a tossed-aside rag doll. "It's dark below," she continued, seizing his attention once more. "You brought your lamp?"

Reed moved away a few steps, grabbing hold of an oil lamp that he lit with shaking hands. The night air was ominously still and he felt a peculiar itching at the base of his skull. "Let me go first, Camilla."

"You're a sweet man, my love… but I should lead the way." The vampire peered down into the gloom, her undead eyes able to make out what lay below. The lamp was for Reed, who was a good servant and whom she did not want to lose. This century was still strange to her and she needed his guidance.

Together, they descended a small set of stairs, emerging into a circular subterranean cellar. Bizarre items lay carefully arranged on bookshelves and on tabletops but it was the scent of death that most caught Reed's attention. He had scarcely noticed it before, as he had been so enraptured by the strange voices in his head, but here it was almost overpowering. He gagged at the sight of a rotting figure with sewn-together eyes, lying nude in the middle of a pentagram.

"Mr. Trench played with zombies, I see," Camilla commented. She wrinkled her nose and moved past the corpse, dismissing it as something beneath her. "Here," she said, nodding towards a box covered with a peculiar kind of leather. Reed wondered if it was human flesh but didn't dwell upon it.

Setting the lamp on the floor, Reed knelt in front of the box and carefully lifted its lid. He expected to see a heavy leather-bound book, closed by a large metal clasp. It was a tome written long, long ago by an Arab mystic that many thought mad. But it was not a natural madness he possessed, for he had been in contact with the Old Ones themselves, ancient entities from the stars who roosted in the dark nether-places of the Earth.

But there was no book to be seen.

Camilla emitted a small cry of rage. "Where is it? You told me he had a copy of the cursed book!"

"I… that's what I was told," Reed stammered. "I don't understand."

Camilla shoved him aside, knocking him onto his rump. She leaned over the box, sniffing noisily, like a dog. The way her neck twitched to and fro made Reed uneasy. "We aren't the first ones to come here, beloved." She turned to face Reed, eyes blazing. "The book was stolen by another… but I have their scent."

"What are we going to do?" Reed asked, rising to his feet and brushing dirt off the back of his slacks.

"Find them, of course." Camilla laughed coldly. "Then I'll rip their throats out and take the Necronomicon for myself."

Chapter V
A Figure of Ice and Steel

The plantation that was now home to Max Davies and his wife was built in the 1820s and still retained much of its luster from the days when cotton was king. A burly farm hand named Joshua and a matronly woman named Nettie ran the place, keeping everything running smoothly during Max's many trips away. Both of them met Max when he drove his car up to the main house.

"Miss Evelyn's not with you?" Nettie asked with concern. An elderly black woman with skin so taut that you could see the bones poking against the flesh in places, Nettie was a devout Christian and a perpetual worrier. "You and she didn't have a fight did you?"

Josh exchanged an amused look with his employer as he began to get the bags out of the car.

Max shook his head. "I dropped her off in town to meet with a producer."

"Not proper for a married woman to be dining alone with another man," Nettie sniffed reproachfully.

"Who said they were dining together? It's a business meeting." Max kissed Nettie on the cheek, who accepted it with a harrumph. "It's good to be back."

"Mr. Davies," Josh said, stopping Max as he started for the front door. "A man's inside. In the study. Says he's a friend of Mr. Grace, from New York City."

Max frowned slightly. Leopold Grace was one of his dearest friends and the current president of the Nova Alliance, an adventurer's guild of sorts. "Did he give a name?"

"Yes, suh. Says his name is Benson."

Max nodded, moving inside. He'd heard that name before, though he wasn't quite sure where. Perhaps Leopold had mentioned him at one of the Nova Alliance meetings? He moved to the study, removing his hat and overcoat as he did.

The man who waited for him was like no man that he'd ever seen before. Not particularly tall or wide, but possessed of a rugged strength that spoke of many physical pursuits. But it was his face that seemed so striking. It was as white and dead as a mask from the grave. Pale gray eyes flicked over Max, moving up and down, as if sizing him up from within.

Benson rose as Max entered, nodding curtly. When he spoke, his voice was clipped and businesslike. Overall, he had the manner of one who simply lacked the time for niceties. "I've come with an offer," he stated.

Max shut the door behind him. He trusted both Josh and Nettie with his life, but neither of them knew about his business as the Rook. "Something related to the Alliance?"

"You might say that. It's come to my attention that your nocturnal pursuits have made you an enemy of the law."

Max didn't bother pretending ignorance about Benson's meaning. Obviously, he knew about the Rook and there was nothing to be done about that. "They see me as a vigilante."

"As well they should," Benson answered. "But you and I both know that there are men in this world whom the law can't touch. And they must be stopped before more innocents are harmed."

Something suddenly clicked in Max's memory and he pointed at Benson. "I recognize you now, even with the change in your features! It was in all the newspapers! Your wife and daughter went missing on a plane flight and…."

"They were the victims of a criminal conspiracy. Those responsible are dead."

"So you're like me. A vigilante."

"Not quite. I choose not to kill… my enemies usually die by their own hands, not mine. This has allowed me to function quite well with law enforcement authorities. In fact, I've created an entire team of like-minded individuals who are willing to assist me."

"I'm not looking to join," Max said, finally taking a seat. When he did so, Benson returned to his own chair. "If that's what you're here for."

"It's not. Leopold Grace asked me to give you assistance in resolving your problems with law enforcement."

"You can do that?"

"I already have. All ongoing investigations into the Rook have ceased."

"How….?"

"It's not important." Benson leaned forward and his steely eyes glinted. "If you'll agree to change your tactics somewhat, I'll provide you with continued protection from the authorities."

"You don't want me to kill the men and women I pursue." Max pursed his lips. "It's not that simple. I have… compulsions."

"Are you saying you're insane?"

"No!" Max ran a hand through his hair. "It's complicated."

"I'm sure. Regardless, all I'm asking you to do is make an effort to take your enemies alive. If things don't work out that way, I'll understand. But we must hold ourselves to a higher standard than the criminals do."

"Very noble," Max countered. "But I'm not always facing mobsters. I'm dealing with cannibals, wizards and the walking undead."

Benson nodded, a smile briefly flashing in his eyes. His face, however, remained rigid and unmoving. "And I wouldn't argue that the undead shouldn't be stopped by any means necessary. I'm speaking about flesh and blood beings, not the supernatural." He stood up, producing a small card that he held out for Max. "Call me if you need assistance with the police."

Max said nothing as Benson left the room, abruptly ending the conversation. He stared down at the card, which bore an address in New York City: Bleek Street. "Leopold… what have you gotten me into now?"

Chapter VI
The Rook Takes Flight

Since the strange visit by Benson, the Rook had focused his attention on learning as much as possible about Reed Barrows and his wife. Mr. Barrows had married a woman of means early in his life, but she had perished under mysterious circumstances not long ago. Within a shockingly short period of time, he had moved on, marrying a pale young woman named Camilla. Of her, there was no trace whatsoever. Given what Max knew about her nature, that wasn't surprising, he supposed. Barrows, who had always lurked in the black market for antiquities, had recently gone into overdrive. Most of his inquiries had to do with the frightful book known as the Necronomicon.

The Rook parked his specially made car along the side of the dirt road that led to the old Matthews Plantation. The car was painted with a unique paint that absorbed light to an astonishing degree. In the black of night, it was virtually invisible. The windshield was covered with a thin layer of "night glass," yet another of Max's inventions. It allowed the driver to see in complete darkness, rendering the use of headlights obsolete. And the engine had been modified to that it was as silent as a fox. All of those creations could have afforded Max many millions of dollars, but he kept them to himself, preferring to utilize them in his war on crime.

The Matthews place was, along with Max's current home, amongst the only major plantations to escape Sherman's march relatively intact. There had been only minor damage done to the place and the intervening years had been kind, giving both homes a melancholy appeal.

As Max crept up to one of the well-lit windows, he took note of the fact that the fields were lying bare. Apparently, the Barrows were still living off their sizable personal incomes rather than using the grounds as a subsidy to their accounts.

With gun in hand, the Rook peered in through the window. He wore his customary garb – long trenchcoat, domino style mask with a small birdlike "beak" and low-brimmed hat. Inside the room he saw Reed Barrows, pacing about like an expectant father. There was no sign of Camilla, but Barrows was talking to himself, rubbing the palms of his hands together anxiously.

Max reached into his coat and retrieved a small listening device, which he pressed against the glass. A small wire led from the device to an earpiece, which he put into place. Immediately, Barrows sounded as clear as if Max were in the same room with him:

"It's dangerous. Too dangerous. We shouldn't… we should let it go. Just let it go."

When the words only continued to repeat for close to a minute, the Rook removed the listening device and moved on. Something was obviously agitating Barrows, but there didn't appear to be any clue to be found from the man himself – and Max wasn't yet ready to break in and begin questioning him. Not without making sure that Camilla wasn't about….

He suddenly wished that Evelyn had been able to come with him, but at the same time he was glad she wasn't. He feared for her safety on nights like this, but she also had a way of making his mission seem not nearly so lonely.

Around the back of the house, he found an open storm cellar. The door lay thrown back and Max heard hushed voices down below. He crouched, catching bits and pieces of a conversation between a man and a woman.

"Aye, I know who has the book. He's had folks translatin' it for 'im into other tongues. Plans to spread it the 'ole world wide. When he has enough people to help 'im, he's going to raise the sunken city."

"I don't care what his plans are. I want the book for myself," the woman replied. Her accent was European in origin and she sounded quite lovely. *Camilla,* he realized. A part of him wanted to rush in with guns blazing, but from the sound of things, Camilla had failed in her attempt to get the Necronomicon. If it was in the possession of another, Max wanted to know who it was.

"It won't be cheap," the man replied with a laugh.

"Money is no object, Guthrie," she answered. "Kill him, destroy all the copies he has made and bring me the original."

There was a sound of paper exchanging hands before Guthrie spoke again. "We'll do as you say. But there'll be a bonus for every man we lose. Our kind are slow to develop and I can't afford to lose even one." He cleared his throat. "Truth be told, I'm a bit surprised you'd even want our help. You types usually look down on the hard workin' sorts like me."

"I have only recently risen. I have not yet returned to the peak of my power… eventually men like Klempt will pose no threat to me."

"But until then, you want me and my kind to die for you. Real kindly of you." The man began to walk up and out of the storm cellar. The Rook pressed himself flat against the side of the house, staying out of sight. Guthrie was emaciated-looking, dressed in a green turtleneck sweater with black coat and pants. He wore a small derby atop his head and a growth of red hair peeked out from beneath. A spray of freckles covered a mean face. "I'll be in touch," he shouted behind him.

The Rook waited for him to get a small distance away and then began following him. In a small grouping of trees about a mile down the way, a car waited with two other men within. Each of them looked just as dangerous.

"Did she pay you?" one of them asked the approaching Guthrie.

"Aye. And she's a pretty one," he answered. "Wouldn't mind playin' a bit with her when the work is done."

"Like she'd let your muzzle come anywhere near her body," the other man retorted.

The Rook had heard enough. He sprang from the darkness, landing atop a started Guthrie. A stout blow to the back of Guthrie's head sent him toppling over, while the Rook drew his revolver and pointed it at the others. "Stay where you are. Hands up."

The men glanced at one another before responding. Slowly, they raised their hands, though Max wondered at the amusement he saw in their faces. "Sure, mister… no need for gunplay," the third man said.

"I have questions that need answering," the Rook continued. "This man… Klempt… where is he?"

"He's gonna be in hell soon enough. Why don't you go on ahead and wait for 'im?" Guthrie laughed from below.

The Rook glanced down and gasped. Before his startled gaze, Guthrie's body began to change. Hair sprouted from every pore and his face began to distend with a horrible popping sound. The clothes he wore ripped and tore, leaving him naked and covered in fur. His ears lengthened and came to tapered points.

A werewolf!

The Rook whirled about, confirming his worst fears. The men in the car were moving out now, also shifting into horrible half-man/half-wolf monstrosities.

Guthrie rose to his full height, snapping at the air with razor-sharp teeth. Saliva dripped from his maw as he turned yellow eyes on the Rook. "Questions, you say? Ask away, masked man… and perhaps I'll answer them before we feast on your belly!"

The Rook refused to take the bait. The creatures before him were only toying with him, hoping to distract him while they spread out and flanked him on three sides. He pointed his pistol at one, using his free hand to draw forth a golden dagger… it was a trophy from a previous case involving a mad geneticist named Felix Darkholme. The dagger was possessed of unknown properties, but it had proved essential in his victories over Christian Rosenkreuz and Jacob Trench.

Guthrie hung back as his men lunged forward. Max blew the head off one of them, startling the two remaining werewolves. The Rook's guns rarely ran out of ammunition and were capable of piercing the strongest armored tanks in the world.

Before the second attacking werewolf could react, the Rook threw the dagger with unerring accuracy. It bit deep into the beast's throat, sending a spray of blood into the air. The creature fell to the ground, writing in agony. He attempted to pluck the dagger out but he howled in pain whenever he tried to touch it.

The Rook felt something slam into him and he fell to the ground with Guthrie atop him, snapping and biting. Max threw his hands up, locking them around Guthrie's throat. He barely held the werewolf in check, keeping his mouth from locking down around his own face.

"Those were my brothers, ya damned murderer!" the werewolf howled, spraying spittle with every word.

The Rook grunted, feeling the thick muscles beneath the monster's flesh. He wouldn't be able to hold him off for long....

Max forced himself to calm as much as possible. When he'd fought Trench's demon in Germany, he'd learned to make contact with minds around him. It wasn't something he was very well practiced at, but he tried it now. At first there was nothing, not even a trace of Guthrie's consciousness. But then, feral and wild, it emerged into the Rook's mental vision.

The Rook had no time for anything fancy, so he projected a single thought with all his might.

Guthrie backed away, looking around in confusion. He'd been positive that his brother Luscious – the first to be killed this night – had called his name in desperate need. But there lay the corpse of his brother....

In that moment of distraction, Guthrie fell prey to the Rook. Max jumped from his back, smacking the werewolf on the back of the head with the butt of his pistol. He did it repeatedly, until his weapon was bloodied and Guthrie had fallen to the ground, silent forevermore.

Panting, the Rook fell to his knees, heart hammering. After a moment, he noticed that the three men had begun to revert to their human forms, leaving behind no trace of their lycanthrope natures. The Rook staggered over to the remains of Guthrie's clothing, rummaging through until he came upon a white slip of paper with a name and address written on it.

Gerhard Klempt was in Milledgeville, Georgia.

Chapter VII
The Mad Doctor

"Milledgeville? Where is *that*?"

"You're showing your Yankee upbringing again, Evelyn." Max sat in the basement beneath his house, surrounded by the weapons and inventions that aided him as the Rook. He was clad only in slacks, having removed his shirt so that Evelyn could doctor a few bruises and scratches he'd received. Luckily, none of them seemed likely to carry the werewolf plague. "Milledgeville," he continued, using that lecturing tone that so annoyed his wife, "is the former capital of Georgia. It wasn't moved to Atlanta until after the War Between the States. It's a quaint little town, renowned these days because of the insane asylum located there."

"Sounds simply divine," Evelyn murmured. She was in her bedclothes, having rushed downstairs when she'd heard her husband returning from his scouting mission. "And why are you going there again?"

"Because a man named Klempt has a dark book that Camilla covets. He's making copies of it… everything I've read about this text says that it bears evil imprinted into every single word. Even viewing it drives some people mad. If it were readily available to hundreds or thousands… I can't imagine the horrors we'd face."

"And do you know where we'd find this Klempt person?" she asked, putting away the rest of the spare bandages.

"So you are going with me, then?"

"I don't like you leaving without me," Evelyn commented.

"I thought you had that script to *Perils of Gwendolyn II: The Lost City* to read over."

"It can wait. And you're avoiding my question about Klempt."

Max sighed, though he was smiling as he did so. He was hoping she'd come with him. "He's a doctor. A psychiatrist."

Evelyn turned to stare at him, hands on hips. "He's not."

"What?"

"He works at that asylum, doesn't he?"

"Yes."

"It gets worse all the time," she said with a shake of her head.

"He specializes in electro-shock therapy as a means to combat mental illness."

"Sounds to me like he's the mad one," she whispered. "Or maybe it's us for going after him."

Max moved behind her, kissing the back of her neck. "Just think of all the history to be found there. The city's a mix of the old south and the new… with the old greatly outweighing the new. It'll be like stepping back in time!"

"They probably have a five and dime as the center of town life," she responded, though she was beginning to warm to the idea. "I'll go pack."

"Can't we relax a bit first?" he teased, pulling her against him.

With a laugh, she turned to kiss him. "Forget the werewolves, Max. *You're* the ravenous beast!"

"**P**lease restrain the patient," Gerhard Klempt said. He was tall and handsome, with more than a passing resemblance to Errol Flynn. But there was none of the goodhearted kindness that the great actor displayed to be found in Klempt. His was a face not meant for smiling, for it was deeply etched into an expression of serious disapproval. His eyes were like cold fortresses, refusing to reveal anything of the soul within.

The orderlies held the thrashing woman down on the table, showing no mercy as they strapped her into place. She was in her thirties and suffering from a number of mental ailments, most of which were the result of the things Klempt had done to her over the past few months. Having a hospital full of the deranged gave him great freedom to include them in his personal experiments. If they went mad or managed to tell their tales of horror to someone, they were dismissed readily enough. They *were* in an asylum, after all.

"That will be all," Klempt said. "Leave us."

The orderlies stepped out, having grown familiar with the fact that the German doctor liked to work alone. There were many stories about his unusual techniques but no one inquired more than was necessary. Some things it was simply best not to know.

Klempt put on a pair of rubber gloves before smoothing down the crisp white medical gown he wore. He moved to stand next to the woman, whose eyes were wide with fright. "Miss Thomas, please. Calm down." He patted her leg, slowly letting his fingers trace upwards until he reached her inner thigh. "It will all be over in just a few moments. And then you can return to your room and take your medication."

Tears formed at the corners of her eyes. She wailed against the cloth that muffled her cries.

Klempt pushed her gown up, revealing her female parts. She wore nothing beneath the gown, which wasn't unusual. Many of the patients soiled themselves so frequently that Klempt had begun dispensing with undergarments as an unnecessary expense. A small amount of dried blood showed around the entrance to her vagina. "Have you been keeping our little friends warm and healthy?" he asked, eliciting more cries from her. "Nurse Whitley tells me you tried to stab yourself down here. Said you seemed to want to tear out your own womb. We simply can't have that." He smiled coldly at her. "Not yet anyway. When the deed is done, your womb will be worthless enough that you can do with it whatever you please… but for now… no."

Without the use of lubrication, he began working his fingers into her. She screamed, which only made him work all the harder. He felt about inside her until he felt one of his prizes, grown fat and slippery. He tugged on it and it dug into her inner flesh, tearing at it in a futile attempt to remain nestled in its hiding place. Klempt yanked hard until it came free.

A yellowish-red worm about three inches long and so fat it looked fit to burst was revealed. Klempt held it up to the light, marveling at its segmented body and the sharp sucker at its head, with its rows upon rows of sharp needlelike teeth. "Oh they're coming along just fine, Miss Thomas. All our little babies are growing up, right on schedule. In another or week or two your stomach will begin to bloat a bit… at that point, questions will be asked. I'll examine you and say that you must have been a bit loose with the guards or another patient. Given that you're not fit to be a mother, I'll deal with the pregnancy in the usual fashion… though you and I will know that's not quite true. Nothing about this is usual, is it?" For the first time, he laughed. It made his patient close her eyes and pray for death. Inside, she felt things wiggling about madly, hoping to avoid whatever had happened to its sibling. She sometimes thought she could hear them, singing to each other in some buzzing tongue, making her belly vibrate.

Klempt caressed her face with his bloodied glove, making her look at him. "This one can't go back in. It's a shame to sacrifice one just to check on their progress. It will die… it's not strong enough to survive for long like this, not in its immature form. But I won't deny you at least one mother-child moment."

The woman began to scream as she saw Klempt begin to attach the worm to one of her nipples. It chewed in hungrily, suckling and swelling before her eyes.

Klempt turned away, ignoring her sounds, which were almost matched by the wet sucking sounds of the worm. He opened up a small satchel, gazing down at the leather-bound book that had been coveted by so many. He had some of the other patients, the brighter ones – for now – working on translating it into other languages. They worked until their fingers bled and their eyes bulged, or their brains began to slowly turn inwards from the sheer force of the knowledge being given them.

Klempt raised the book to his face, inhaling its scent. So much blood. So much death. All locked away in these pages.

When the Old Ones returned, they would reward him.

Chapter VIII
A Gathering of Shadows

Reed Barrows wiped the sweat from his brow, panting from exertion. "They're buried, Camilla."

The vampire watched him without comment for a long time. She hated being out in the daylight, but with great effort she could abide the sun's rays for a time. There were many falsehoods about her kind, most of which had been spread by the vampires themselves. That afforded them some protection from the occasional vampire hunter, who would come in armed with knowledge that was faulty at best and ridiculous at worst.

Camilla stood under shade of a tall tree, beside which the werewolves' car remained. She held an umbrella over her head, further shielding her from the sun. "Who did this, beloved? Who knows of our plans?"

Reed shrugged. He was exhausted and his hands bore blisters from the shoveling he'd done. Hiding bodies was a new experience to him and not one he cared to repeat. But he knew that he'd probably grow used to the task… being caretaker to a vampire virtually required that he occasionally assist in the hiding of her victims. "I'm not sure. I've heard rumors about a vigilante in the area. Calls himself the Rook. They say he killed both Trench and Felix Darkholme." Reed noticed a small piece of paper on the ground and plucked it up. It was a calling card of some kind – a white background upon which rested the silhouette of a bird.

"Why would he involve himself in our affairs?"

Reed struggled to find an answer. "Maybe he collects mystical artifacts, just like I do. He killed Darkholme and stole something from him. Maybe he did the same to Trench."

"The werewolves didn't have anything for him to collect," she pointed out.

"Ah, but they did." Reed stuck the point of the shovel back in the earth and leaned his weight against it. "They had a name and an address on them."

That made Camilla's eyes flash with anger. Her bosom rose and fell in a mockery of human breathing. "The Necronomicon. This Rook wants it, too."

"That's my guess. If he were interested in you or I, he would have struck at us. He had the opportunity to do so. But he didn't."

Camilla moved towards him, the umbrella casting her features in shadow. She smiled at him, the redness of her lips standing out in stark contrast to the pale white alabaster of her skin. "You are such a clever man, my love. Destiny truly rewarded me the day you came to awaken me."

Reed puffed up in response to the compliment. "So now we just have to decide what to do about it."

"I would have thought that would have been obvious," Camilla responded, reaching out to caress his face while she spoke.

"What do you mean?"

"We have to stop him ourselves. We go to Milledgeville and we kill this Rook. Then we tell Dr. Klempt that he either gives us the book or he dies, as well."

Reed swallowed. "Klempt's dangerous. You might be hurt." He clasped her hand in his own. "Let me go by myself."

"I would never let you do that," she responded. "We do this together, you and I."

"When you've used that spell from the book," he whispered, his voice quavering just a little. "Will you still need me? Or will one of those other vampires become your lover?"

Camilla parted her lips, revealing her sharp teeth and the pink of her tongue, which darted along the tips of her canines. She was all too familiar with her mate's concerns, for he knew of the stories… the stories of one who lorded over all vampires, appearing as a man of unspeakable, hideous beauty. Reed feared this figure, for he was sure that Camilla desired this Lord of Vampires. "When the Kingdom of Blood has risen… you will live as my King."

Reed groaned as she leaned in, sinking her teeth into the flesh of his neck. The pain faded quickly, replaced by a pleasure so intense that he dropped the shovel from his grip and clung to her. She could have finished him if she'd wanted, drained him dry… and he would never have resisted. But she always pulled away, avoiding taking too much, avoiding taking the steps necessary to make him one of her own, one of the undead.

"I love you," he said, holding her close. "Forever."

Chapter IX
A Place of Old Glories

"**Y**ou have to admit, it's a beautiful theatre."

Evelyn pursed her lips before speaking. She and her husband were standing outside the Campus Theatre, a wonderful bit of culture that had been opened to the citizens of Milledgeville in 1935. So far, her impressions of the former state capital had been uniformly negative, from the poor state of the roads to the dingy houses they'd passed on the way into town. But the Campus… that changed her mind a bit. "It is nice, Max. I wonder if we'll have time to see the interior."

"Hopefully, we'll be finished with our work here quickly and can enjoy the sights. The Governor's Mansion is just down the road from here."

Evelyn nodded, refraining from saying anything that would ruin her husband's enthusiasm. He was an explorer by nature, enjoying nothing so much as finding a new place to wander around in. She shared his appreciation for that, but their tastes in what could be defined as interesting varied wildly. "There's a man walking towards us," she whispered. She put on her most dazzling smile as an officious-looking man in a dark suit stopped just short of them. He was sweating profusely, which didn't surprise her – Milledgeville, like Atlanta, was a hellish place to be in the summer.

"Hello," the stranger said, his voice dripping with southern charm. "I recognize you, Miss Gould. I've watched a number of your films."

Evelyn blushed on cue, as she always did when she met a fan. "Why, thank you. And you are–?"

"John Oden, Miss Gould." John took her offered hand and squeezed it warmly. "It's a real pleasure."

"You're the superintendent of the Milledgeville State Hospital, aren't you?" Max inquired, interrupting the spectacle before Evelyn could get around to asking John what his favorite film of hers was. "Pleasure to meet you."

"I was surprised when you called me," Oden admitted, "but not displeased in the least. It's not often I hear from two such important people."

"You're too gracious," Max responded. He'd picked up on Evelyn's curious glance. She was slightly annoyed that he hadn't told about phoning Dr. Oden. He knew it was wrong of him, but he still enjoyed having the upper hand over her on occasion. "Could we buy you lunch?"

"I've never turned down an offer like that, Mr. Davies." Oden's eyes twinkled as he looked at Evelyn again. "*The Perils of Gwendolyn* is my favorite."

"That was one of my most understated roles, I think." Evelyn turned on the charm, keeping Oden laughing and smiling all the way to the corner café. Max could smell the cheese grits before they'd ever entered the door and it made his stomach rumble.

Oden was apparently well-acquainted with the owners of the establishment for they greeted him by name and escorted him to a table set next to an open window, allowing him the luxury of a soft breeze every now and again. "So, Mr. Davies, you told me you have questions about one of my doctors?"

Max nodded, casting a quick glance at the menu before responding. He ordered for himself and Evelyn, feeling a twinge of amusement when Oden ordered the most expensive dish that was offered for himself. "Dr. Klempt. How long has he worked at the Hospital?"

Oden's face paled noticeably and he leaned across the table to whisper, "Is he in some sort of trouble with the law?"

Max stared into the other man's eyes. "That wouldn't surprise you in the least, would it?"

"He's an odd one," Oden admitted. "And he and I don't see eye to eye on a great many things. But he has connections… when I attempted to reprimand him several weeks ago, I received a number of threats to my office until I finally relented."

"What was he being reprimanded for?" Evelyn asked.

"Some of his work… is eccentric." Oden pursed his lips. "To be honest, I don't like him. Not a bit."

"What is his specialty?" Max pressed.

"He works with our most severe cases, using shock treatment and other radical therapies to restore a sense of equilibrium in their brains."

"I'm not sure that electric shocks would restore much of anything," Evelyn whispered disapprovingly.

"I would tend to agree with you," Oden replied, "but there are many who profess to have seen its beneficial effects."

"Does Dr. Klempt live on the grounds of the hospital?"

"Of course. Almost all our doctors do." Oden swallowed hard. "At first, I was disinclined to meet with you on this matter, Mr. Davies. But the number you gave me to verify your intentions… well, the man on the other end of the phone was most persuasive."

Max didn't reply to that, though he was gratified to hear it. He'd made the decision to test Benson's claims, offering up the man's number to Oden. Now that he knew that Benson did have sway over people in power, he felt much better about the fact that Benson knew his identity.

"The next few days might seem a bit odd to you, Mr. Oden. You might hear some unusual rumors… but it's essential that you not let Klempt know that he's being observed. Do you understand?"

Oden laughed. "If this means that Klempt might end up leaving the staff, I'll turn a blind eye to almost anything."

You might just have to do that, Max thought to himself.

Chapter X
The Devil's Library

The retarded and the insane worked side-by-side. Klempt stood in the corner of the room, watching them as he sipped an ice-cold glass of tea. He'd hated iced tea when he'd first come to the South, but it had grown on him over time. It was almost impossible to avoid having to drink the stuff, really, so it was all just as well.

Some of the patients moaned while they worked, their heads aching. One of them, an Asian, had begun bleeding from his ears. It spilled down his cheeks, dripping to the workbench that he was hunched over. Klempt didn't mind, as long as the blood didn't stain the pages he was working on. Each of them had several pages of the Necronimicon and were busy translating it into languages they were familiar with. Those who spoke only English were merely making more copies of the text in that language.

Klempt set down his glass and moved amongst the patients, examining their work. Here and there, he saw meaningless scribbles alongside the text, but he said nothing in disapproval. The rantings of the mad might actually give the pages added power – and that was crucial to what he had planned. The eventual return of the ancient entities who had ruled this world when man was young would be made easier if chaos and madness became prevalent, for such things weakened the barriers that had trapped the Old Ones in bondage.

A knock at the door made Klempt pause in his examinations. As far as he knew, there should have been no one else in this building at this hour. At seven o'clock each evening, he sent the orderlies to other buildings so that he could engage his patients in 'group therapy.' Striding towards the door with an imperious air, Klempt made a mental promise to wreak his revenge on whoever had disturbed his work.

He was thrown for another loop when the face he saw peering through the crack he made in the door was John Oden. "Superintendent… this is quite a surprise." He forced a smile on his face, well aware that under no circumstances could his employer be allowed into this room… if Oden pressed the issue, Klempt would simply have to kill him and blame the act on one of the patients. "What can I do for you?"

"I was hoping you might come down to my office for a few minutes, Gerhard."
Oden tapped a small notebook he held in his hand. "A few special cases are being
brought in – the types you usually do so well with."

"I'm in the middle of an important session," Klempt replied, trying to keep his
tone neutral. Oden was a nuisance, but it wouldn't do to tip his hand too early.
"Could you leave the reports with me and I could discuss them with you in the
morning?"

"Afraid not. These patients come from very wealthy patients and will arrive
before noon tomorrow. We simply must have plans in place."

Klempt sighed, seeing that there was no way out of this at the moment... not
unless he wanted to do in the superintendent once and for all. "May I have a few
minutes to get the patients back to their rooms? Then I'll join you."

"Do you need assistance? I could help and there's always the orderlies...."

"No!" Klempt snapped. Recovering, he lowered his tones and continued, "I can
manage on my own. My patients must see me as their primary caregiver if the
treatments are to take hold."

Oden backed away. "Very well. But be quick about it."

Klempt shut the door and unleashed a small string of curses. He stormed
through the patients, gathering up their materials before lining them up to return
to their rooms. Each of them was given a small wafer to eat, laced with a powerful
drug whose origins in Africa was unknown to most Western scientists. It made
their recollections of the night's events so blurry as to seem indistinguishable from
dreams. If they did decide to tell anyone, their rantings would appear appropriately
confused and insubstantial. He'd avoided giving any of the drug to Miss Thomas,
however, as the substance might harm the delicate life forms growing within her.

After Klempt had placed the pages in several drawers and led the patients
out of the room, silence descended upon the building. Small rays of moonlight
illuminated the place, but it was just enough to give it an eerie air.

A small scraping sound grew louder and then one of the windows suddenly
popped out of the frame, drawn back by feminine hands. A moment later, Evelyn
was squeezing through the opening, followed by her husband. Like the Rook,
Evelyn wore a dark bodysuit that absorbed the light around her. Her auburn-
colored hair was wore up in a tight bun, hidden beneath a wide-brimmed hat. A
small domino mask and gloves completed the attire, making her appear no more
substantial than a wraith. "It smells," she whispered.

"Some of these poor souls can't control their bodily functions," the Rook
replied. He and Evelyn had been crouched outside the window for nearly twenty
minutes and he now moved directly towards the hidden pages. He pulled them
out, holding them gingerly, as if he was afraid they would burn him. Indeed, they
pulsed with a power that made him feel faint. "This isn't the entire book. Only
select pages. He must only bring a few sections at a time in here."

"If we take these, is it enough to make the rest of the book worthless?"

"Hardly. Every one of these has enough power to cause harm, even if it's as
little as driving a single person mad." The Rook carefully folded them in half, not
fearing that he would damage the ancient manuscript. These pages had survived

fires, water damage and numerous attempts to destroy them. "We need to go to his house."

"That's what I said," Evelyn pointed out, keeping her voice low. "I said we should split up so one of us could come here and the other would check out his home."

"Too dangerous," the Rook answered. "We shouldn't split up on something like this. You don't have enough experience." Max touched his temples, massaging them. A pressure was building behind his eyes....

"Oh. So that's what this comes down to, is it? You think the poor little actress is safe enough with you, but not on her own?"

"Evelyn, please." The Rook pushed past her, scanning the room. "I think he left behind a watch dog."

"Where?" she asked, glancing about. "I haven't seen or heard anything."

"There," the Rook replied, drawing forth his mystic dagger. His guns were specially made and rarely ran out of bullets, but against foes like this one, it was best to fight back with enchanted weapons.

Evelyn followed his gaze, holding back a small gasp when she spotted the source of Max's concern. Huddled against the wall was something that resembled a large, oversized maggot. At one end a hungry maw gaped open, dripping saliva onto the floor. It was about the same size as a small housecat and was moving towards them with surprising speed, leaving behind a trail of slime. "What in the name of God?" Evelyn whispered.

"That has nothing to do with God, Evelyn. At least not one with which we're acquainted." The Rook moved forward, keeping himself in a crouch. He swung the blade in the moonlight, letting the rays play across the blade's length. The worm seemed to sense its power but its unnatural hunger propelled it forward despite the danger.

The worm struck first, clenching up its body and then springing up towards the Rook's body. Max caught it in one hand, feeling the soft rubbery flesh give a bit beneath his fingers. The head twisted this way and that, seeking some flesh upon which to purchase. Max felt a sense of relief that this was obviously an immature version of the creature. He drove his dagger into the thing's side, twisting cruelly. The worm howled in pain, disturbing anyone who might have heard its death cries.

The Rook tossed the carcass aside as it suddenly began to smoke and then flame. "Klempt might be heading home as soon as his meeting is over, Evelyn. We have to make haste."

Evelyn stared at the smoking worm for a moment, revulsion filling her soul. When she finally found her voice, all trace of her earlier anger had been burned away. "Yes, dear."

Chapter XI
The House on the Hill

Reed stifled a shiver, reaching inside his dark coat to retrieve a silver flask. He unscrewed the lid with shaking fingertips and hurriedly took a hit of the burning liquid, scowling as it sizzled its way down his gullet. He was not normally prone to drinking, but in recent months he had found himself turning to the spirits more and more often. It seemed that something inside of him was dying a little more each day, even as his affection for Camilla turned into something bordering on obsession.

Reed crept from his dark-tinted car, moving up the cobblestone pathway leading to the small house belonging to Dr. Klempt. Less than a mile from the main campus of the asylum, the house was a sterling example of the Federal style of architecture, which was common enough in this city. But there was definitely something more sinister about the place, something that made the shadows cling to its walls just a little bit more than was natural.

Reed moved to the front door, having placed the flask in his hip pocket and exchanging it with a small pistol. He rapped on the door, heart hammering in his chest. If the doctor had the misfortune of being home, a swiftly delivered bullet to the head would clear the way for Reed's entry. Though he'd become more comfortable with death over the course of his association with Camilla, he still hoped that he would be able to get in and out of this house without killing anyone.

He relaxed slightly when no one stirred within the home. Camilla was out feeding, having given him strict warnings to wait for her assistance. Reed had disobeyed her, however, fearing for her safety. It was sure to bring about her wrath later on, but he would rather face that than have this Klempt harm her. If half the stories he'd heard about Klempt were true....

Reed knelt before the door, hurriedly working to pick the lock. He'd made good progress when the hairs on the back of his neck began to rise. Looking over his shoulder, he saw that a shadowy figure was emerging from the nearby woods. Fearful of being seen, Reed moved to the side of the house, peering out from behind a set of bushes. The figure wore a dark suit that seemed to absorb the moonlight, devouring it like a ravenous beast. A small bird-like mask hid his features and sent another surge of concern through Reed's spine. "The Rook," he whispered.

The nocturnal avenger paused in mid-step and for a moment Reed worried that he had been overheard. But then the Rook resumed his silent march, stopping only to attach a small device on the front door's lock. Reed heard the tumblers slipping into place and a moment later, the door opened with a small creak.

Reed glanced around, making sure that no one was traveling with the vigilante. Satisfied that they were alone, he made to follow the Rook, his pistol held at the ready.

He never made it very far. Just a few steps into the foyer, he was suddenly wrapped up tightly in a viselike grip. The Rook's words hissed in his ear. "Mr. Barrows. This is a surprise."

Reed moaned aloud as the pressure on his neck increased. He dropped his pistol the floor, trying in vain to catch a glimpse of his attacker. The foyer was wide and led to a set of stairs and two doors, one on the right and one to the left.

"You're not going anywhere, Mr. Barrows. So don't waste your time looking for escape routes." The Rook pulled Reed roughly to the room on the right, which was a small den lined by bookcases. A fireplace, cold and unlit, dominated the far corner. "Where is she?"

"I don't know what you're talking about," Reed answered. "Let me go... please!"

"Don't lie to me. I know that you've been helping her. I know why she wants the book. What *is* the Kingdom of Blood, Mr. Barrows? Do you even know?"

Reed began to twist and fight, though he made no headway against the much stronger man. Finally, he sagged limply in the man's embrace, knowing that he had failed his beloved. "There's a spell," he said between great gasps of air. "It will awaken all the slumbering dead... the ones she calls The Noble Dead."

"What are they?"

"Vampires, like her. But there are different types... Nosferatu are basically nothing more than animals, feeding indiscriminately. The Noble Dead are beautiful and powerful, lording over humanity throughout the ages. When they're all awake again, they'll unite the lesser vampires under their control and establish the Kingdom of Blood. It's one of their myths: a form of heaven on Earth."

"Or Hell," the Rook replied. He tossed Reed onto the couch, staring at him with barely veiled disgust. "And you're selling out humanity to help her?"

"You don't understand."

"You're right. I don't." The Rook drew one of his pistols and aimed it directly at Reed's chest. "Do you know where the book is hidden?"

Reed stared at the barrel of the gun, fearful of dying. "No. I was... going to look for it."

A tickle in the back of the Rook's brain made him pause for a moment. He'd felt it when he'd first approached the house, as well: a sense of grave foreboding that made him long for sunlight. "Give me one reason why I shouldn't do the world a favor and end your life right now."

"Because... right now we both want the same thing. We both want the book. Let's look for it together and then we can sort it out afterwards." Reed spoke quickly, the words spilling from his mouth. "Two could search much more quickly than one."

"Not good enough." The Rook pulled the trigger.

Reed fell back, arms flying out from his body. The Rook moved towards him, checking for a pulse. It was there, strong but fast. The shot had gone intentionally awry, missing him by more than a foot and leaving a nasty looking hole in the fabric of the couch. But it had been enough to cause the terrified man to pass out.

Confident that Barrows wasn't going to interfere anytime soon, the Rook began searching the lower floor of the house. He knew that Evelyn was waiting in the car not far away, probably growing more concerned by the minute. Though her fright had allowed him to convince her to stay behind after all, her curious nature meant that she could come after him at any moment.

Spurred on by that thought, he sprang up the stairs and felt another burst of fear rush through him. Something in this house was causing his latent mental powers to send out an alarm. Instead of fighting it this time, he allowed the pulsing in his skull to serve as a tracking device, leading down the long corridor at the top of the stairs. He ignored all rooms save for one – for that was where the sensations seemed to be concentrated.

The door opened easily to his touch, though the doorknob was so cold that he winced from the contact. Once he'd stepped inside, the tickle began a loud buzzing in his brain, making him stumble slightly. It was hard to keep focus and his surroundings seemed to fade in and out of existence. He was in some kind of study and the book of the damned lay open atop a desk. He reached for it, hand shaking as he fought through the pain that made him grit his teeth.

Something powerful slammed into the back of his head and he tumbled forward, striking the side of the desk with his temple. Blood gushed from the wound and the buzzing began to fade, though what was left in its place was just as awful. He looked up into the beautiful features of Camilla, who looked at him with cold fury.

"You harmed my pet," she said simply. She then raised a fist high above her head and brought it crashing down on the Rook's skull.

Chapter XII
Captured!

Klempt had been furious as he strode out of Oden's office. The entire meeting had been a waste of time, with Oden saying nothing of real interest. The whole affair seemed to smell wrong to Klempt, as well, and the negative feelings had only intensified when he'd returned home to find his front door standing wide open. There were signs of a struggle in the den, where a bullet hole in his couch caught his eye. He'd fled up the stairs, fearful that something might have happened to his book, only to have his most dire concerns proven true. In his study, a gorgeous young woman had been tending to a man wearing a mask. Klempt had virtually ignored them at first, however, instead focusing on the blank surface of his desktop.

A fury had seized him then and he'd burst into the room, possessed of an almost preternatural strength. His unexpected entrance had startled the girl and he'd grabbed her by the throat, throttling her until she'd passed out from the strain. Still seething, Klempt had then drug both man and woman down the stairs, being none too gentle with them. He'd locked them in the spare bedroom, being careful to search each of them first and then binding them to chairs. The man had been sporting a wide variety of weapons, including a dagger that caught Klempt's eye. Those objects were now strewn across the kitchen table, where Klempt studied each in turn. His guests were bound to be waking any moment now and he was still uncertain what he wanted to do with them. It was apparent that they'd been in a struggle – and lost – with some unknown beings. But that did little to convince Klempt that they could be trusted.

Finally calming himself somewhat, he smoothed down his jacket and re-entered the bedroom. They were both conscious, though the girl looked somewhat dazed. "You broke into my home," Klempt began. "And there are items belonging to me that are missing. Where are they? And who are you?"

"Tourists," the Rook replied. "And your items were stolen to begin with, so they never truly belonged to you."

Klempt backhanded him, causing a fresh trickle of blood to begin oozing down. The man's head wound had only recently ceased bleeding. "Do you always dress like a bird?" Klempt asked. "Or did you just come from a masquerade?"

"It's part of my uniform," the Rook spat. "Let the girl go and I'll tell you what you want to know."

"You'll tell me who took the book?" Klempt pressed.

"Yes."

Evelyn glanced at her husband, shaking her head. "Don't," she whispered.

"I know what I'm doing," the Rook replied without looking at her. He kept his eyes on the sadistic doctor. "Do we have a deal?"

Klempt sneered at him. "No. A deal is only required when we are on equal footing. I hold all the cards here... so I have no need of deals. You will tell me what I want to know... or I will cut her ear off." The harsh words were spoken in a matter-of-fact manner, which made them all the more terrifying. Klempt reached up to smooth down his pencil-thin moustache. "Do you understand?"

The Rook nodded, having no doubts that the doctor would do exactly as he said. "A vampire named Camilla has taken your book."

"A vampire?" Klempt momentarily lost some of his menace and instead seemed honestly confused. "You're certain?"

"Very. She's the one who clocked me from behind." The Rook quietly worked at his bonds, becoming aware that the doctor's skill at knot tying left a lot to be desired. Given enough time, the Rook would be free....

"And who do you work for, if not her?" Klempt was watching them both with suspicion. "How did all of you find out that I even had the cursed tome?"

"I'd feel more comfortable talking with you if you'd let the girl go."

"Again with the concern for her. She is quite pretty, isn't she?" Klempt moved closer, leaning forward to stare into the Rook's eyes. "It would be a terrible shame to mark her face… but I will do it if necessary. Tell me more about the vampire, please."

"She works with a man named Reed Barrows. They've recently moved to Atlanta. She wants to bring about something called the Kingdom of Blood. It's supposed to be a golden age in which the Noble Dead rule over humanity."

Klempt tapped his chin with one slender finger. "Intriguing. And you?"

"I want it so I can make sure it's not misused… by people like her. And you."

"Ah. A hero, then." Klempt laughed softly and contemptuously. "I've heard about you so-called 'mystery men,' with your costumes and gadgets. Are you a killer like the one who calls himself the Spider? Or a more merciful sort, like Mr. Savage?"

"I'm my own sort, Doctor. I've killed often enough to know that sometimes it's the only way to end things properly. But I'll avoid it as much as possible."

Klempt studied him for a moment and then nodded. "I believe you. Tell me one thing more – do you know where I can find Camilla and her servant?"

"Yes. But I'll only tell you if you promise to let her go."

"Again you pretend to have some sort of bargaining ground. You've told me they're in Atlanta. What makes you think I cannot find them on my own if I have to?"

"If you thought you could, you wouldn't be wasting time by asking me for directions."

"Touché." Klempt spun on his heels and left the room, returning a moment later with the Rook's weapons in his hands. He threw them at Max's feet, the dagger clattering loudly on the wooden floor. "You have told me enough, I think. Time grows short – and I am on a schedule of sorts. I wish you and your lovely companion a quick and painless death, though I suspect that it will be anything but. I'm going to set this house afire, you see… I hate to leave my home but I simply must have that book. Oden's deception of earlier this evening makes perfect sense now – he was stalling me while you ransacked my home, eh? So that means he is on to me."

"You'll never get away with this," Evelyn murmured, her strength returning quickly. "Even if you kill us, someone else will stop you."

"Perhaps. I am willing to take that chance." Klempt withdrew a small canister from his pocket, along with a set of matches. The canister's contents were sprinkled liberally around the room, giving the area the distinct scent of brimstone. "This is deadly stuff, my friends. Forged by occultists long ago and put to good use by more modern men such as myself. It burns hot and fast."

The Rook waited until Klempt was finished before speaking again. "If I do die here, Doctor, I promise you this: I'll be waiting for you in Hell."

Klempt shook his head. "I think not. There's a special type of Hell reserved for idealists like yourself. I wouldn't fit in there. Goodbye, my friends." As he stepped from the room, Klempt tossed a lit match onto the floor. The effect was startling in its abruptness. Great plumes of flame suddenly rose up, casting the room into an inferno of heat and smoke.

The Rook slipped one hand free of his bonds, using it to untie the remainder of the ropes holding him to the chair. He moved to Evelyn next, who stared at him in surprise. She obviously had no clue that he'd been working to free himself the entire time. As she rose to her feet, Max knelt and retrieved his weapons, shoving them into his pockets. "The window, Evelyn – it's our only hope!"

To her credit, Max's wife remained outwardly calm. She covered her mouth and nose with one hand, jumping over flames until she stood next to the window. Evelyn cried out when she touched the sill, however, for it was red-hot.

The Rook pulled her aside, aware that Klempt was probably already out of the house and fleeing into the woods. For the doctor to lose all the items and books in this house… his obsession with the Necronomicon must have made everything else seem replaceable. Max pulled his jacket off and wrapped it around his gloves. Then he gave a mighty yank on the window, pulling it open. The fresh Georgia air that rushed in was an amazing thing and he immediately felt revitalized. Gripping his wife's hand in his own, he led her out the window, standing perilously on the second-floor ledge. "Wrap your arms tightly around me and don't let go!"

Evelyn nodded quickly, squeezing hard as her husband threw himself from the ledge. He landed first, rolling to soften the blow. Somehow he managed to angle his movements so that Evelyn was cushioned on top of his own body.

Behind them, the house was going up in flames, dark shapes writhing about in the smoke-filled shadows.

"Are you okay?" Evelyn asked, pushing herself to her feet. Her uniform was smudged with dirt and grime, along with no small amount of her husband's blood.

"I'm fine," the Rook answered, though his fury grew by the second. This entire evening had been a massive failure, with the book now in the hands of Camilla and Klempt still on the loose. "We need to get back to Atlanta," he said.

"I love you," Evelyn whispered. "We'll get them back, I promise."

The Rook felt his anger dissipate within seconds of seeing her concerned expression. He grinned and reached out to take her hand. "You're the prettiest partner I've ever had, you know."

"I'm the *only* partner you've ever had."

"Doesn't change what I said." The Rook led his wife away from the raging fire, his mind already turning to what would come next. He needed to know more about the Kingdom of Blood and how soon he could expect Camilla to use the spell. Would she return to her house? Or would she know that the security of that place had been compromised? Either way, she had to be stopped… and so did Dr. Klempt.

Chapter XIII
A New Ally

Josh sat on the front porch of the plantation house, sipping iced tea and enjoying the smell of a freshly plowed field. He'd worked hard today, using his mighty muscles to do the work of three men. He didn't mind the exertion, especially not when it was done in the service of a man like Max Davies, who treated his employees as equals, no matter what color skin they had.

"A police man is on the way up," Nettie warned, emerging from the side of the house with a bucket of water held tightly in one hand. Though she was so thin that her bones rubbed against the leathery covering of her skin, Nettie was a tenacious woman. "You best not be seen out on the porch like that."

"Is it the sheriff?" Josh asked, not yet rising from the chair. "If it is, I'll budge… but if it ain't, I'm comfortable where I am."

"Uppity, that's what they call men like you." Nettie set the bucket down with a thud, looking towards the dirt path that led to the road. A police officer's vehicle was bouncing along the way, its headlights dancing across the cornfields. It was well past nine in the evening and both Mr. Davies and his bride were upstairs in bed already. "I better go and wake 'em," she murmured. "They's goin' to be terrible upset. They looked tired as can be when they came back from Milledgeville."

Josh stood up, even though it wasn't the sheriff. It was the young chief of police, the one who'd only been on the job for a month or so. William McKenzie, son of the police chief in Mobile, Alabama. When the policeman stepped from his vehicle, Josh was taken by how broad-shouldered the fellow was and how dark his hair and eyes were. He looked about twenty-two, but Josh had heard he was closer to thirty. Either way, he was the youngest police chief in Georgia. "How can we help you, sir?" Josh asked.

McKenzie strode towards the front steps, taking in the massive physique of the man before him. He smiled and removed his hat. "Just paying a visit to Mr. Davies. Is he in?"

"He's sleepin'," Nettie said, moving to stand beside Josh. "I can go fetch 'im for you."

"No need," someone said from behind her. The sudden appearance of Max made Nettie nearly jump from her skin. He was dressed in a soiled white shirt and dark trousers, his hands covered with grease. Nettie realized that he hadn't been sleeping at all – he'd been tinkering in that workshop of his. "Good evening, officer. I hope there's no trouble."

"No, nothing like that. Could I come inside and speak with you in private, though?"

Max nodded, moving to open the door for the officer. He winked at Josh, making it clear that he'd appreciate if the big farmhand stayed nearby on the porch. Once inside the house, Max led McKenzie into the sitting room and offered him a drink.

The police chief declined, but did accept a seat when it was mentioned. "Brought along some information that you might find useful," McKenzie began, removing a small envelope from his left hip pocket.

Max sat down across from him, accepting the envelope but not yet opening it. "What sort of information?"

"Mr. Benson suggested that you and I become familiar with one another."

"Oh." Max felt a heat rush across his cheeks. Had Benson compromised his identity with someone else?

"Don't worry," McKenzie whispered, sensing Max's thoughts. "I'm on your side. My brother was murdered when he was sixteen. Gunned down in the middle of a crowded street… and the man who did it walked away scot-free. Not even my daddy's connections could touch him. I know damned well that sometimes the law can't touch the real criminals of the world. Sometimes it takes people like you and Mr. Benson to set things right."

Max pursed his lips but said nothing. Instead, he ripped open the envelope and peered inside. He scanned the words on a property deed, his eyes narrowing. "Mr. Reed Barrows owns more property than I thought," he said.

"That's right. Nobody's been in their main home for several days, but I dug that out of the records for you. A smaller place, well outside the city limits. Has a huge cellar and it's located next to an old cemetery that was abandoned years ago." McKenzie scratched at the dimple in his chin. "Nobody makes it out there unless they're going there intentionally. You can't get anymore out-of-the-way than that."

"Do you know about Dr. Klempt?" Max asked.

"No."

"He's a sadistic madman. He'll be looking to find Camilla and Reed – I've managed to find out that he's got a room at the Manzini Hotel downtown. I was going to check it out… but if you are willing to help, I'd love to pass that on to you so I can drop in on Mr. Barrows during the day tomorrow."

McKenzie smiled eagerly and Max was suddenly seized by the image of the police chief as an eager puppy, ready to please. "Hell, I can be there tonight if you want."

"No. He's too smart to go after Camilla at night. He'll wait for daylight, just like I want to. Make your move at dawn and you'll catch him unawares." Max sighed, rubbing his temples. "So… how much do you know?"

"Mr. Benson helped me through a bad time in my life, Mr. Davies. He says you're aces with him and that's more than good enough for me. So I don't know if you're the Rook, but it wouldn't take a genius to figure maybe you were. He's the only mystery man operating in these parts, after all."

Max studied him, finding no trace of deception in his eyes. "Camilla Barrows is a vampire," he said, amused to see a brief flare of disbelief from McKenzie. The police officer shoved away his doubts, however, and merely nodded for Davies to continue. "Klempt is equally dangerous. He's an occultist and will very likely have some nasty surprises waiting for you. In fact, it might be too dangerous to have you go after him at all...."

"I can handle it," McKenzie assured him.

"I don't doubt that you're capable enough. I want my partner to go with you, though – just in case."

"What's his name?"

"He's a she, actually. And she hasn't taken an adventuring name yet. I've trained her well, however. She can help you."

McKenzie thought it over and nodded. "Can she meet me at the hotel around 5 o'clock?"

"She'll be there," Max answered, though he knew that Evelyn would despise rising so early. "And thank you, Mr. McKenzie... it'll be nice to have someone in law enforcement on my sde for once."

"**G**oodness, you certainly don't give a girl much time to rest, do you?"

Max patted his wife's knee as he sat on the edge of their bed. Her silken nightgown fit her enticingly but he was too tired to pursue anything physical at the moment. "I think it's better for you to handle Klempt."

"You don't think I can stand up to the vampire?"

"The vampire's going to be asleep, hopefully. Even if she is awake, she'll be weakened. We both know how horrible Klempt can be... I wouldn't be sending you if I didn't think you were capable of stopping him."

Evelyn drew her knees up and smiled. "It's the first time I'll be going out on my own..."

"Nervous?"

"Excited, actually. Like the first day on a new movie set."

Max leaned over and kissed her cheek. "Break a leg."

Chapter XIV
The Infernal Doctor

Klempt rose at four, washed himself in a basin of cold water, and began to dress. He wore a dark suit, each of the pockets containing the items he thought he would need to destroy Camilla and her servant. A pistol loaded with silver bullets, several crucifixes, a vial of holy water and a knife soaked in a virgin's blood… these things would do the trick, he suspected. Just in case, a sturdy wooden stake and mallet completed his arsenal.

He took a long time fixing his hair, smoothing it back just so… before moving on to wax his moustache. Klempt was vain enough to acknowledge his attractiveness, so he enjoyed the primping that was part of his morning routine. Regret still lingered in his heart, however, making him long for his home in Milledgeville. He had grown comfortable there, believing that he was finally closing in on the end of his long trek towards absolute power. Now, he was on the run, seeking to claim what had been stolen from him. No doubt, his machinations back at the hospital would come to light soon enough… assuming the worms didn't devour their way out of their host first.

As the first rays of sunlight streamed in through his window, he stepped out into the hall – and came face-to-face with a dark-clad beauty whom he recognized immediately as the girl who had invaded his home. At her side was a police officer who brandished a service revolver, its muzzle pointed directly at Klempt's face.

"Raise your hands, doctor," the officer commanded.

"What is the meaning of this?"

"I repeat: raise your hands or I will shoot."

Klempt did as he was told, but a smirk played upon his lips. "I'm surprised to see you again, Miss Rook. Does the absence of your usual companion mean that he died in Milledgeville?"

"He's hale and hearty," the woman replied icily. She moved forward and began to search Klempt's pockets, pulling forth his weapons and dropping to the floor. "It would take more than you to kill him."

"You smell like him," Klempt hissed in her ear. "Does he rut with you? Is that the key to your success, my dear? Sleeping your way into his good graces?"

"Pig," Evelyn replied. She stepped back and glanced over at McKenzie. "You heard him admit to attempted murder – and he's got enough weapons here that you should be able to put him away for quite awhile."

The chief nodded, gesturing towards the stairs with his pistol. "Get walking, doctor. We're going down to the station. And don't make any funny moves. Two more officers are downstairs, just waiting for you to make a break for it."

Klempt, hands still raised, began to walk ahead of them. "Miss Rook… do you have any idea about the forces I serve? They are older than humanity and their power is so great that the stars themselves bow down before them."

Evelyn tried to ignore him as they began to descend the stairs. There was something in his tone that made her shiver… madness, yes, but also… certainty.

"Anyone who tells you that the universe is not a cold, chaotic place is a liar. There is no purpose… no rhyme nor reason… when we die, our bodies rot and turn to dust. Worms burrow in through our flesh and live in the empty sockets of…."

"That's enough," McKenzie warned.

Down below, Klempt could see two more uniformed men waiting. The frightened hotel clerk peeked out from behind a closed door, eager to have the whole sordid affair over with. Klempt imagined the clerk's one positive impression was that this occurred early enough that most of the guests were still asleep. "No. It's not enough. You're going to arrest me. You're going to put me on trial… and in the end, I'm going to fail my masters. I'll never know their perverse touch… smell their putrefying flesh… or receive the gifts of power over others. That's. Not. Right." Klempt turned around when he reached the bottom of the stairs, dropping his arms. "Look at me, Miss Rook. This is not a game. This is my existence… and yours."

Behind the doctor, the other officers were drawing their weapons. Klempt smiled cruelly, his lips parting.

"Doctor, put your hands up and move towards the exit." McKenzie swallowed hard, sensing that something awful was about to occur.

Klempt, his eyes still locked on Evelyn's, threw himself towards McKenzie. He howled like a banshee and at the last moment Evelyn could have sworn that he deliberately placed his own mouth over the barrel of the gun. When the police chief pulled the trigger, flecks of bone and red-gray matter exploded from the back of the doctor's head. Klempt's body whirled around, jerking like a marionette whose strings had been unexpectedly cut. His eyes stared out above a bloody hole where his mouth had once been and those eyes – full of madness and hate – seemed to somehow follow Evelyn as the body slammed to the floor.

Evelyn's screams were matched by the horrified clerk, bringing the guests bursting from their rooms. The sight they received when the first of them arrived in the lobby was one of sheer chaos.

It was a fitting testimony to Klempt's view of the universe.

Chapter XV
Father's Lament

"Cursed the ground where dead thoughts live new and oddly bodied, and evil the mind that is held by no head."

Max Davies let the words drift through his mind, continually replayed in his father's strong voice. He was seated behind the wheel of his car, driving down the bumpy dirt road towards the Barrows' second home. His car's motor had been specially modified to be almost perfectly silent, making his approach a stealthy one. The quiet also gave him ample opportunity to think about his current situation.

Now that Benson had come into play, the Rook's mission was shaping up quite differently than before. He now had a police officer who would run interference for him and give him ready access to evidence… but it also meant that more people than ever before knew about his dual identity. Should he eventually abandon the mask entirely? The nation's papers were full of stories about men like Benson, fighting the good fight openly. But there were plenty of others who still lurked in the shadows… and given the caliber of foes that Max usually faced, perhaps it would be best to remain hidden lest his friends and family be at continual risk.

"I think that would be for the best."

Max jumped, barely able to keep from swerving off the road. He cast a furious glance at the figure who had materialized in the passenger seat: his father, still wearing the same suit and tie that he'd worn on the day he'd died.   "You nearly frightened me to death!" he hissed.

"Sorry, son. I suppose I should clear my throat before speaking?"

"What do you want?" Max asked, returning his attention to the road before him. The farmhouse was now visible in the distance.

"I've been listening in to your thoughts and…."

"I have no privacy at all, do I?" Max shook his head. "Go on."

"Benson is safe enough, but be aware that Evelyn and McKenzie will be in danger every time you bring them into our affairs."

"Our affairs, is it?" Max snorted. "You used me, turned me into a killing machine so you could get some sort of cosmic retribution. And now you make it sound like we're partners."

The elder Davies looked away, his voice lowering slightly. "Max, I loved you. I did what I thought was best – for you and for the entire world. I'm sorry for all the pain it's caused you."

Max lifted his foot off the accelerator, letting the vehicle slow somewhat. He'd rarely ever heard such emotion in his father's voice and it touched him. "I… missed you after you died. Very much."

"I would have come to you… but the barriers between the world of the living and the dead were too strong. I could only send you messages via dreams. I had to wait until your mental abilities were more pronounced."

Max rode in silence with his father for a moment, feeling oddly at ease with the ghostly presence of the man who had shaped his life. "I'll be careful, father. I won't put anyone at risk if I can help it."

"I trust you to do the right thing," his father replied. "You've been giving that warning I gave you some thought, eh?"

"The terribly vague one?" Max responded with a smile. "Yes. Care to give me anymore details on it?"

"No," his father answered. "I can't. Things are still unclear to me… but I know this: dark things are looming in your future. The Kingdom must be stopped."

Max pulled off the road, reaching under his seat to retrieve his coat and mask. "I'll do whatever it takes. Hopefully, I'll catch Mr. Barrows unawares and Camilla sleeping. Thanks for the talk, by the way. I…."

Max let his words come to a stop. His father was gone, as if he had never been there at all.

"To work I go," Max whispered. He placed his mask over his eyes and nose, allowing himself the briefest of moments to treasure the first real man-to-man talk he'd ever had with his father.

Chapter XVI
Dead Thoughts Live New

The house was eerily quiet, though the bright sunlight robbed the place of any terror it might have otherwise induced. The Rook crept about the outside of the house, but heard no sounds of habitation within – nothing save for the slow, steady rocking of a chair in the main parlor. The ground outside was well trampled and by many feet – Max counted at least twelve distinct sets of prints.

When he finally steeled himself to enter the home, the Rook made sure that he held a pistol in both hands. He burst in through the unlocked front door, bellowing "Barrows! Stand down or I swear to Heaven, I'll blow your head off!"

"You're a bit late," Barrows said, his voice echoing into the central hallway from the parlor. Max noted that there was a peculiar quality to Reed's words…

like someone whose spirit had been battered repeatedly and finally broken had voiced them.

The Rook strode into the parlor, guns at the ready. "Where's your mistress?" he demanded, though he came up short upon seeing the figure seated in the center of the room. Barrows was there, looking pale and wan… his neck was heavily bandaged and he held a small ring box in his lap. He turned sunken eyes upon the Rook, displaying red-tinged gums as he smiled.

"She's gone away," Barrows said, his words taking on the sing-song quality of madness. "But she left me behind, to give you words of warning."

The Rook lowered his weapons and knelt beside Barrows, reaching up to examine the man's wounds. His neck had been torn asunder by multiple bites… and his shirt was stained red with his own blood. "Tell me where she is, Reed."

"Don't bother dressing my wounds. They drained me dry."

"You'll be fine," Max whispered, though he was concerned by how much blood had been lost. Against Reed's objections, he removed the bandage around the man's neck and began applying some ointment that he carried in his pocket. "Tell me what she said," he prompted.

Reed closed his eyes, looking forlorn. "She activated the spell as soon as we got back. I could feel the air around us changing as she spoke the words… and then *they* started coming. I couldn't believe there could be so many, not so close… she said they were waking up all over the world, but there were over a dozen right here in Atlanta. They came and they talked about the heaven that was to come… and then she offered them a feast. She offered them *me*." This last word was forced out amongst a sudden onslaught of sobs that wrenched at Max's heart. "I loved her. She said she loved me… but it was a lie. All a lie."

Max removed a needle and thread, working to stitch the man's neck. It was difficult work, made all the more so by the fact that Reed kept turning his head away from the help he needed. "You mentioned words of warning," he reminded, hoping that keeping Reed focused on something specific would soothe the man and allow Max to finish his work.

"The Noble Dead. That's what they call themselves," Reed continued. "She said they were going into town, to wait for more to arrive. When there's enough of them, they'll begin a blood orgy. They'll slaughter everyone they can find, using their victims' souls to power the final phase of the Kingdom's spell. Then the air will change and night will rule over day forever… and science will wither and die, leaving only magic in its place." Reed leaned forward, grabbing Max by the collar. "She said that He comes tonight. She said that Dead Thoughts live new and oddly bodied. She said…." Reed pulled away suddenly, rising from the chair so quickly that it fell on its side. "She said that if you oppose her, you will die in the most painful way imaginable!"

"Where in the city is she?" Max asked, reaching out to keep Reed from tossing himself to the floor. "Help me. I know she's hurt you… but you can help me and redeem yourself!"

"She lied to me. She said I would rule as her King…."

"Who is coming tonight? Who is this 'He' that she spoke of?"

"The speaker of the dead. The messenger of madness. The black stranger!"

Max paused, for something in his words was now making sense to him. In his studies of the Necronomicon, he'd been forced to read much about the Old Ones, the entities whose mad designs for power had forged the universe. At the center of it all spun the mad god Azathoth. But most recurring of all was the sinister black stranger who ferried messages from the Old Ones to their human servants. An entity of tremendous power and trickery, one who wore the skin of humanity but had been birthed by no mother. He had been the inspiration for a wealth of human myths, but the one that he clung to most was that of Loki, the Norse God of Mischief. "Are you telling me that Nyarlathotep is coming to Atlanta?" Max whispered in disbelief.

"Yes! Yes, he comes! He is the one who spawned the Noble Dead by lying in vile forms with humanity. He comes to welcome his children to their just reward! He comes to witness the evolution of humanity… as we become cattle to those who lord over us!"

Max saw madness reign in Reed's eyes and he delivered a powerful slap to the man's face. It startled Reed for a moment, but then lucidity returned, ever so tenuously. "Help me, Reed. Help me stop her from succeeding."

Reed licked dry lips and nodded. "I can sense her," he said, touching the side of his head. "All the times she suckled me… *I can sense her.*"

The Rook smiled beneath his mask. "Then we have an advantage that they might be unaware of." He held on to Reed's shoulder, leading him towards the door. "Is there anything else here that might help us?"

"No… there's nothing here worth keeping. Not any more." He looked down at the ring box he still clutched in one hand. Within lay the gold band he'd once removed from his dead wife's finger… the same band he'd once slid onto Camilla's hand with all the attentiveness of a passionate lover. He tossed the ring box into the ashes of the fireplace.

"Nothing at all."

Chapter XVII
The Messenger of Madness

Camilla watched her fellow Noble Dead, writhing naked atop one another. They were beautiful to behold, but it seemed needlessly decadent… they should be planning for the Kingdom to come, not losing themselves in the release of pent-up passions. The tall vampire queen kept to herself, hiding in the shadows of the underground tunnels. This place had once served as a means of transporting people and supplies, but now it served as a lair to the undead… but despite the presence of her fellows, this area seemed dank and oppressive to Camilla. It was unseemly for them to debase themselves amongst filth.

"Your standards are higher than most," a male voice said. Camilla turned to face the stranger, who emerged from the shadows with a smile on his handsome features. He was dark-skinned like an Egyptian, with a small neatly trimmed beard and deep-set eyes that spoke of hidden knowledge. His clothing was dark and fit him well, but it was his scent that caught Camilla's attention immediately. It was the musk of pure masculine sex, an animal scent that set Camilla's blood aflame. "I wish I had been here last evening, when the spell was first invoked. Alas, I was busy in Europe at the time."

"Are you....?" Camilla began, but stopped herself. It was He, of that there could be no doubt. The power that emanated from him was a powerful aphrodisiac and she was barely able to restrain herself from offering her body to him, then and there. "There are nearly twenty of us here now... but many more are coming. The call has gone out. They can all hear it in their souls."

"You have no souls," the man said with a laugh. "You're soulless monsters, sent out to inflict pain and suffering on humanity. Your beauty is only to entice them into a fall from grace."

The words stung Camilla, for they were full of scorn. She had expected him to love his children. Eager to win over his approval, Camilla gestured with her chin towards the writhing bodies of her kindred. "They will help carry the day but none of them are fit to rule at your side."

"But you are, aren't you?" he asked, his eyes traveling over the curves of her flesh in a way that made her tremble. "The female who finally brought about the Kingdom of Blood. You are impressive."

Camilla smiled at the compliment. "There were many obstacles that had to be overcome, but I would not be denied."

"Where is the human who brought you out of your own slumber? Is he not here to enjoy the fruits of his labor?"

Camilla's smile faltered. Had she made a mistake in disposing of Reed? "He was no longer useful to me... so I abandoned him."

"Did you kill him?" Nyarlathotep asked, stepping around her to better view the orgy. "Or were you so stupid that you left him alive so that he could betray you later?"

Camilla flinched at the insult. "He can do nothing! He is weak and helpless!"

"I suppose it was too much to hope for... that you could be as smart as you are beautiful."

"I... I can find him. I will kill him if you want!"

Nyarlathotep looked back at her over his shoulder. His dark eyes blazed with anger. "You've made your mistake. Accept it. When he comes with his allies, then you will have the chance to impress me."

"What makes you think he will come?" she asked, disappointment racing inside of her. She had so looked forward to this moment, to being able to bask in the glow of her master...! But to see the disdain he held for her... it made her feel like a child suffering a rebuke from their parents.

"Because that's the way things work," he said patiently. "Our servants prepare for triumph... and then their enemies gather to oppose them. Sometimes you win, sometimes you lose. That's the way the game is played."

"But this is no game," Camilla whispered.

"Anyone who tells you it isn't… is a fool."

Camilla looked away from him, unable to stand up to his penetrating gaze. "I will win. I promise you that."

The messenger of the dark gods reached out to cup her chin, turning her face back towards his. He leaned close enough that she could smell the death that clung thick and hot on his breath. "You'd better, my sweet. Or else your pain will become something that will be sung of for centuries to come."

Camilla swallowed hard, her inhuman form trembling all the more. "Who will he bring with him?"

"The Rook, of course." Nyarlathotep laughed loudly, capturing the attention of the rutting vampires, who now gazed up at him in confusion. "He has interfered with a number of my recent servants… Felix Darkholme and Gerhard Klempt foremost amongst them."

Camilla's eyes opened wide at the mad doctor's name.

"Yes," Nyarlathotep continued, sneering. "You ruined a plan of mine that was close to coming to fruition. So you'd best be right that you and your army of fiends can deal with the Rook… because I won't abide failure from you. Not again."

"The Rook dies tonight," Camilla replied, steeling her voice with conviction. "I will tear out his heart and offer it to you, my lord."

Chapter XVIII
Council of War

Evelyn sat in the parlor, trying to get the image of Klempt's death out of her mind. It wasn't easy and she could almost hear the gunshot echoing over and over again. She was wearing one of her nicest dresses, a leftover from a film called *Belle of the Ball* that had tanked at the box office. It had been a departure from her usual damsel-in-distress roles, instead offering her up as the lead in a romantic comedy. The financial disaster had sent her scurrying back to the stage for a time afterwards. The feel of the silk against her skin calmed her somewhat, making her feel like a normal woman again.

Max was well aware of his wife's distress. He had seen it clearly enough in her eyes upon returning to the house and hearing McKenzie's detailed account of the situation had only chilled him further. He had not pressed her, however, knowing that she would discuss the matter when she was ready and not a moment before.

"Sorry for the lack of details in the drawing," McKenzie was saying, leaning over a large drawing table upon which lay a map of the underground section of the city. "I had to move quickly and this was the best I could find in our files."

"It'll do fine," Max assured him. He glanced up as Nettie entered the room, carrying a tray filled with glasses of iced tea. The old woman looked around the room nervously, letting her gaze linger on both Evelyn and Reed, who was sitting in the corner, nervously chewing his nails and looking as skittish as a mouse. Max wondered just how far Reed could go without irredeemable madness setting in. "Thank you, Nettie. I'll let you know if we need anything else."

Nettie nodded, realizing that she was being dismissed. She pulled the door closed behind her, but her expression remained one of concern.

"Why don't we go before the sun drops?" McKenzie pressed. It was nearly seven o'clock already and the sun was beginning to recede behind the clouds. The police chief looked none the worse for wear, despite the horrors of the early morning. His uniform was freshly pressed and his handsome features made him look like he'd stepped right off the silver screen. "I mean, the vampires will be asleep now, won't they? We'd only have to deal with any human servants they might have."

"Possibly," Max agreed, "but I think we've all had trying times as of late. I'm more interested in giving us time to rest and regroup than I am in pressing forward when we're not at our peak." The Rook glanced over at Reed Barrows, adding a note of command to his words. "Reed, I want you to come with us tonight. You're our link to finding Camilla."

"What does it matter?" Reed answered, shaking his head. "If the black messenger comes... if all the other Noble Dead come... then Camilla doesn't matter anymore. She's just another cog in the machine."

"A very important cog," Evelyn pointed out. "Because she still has the Necronomicon. Even after we've dealt with this Kingdom of Blood, we still have to find that book and make sure it's not used for foul purposes again."

"There are other copies," Reed countered. "You'll never be able to stop that book's evil."

"Then people will have to use other copies!" Max bellowed. "I don't give a damn whether or not you feel like helping us, Reed – you're going to. Now accept that and start helping us!"

Reed pouted like a petulant child but finally relented, rising from his chair to stand near the table. "There will be many more vampires there tonight. You'll need special weaponry."

"We have the things that Klempt was carrying," Evelyn said, moving to join the men. "Was he on the right track?" she asked Reed, bowing to the man's intimate knowledge of the undead.

Reed thought for a moment before nodding. "Yes... but I'd make sure your necks are well protected, as well. Garlic won't put them off very much, but it does assault their senses and makes them more cautious." He looked at Max. "That dagger of yours will hurt them badly. It possesses powerful magic."

"One of these days I'll have to look into the origins of that thing," Max whispered. He tapped an area of the map. "I say we enter here. McKenzie, I want you and Evelyn to distract the vampires while Reed and I go after Camilla. With any luck, we'll find them all together."

"Should I call in some backup?" McKenzie asked. "I can always draft in some officers, tell them we're going after gangsters...."

"They won't stand a chance," Evelyn said with a shake of her head. Max noticed that McKenzie seemed quite taken by Evelyn's beauty, but he couldn't blame the man: she had that effect on nearly everyone. "If we take some of Max's special equipment with us, we'll be able to hold off these Noble Dead for a time."

"Suicide," Reed snorted. "We're all going to die in agonizing pain."

Max began to roll up the map, ignoring the man's cowardice. "Follow me. I'll take you a place where we can get ready." With the papers held firmly in one hand, he led the group out of the house, walking right by a still nosy Nettie. He unlocked the entrance to the storm cellar and descended into the darkness, lighting a lamp when he'd reached the center of the room. Gesturing for Reed to close the cellar door behind him, Max said, "Welcome to the Rook's Nest."

McKenzie gaped at the sight, taking in a wide variety of beakers, weapons and scientific odds and ends. "It looks like a damned museum… of what kind, I don't know… but a museum of something."

"It's my private Cabinet of Curiosities," Max replied with a laugh. "Mementos, things I'm working on, spare costumes… I store it all down here." He moved to a workbench and pulled out a small box from underneath. He set it on the table and began removing several small spherical objects. "Gas bombs. If you use this," he held up a small device that he demonstrated by briefly slipping into his nostrils, "it will filter the smoke… but anyone who's unprotected will find that their lungs are suddenly on fire. Even though vampires don't need to breathe in the way we do, their internal structure seems much the same and Reed has confirmed for me that they are able to smell, taste and hear just as we do, only at an augmented level. I think this gas will make its way into their lungs just like it would a human… and I'm betting it'll hurt - a lot."

Evelyn couldn't avoid smiling a bit as her husband talked about his inventions. From the first moment she'd met him, she'd known he was different than most men – greater in some ways. But when he talked like this, full of animated excitement, he seemed like a little boy… and it made her wonder what sort of father he'd make someday.

Max caught her eye for a moment and winked.

Chapter XIX
Into the Darkness

The Rook walked at the front of the group, pistols held at the ready. He was remarkably calm considering the fact that there were dozens – possibly hundreds – of vampires waiting for him just up ahead. Max was comfortable with the knowledge of death looming just over the horizon, however – he had lived with danger for so long that it rarely troubled him any longer. His marriage to Evelyn had tempered that a bit, however, and he glanced over at her now, wondering if he should have pressed harder for her to stay behind.

With a wry smile, he pushed that thought out of his mind entirely. Evelyn never would have agreed to play the helpless damsel, waiting at home for her husband to finish the dangerous work. She was a rare person – and he loved her for it.

The tunnels beneath the city were filthy and wet, a steady drip of water coming from above. Several times, he heard Reed slip and catch himself, uttering muffled curses each time. McKenzie brought up the rear of the party, gas bombs strapped across his chest in a crisscrossed fashion. Max noted that the police officer betrayed no fear at the coming battle. In fact, he looked somewhat hopeful of it.

He's an odd one, Max mused. *I'm glad Benson sent him my way, though. I trust him like I've known him for years.* Once again, he was reminded of how lonely had been before moving to Atlanta – and how he'd tried to avoid bringing others into the dangerous life he lived. *I'll never go back to that kind of solitary existence,* Max thought. *Not after I've seen the alternative.*

"Max," Evelyn whispered. She reached out and touched his arm, the small lantern she carried casting flickering, distorted shadows along the walls. "Do you smell that?"

The Rook paused, inhaling deeply. At first all he noticed was the scent of decay and rotting vegetation... but mixed in with those awful odors was something else: something peculiar and foul. "Reed. What do you think is causing that smell?"

The thin man moved to join him, looking distressed. "It's the Noble Dead. Camilla told me that the ones who've been asleep for a long time sometimes begin to rot. It takes multiple feedings to revive them and get rid of the smells of the grave." Reed sighed. "It also makes them weaker until they've finishing healing... which is the only hope we have of not being killed in the first few minutes of fighting."

The Rook ignored the man's dire attitude. He moved forward, leading the group down further into the darkness. After several moments, the walkway began to take on an incline slope and they emerged into a rounded chamber from which three exits could be seen – each of the tunnels were too dark to reveal anything about where they led. The smell of death and blood was overpowering.

"We're not alone," McKenzie warned, pointing his own lamp at one of the tunnels.

The Rook watched as Camilla emerged, flanked by four vampires who appeared in reasonably good health. Each of them showed some signs of recent emergence from the ground, but they were strong and deadly. Before anyone could speak, more vampires stepped out from the other tunnels... and worst of all, Reed's terrified squawk alerted Max to the fact that there were vampires behind them, as well. Somehow they had watched them enter the tunnels, using sentries to warn Camilla and the others that enemies were approaching. *So much for all my detailed planning,* Max thought.

"Hello," Camilla purred, her eyes flicking from one member of the group to the next. Her gaze fell last upon Reed and for the briefest of moments her demeanor seemed to soften. But the weakness was gone so swiftly that none could truly say that it had been there at all. "I must admit... our prey don't usually come rushing into our laps like this."

These comments made the vampires laugh raucously, baring their fangs. Some of them were covered in blood already, giving ample evidence to the fact they'd been feeding in preparation for battle. Thankfully, several of them were little more than skin and bones at this point, still needing days or weeks to recover fully from their long slumber.

The Rook pointed his pistol directly at Camilla's head. "I find the undead particularly disgusting… but I'm willing to work with you. Give us the Necronomicon and we'll let you leave here, as long as you promise to abandon this Kingdom scheme."

"You must be joking," Camilla responded, impressed by the man's bravado but finding herself quite certain that he must be mad. "You're outnumbered and overmatched… and the Kingdom is coming. We are its harbingers."

"I was afraid you were going to say that," the Rook replied. He knew that Camilla was too fast for him to hit cleanly, even at this close range, so he spun about and fired instead at one of the vampires to her left. The bullet, soaked in holy water, sliced through the center of his forehead, exiting out the other side. "No mercy!" he shouted at his companions and they joined the battle in earnest, striking without hesitation. Even Reed was in the thick of things, though Max suspected that the man's sense of self-preservation had kicked in where bravery would not.

Evelyn found herself surrounded by several of the vile creatures, each of them reeked with the grave. She fought well, using every trick taught to her by her husband. A swift kick to the head sent one of the vampires tumbling away from her and she tossed one of the smoke bombs directly into the face of another, sending him gasping in pained terror. She lost track of her husband in the melee, but was far too busy to worry about his safety.

McKenzie, likewise, was engrossed in defending himself. He shoved a wooden stake through the heart of a female vampire, one whose beauty was so beguiling that the officer had almost lost his will to fight. He cried out when one of the males raked his cheek with sharp dirt-stained fingernails, drawing blood. McKenzie backed up against a wall, drawing his pistol and firing again and again, his perfect shots leaving one foe after another with gaping wounds in their heads and torsos.

Camilla watched in shock as the small band laid waste to the Noble Dead… even the power of the ancient beings seemed to pale beside the heroic energy of their attackers. Feeling a cold certainty that they were doomed, she turned to flee to the safety of Nyarlathotep… only to find that the Rook was ahead of her, hurrying down the center hallway from which she had come. Hissing in anger, the vampire queen set off after her foe, moving so quickly that her feet seemed to glide across the tunnel floor. "Bag of meat! Bag of blood!" she shouted, landing atop the Rook's back, sending him to the floor. She allowed him to roll about beneath her, eager to bury her fangs in his neck.

When the man did turn to face her, he seemed oddly composed for one whose death was so imminent. "You've lived a long time," the Rook said, staring up into her eyes. "Do you really want your existence to end down here? Is this tunnel where you want to have your remains scattered for all eternity?"

Camilla paused, holding her prey down with a strong grip on his shoulders. She leaned close to him, smelling his aroma and allowing her pink-tinged lips to part in a grin. "How is it that you can remain so… confident… when I'm seconds away from ripping your throat open?"

"Because you don't know anything about me.You're assuming that all I am is a nut who wears a bird mask and carries a gun."

Camilla laughed softly."And you're more than that? Tell me, Mr. Rook... what *are* you really?"

"I'm someone who's capable of *this*."Max reached out with his mind, performing the same type of telepathic assault that he'd done before... during those frightening days in Germany, when Jacob Trench had come so close to unleashing ultimate evil upon the world. Camilla let out a surprised sigh as Max's mind sliced into hers, tearing and ripping like a weapon. It was painful to Max, as well, and disturbing on even deeper levels... for it felt like a particularly nasty form of rape.

The vampire queen screamed, pulling her hands away from Max and using her nails to scratch at the sides of her head. When that failed to stop the pain inside her skull, she began beating at it, using such force that blood began to ooze from the inside of her nose and eyes.

Max shoved her away from him, dusting himself off. He pulled his mental attack back a bit, slowly easing his consciousness out of hers. She whimpered on the ground, curling up into a fetal position and Max felt a twinge of sympathy for her. He'd seen many awful things when he'd visited her mind, though, and the depths of her actions made him feel secure that he'd done the right thing.

The Rook moved to stand over her, planning to end her threat once and for all...but was stopped by the sound of Reed's voice.

"Don't," the other man said, moving into view. He was bleeding badly and one of his ears had been torn away, leaving only red meat in its place.

"You should be helping Evelyn and McKenzie," Max said, kneeling so that he could place the barrel of his gun against Camilla's head."And you don't need to scc this."

"Let me take care of her. Please." Reed moved forward, gun in hand.

The Rook pointed his gun at Reed, halting him in mid-step."I know you loved her... and I know a part of you wants to save her, even now. But I can't let you do it. She's evil."

Reed looked away, his body shaking."Don't kill her... she's so old... so beautiful. Can't we just let her leave?"

Max sighed."She'll kill more innocents. She'll try to restore the Kingdom. You know that."

Reed turned away, staggering back up the hallway, back to the sounds of violence."Be quick about it," was all he said, but the emotion behind the words was heartbreaking. He'd coveted something far lovelier than he'd ever had a right to have... and in the end, he'd found himself all the worse for having possessed it, ever so briefly.

The Rook looked down, into the face of a murderer. Once again placing his pistol against her temple, he ended her threat once and for all. Max then staked her through the heart and used his golden dagger to behead her. The final act was the most important, as he doused her with a flammable fluid and set the remains aflame.

Confident that Camilla no longer posed a threat, he began moving again, eventually stepping out into a larger chamber that contained a number of dead bodies… prey for the refueling vampires, he realized. The faint odor of sex hung in the air, mixing with death, but it was the man who stood in the center of the room, Necronomicon in hand, that chilled the Rook's blood.

"Hello, Max," the dark-skinned man said, reaching down with one hand to smooth the fabric of his finely cut suit. He wore a red signet ring on the little finger of his left hand. "Welcome to Hell."

Chapter XX
A Mind Held By No Head

The Rook stared at the man in disbelief, for there was something eerily inhuman about him. It wasn't obvious in the man's form, for he appeared normal enough in that regard… but rather it was in his presence and bearing. "Are you the messenger?" he asked, remembering what Reed had said about an elder entity that would be summoned by the Kingdom's arrival.

"I am indeed," the stranger replied, taking a step towards the vigilante. "But I have many names, though the one I favor the most is Nyarlathotep."

Max frowned, suddenly feeling that he had finally delved too far on his own… and that he now faced a being quite capable of destroying him utterly. Rather than turn and flee, the Rook merely drew forth his golden dagger and held it at the ready. "Camilla's dead. The plan has failed."

"As I knew it would… though you're far too hasty in assuming that everything is completely resolved. The summons was sent out and the Noble Dead now walk the earth in numbers that haven't seen in centuries. Chaos will reign for quite some time, Mr. Davies."

"Is that what you're after? Chaos?"

"It's the master that I serve," Nyarlathotep replied. "What master do *you* serve, Mr. Davies? Do you even know?"

"Hand over the book," the Rook answered, not wishing to be drawn into any kind of conversation with an entity like this. Though it wore the flesh of a man, this was something else… something older and far more deadly.

Nyarlathotep glanced down at the knife and sneered. "You took that from one of my pets, didn't you? Mr. Darkholme. His loss pained me greatly."

"I've noticed that beings like you don't like its touch," the Rook warned, slashing at the air for emphasis. Somewhat to his surprise, Nyarlathotep took a step away, avoiding the weapon.

"Darkholme was going to destroy it," Nyarlathotep hissed. "It's a vile thing and has no place in this world!"

The Rook wondered at the being's words… he knew so little about the weapon but if Nyarlathotep feared it and Darkholme had wanted to destroy it, the weapon must be of supreme importance. Once again, he promised himself that he'd delve into the mysteries of the blade if he survived this affair.

Returning his thoughts to the present, the Rook pressed the issue again. "Are you going to turn over the book or do I have to take it?"

"Foolish mortal," Nyarlathotep whispered. "Do you think I would sully my hands by touching you in combat? Never! I merely wanted to inform you that from this moment forth you are *marked.*"

Before Max could ponder what that meant, a searing pain developed in the palm of his left hand. He howled, almost dropping the dagger in his haste to remove the leather glove that covered the inflamed area. There in the center of his palm was a blasphemous looking black circle, one that twisted occasionally and oozed a small trickle of some vile tar-like substance. "God above," he whispered, staring at the bizarre wound. He looked up when Nyarlathotep began laughing and in his sudden fury he launched the dagger at his foe, sending it whistling through the air. The blade embedded itself in Nyarlathotep's throat, driving him to the ground with a thump.

The Rook pounced upon the man, only to find that his skin was as loose and empty as a discarded set of clothing. Inside were no bones, nor any trace of the entity that had inhabited the form. The Necronomicon was lying there, however, and the Rook pulled it into his grip hastily, still reeling from the pain in his palm.

"No longer will you be able to sneak up on my pets," a bodiless voice intoned. It was Nyarlathotep, no longer bound by a physical form. He was now a mind held by no head, an astral wraith. "From now on, you will stand out like a beacon to them... they will sense an enemy is present... and they may strike first, rather than allow you to pursue them. This is your punishment, Rook... and it will prove a most foul one, for no one who is near you will be safe from the wrath of those you'd hunt!"

The Rook pulled his glove back into place, rising from his kneeling position atop the skin of Nyarlathotep. He had to leave this place... check on Evelyn and the others... and think about the price he would have to pay for his actions.

Chapter XXI
Back in the Nest

"I've had an alert out on Barrows for the past two days and nobody's spotted him," McKenzie said, sitting in a comfortable chair in the Rook's Nest and nursing a cold beer. He had a number of scratches and bruises from the battle beneath the city, but the worst of his wounds was a horrid looking scar on his neck that had required a fair number of stitches to close up. "With the way he was bleeding from that ear of his, I can't imagine he got very far."

Evelyn fingered one of the buttons on her silky overcoat and looked thoughtful. A script for a new play was set out in front of her, but she'd barely paid any attention to it. "I can't help but feel sorry for him."

"He had that vampire kill his wife, remember?" McKenzie pointed out. "Maybe he did love this Camilla... but it doesn't excuse all the actions he took in her name."

Evelyn nodded, though her sense of regret remained intact. She looked over at the entrance to the lair, where her husband was descending the stairs. He looked older somehow, as if he'd aged several years down in the tunnels. A thick bandage was wrapped around his left palm and a dark stain was beginning to seep through. "Did you speak to Mr. Oden?" she asked.

"Yes. The worst of the cases was a woman named Margaret Thomas. Klempt had done... terrible things to her. She's going to survive, they think... but it's going to be touch and go for awhile. I'm paying to have her transferred to some friends of mine at Miskatonic University. They're experts in these sorts of things."

"What about the Noble Dead?"

Max shrugged. "Still out there... but they'll have sensed what happened. I imagine they'll go into hiding, spread out over the world... try to reassert their old dominance from the shadows."

"And that wound of yours?" McKenzie prompted. He'd been the first to see Max's hand and the memory of it had kept him awake for over an hour last night. It looked... demonic, in every sense of the word.

Max glanced down at it, choosing his words carefully. "It's stopped hurting... but I suspect it's going to cause me trouble for some time to come." Forcing a smile on his face, Max looked back at McKenzie. "Thank you for helping us."

"Thank Mr. Benson. If it wasn't for him, I wouldn't have known you from Adam." McKenzie stood up, setting his now empty bottle of beer on a table. "I better be heading back home, folks. Anything looming on the horizon, adventure-wise?"

Evelyn stifled a grin. McKenzie seemed particularly gung-ho about his role in their little party... which she didn't mind all that much, actually. She and Max needed all the help they could get and it might mean that the Rook wouldn't be flying solo while she was away filming her next movie.

Max pursed his lips. "Nothing yet... but I'll call you. And you keep an eye out for anything that seems beyond normal police work. I think I'm going to enjoy having you around to offer me 'official' lines of information."

McKenzie smiled at the compliment and gave a gallant tip of his head to Evelyn. "Don't stay up too late, you two."

After he was gone, Max moved to take his seat next to Evelyn. He held up his bandaged hand, saying, "This might cause some problems. Nyarlathotep said that some of my enemies might strike at us... at those close to me."

"Then they'll be making quite a mistake, won't they?" Evelyn leaned close and kissed his cheek. She'd fared quite well in the battle with the vampires, escaping with only one long scratch on her stomach. It was healing nicely, which meant she'd be back to wearing her skimpy outfits onscreen soon. "I know that you're worried about me... and Nellie and Josh, too. But we'll be fine."

"I wish I could be so sure."

"You know… that honeymoon of ours ended a little abruptly." Her eyes twinkled mischievously. "Maybe we could pretend we were still on it."

Max studied her face, a heat growing in his cheeks. "I was so lucky to have found you… for so long I thought I was cursed, but I was wrong. I'm blessed."

Their lips came together, slowly and softly at first but with growing intensity as the seconds passed.

Warren Davies watched from beyond the veil of death, turning away only when it seemed improper to watch his son and daughter-in-law any further. He was glad that his son had found some measure of peace, but he also knew it would be short-lived… for the Rook would have to fly again, and soon. For him, there would be only a lifetime of adventure… it was the road to which his father had tied him and there could be no escaping his destiny.

Warren felt the pangs of regret but he ignored them. He had done the right thing, no matter how awful it might have seemed. He had helped transform his son into a killing machine, a weapon against the evil that plagued the world. The recent battles against Trench and Camilla had helped harden the Rook, but there were more tests to come…

Warren stared hard into the future, straining to see past the haze of time. War was coming, a war that would plunge the entire world into a nightmare that would consume millions. Warren wasn't sure who the true threat was, though he suspected it had something to do with the madman who had risen to power in Germany.

Be strong, Max. The world is about to need you – and men like you - more than ever before. I just pray you're ready for what's about to come.

THE END

THE GASPING DEATH

Starring
the Rook and the Moon Man

THE HEROES

Moon Man: *Modern Robin Hood of crime, the Moon Man is actually police detective Stephen Thatcher. Donning a midnight black cloak and a domed helmet of Argus ("one-way) glass, the Moon Man steals from underworld kingpins and high society alike, passing on the spoils of his victories to the needy citizens of Great City. Aided only by his loyal assistants Sue McEwen and Ned "Angel" Dargan, the Moon Man is hunted by police and underworld alike!*

Rook: *Wealthy socialite Max Davies inherited the family fortune after his father was brutally gunned down by criminals. Afflicted with painful visions of future crimes, Max traveled the world, learning every fighting art known to man while simultaneously mastering the sciences. Wearing a dark cloak and a strange birdlike mask, the Rook began slaying criminals throughout the United States and Europe, leaving behind only a playing card to show his presence. Eventually moving his operations to Atlanta, the Rook married actress Evelyn Gould and became embroiled in an ongoing feud with the messenger of the gods of chaos, the dark wanderer known as Nyarlathotep!*

Chapter I
Theft!

Merv Sanford had worked at the Great City First National Bank for almost twenty years. When he'd started out, he'd been a fresh-faced veteran of the Great War, one who was stuck with a permanent limp after a German bullet had pierced his left leg. Merv's uncle had worked for the local police force and had helped his nephew get a job as a security guard at the bank. It was good, steady work and Merv enjoyed it.

He tipped his cap to Mrs. McGreavy as she entered the bank, carrying a small paper bag filled with coins. She came in every Wednesday at 4:30, creeping along at a snail's pace. She smiled at him, her wrinkled face brightening when she saw him. She took a spot in line just behind another regular, Larry Thompson. Mr. Thompson was a stock broker, one who'd nearly lost his shirt during the Big Crash of a few years back, but he was slowly crawling out of the hole he'd found himself in – just like the rest of the country was doing.

Merv chuckled a bit as he leaned back against the wall. Life was good, he had to admit – the ache he used to get in his leg was almost gone and he'd become enough of a fixture at the bank that he didn't worry from month to month about keeping his job. He reached out and picked up a newspaper from a nearby table, scanning an article about the notorious Moon Man and the police force's ongoing attempts to capture the criminal. Merv's uncle knew that man in charge of the investigation – tough as nails Detective Gil McEwen – and it was common knowledge around the Sanford household that the Moon man's days were numbered.

Merv coughed as he turned the pages, eager to see whether or not the Great City baseball team had righted themselves after their last three-game losing skid. Before he'd even reached the sports pages, another cough had wracked his body… and this one hurt. Merv looked around and noticed that others in the bank were beginning to double over, hacking like a bunch of sick cats. Mrs. McGreavy fell to the floor, clutching at her throat and wheezing.

Merv's vision began to cloud and a terrible heaviness settled in his chest. It felt a bag of lead weights had settled into his lungs, weighing him down.

As the war veteran turned bank guard slid down the wall to the floor, his head beginning to throb painfully, the doors to the bank flew open. Several men wearing gas masks ran in, dancing amidst the fallen bank tellers and customers. Each man wore all-black uniforms and carried small sacks in one hand, while the other brandished dangerous looking rifles.

Merv struggled to reach his gun, despite the fact that he never kept the revolver loaded. It was used mainly to give little boys a thrill when Merv would show it off to them… but as he felt his life ebbing away, Merv had only thought in his mind: stop these thieves from looting the bank.

A final figure emerged into the guard's fading vision, a figure draped in a form-fitting black suit and a long cloak that swirled about glossy leather boots. This figure, too, wore a gas mask, which looked all the more bizarre with the wide-brimmed hat he wore above it. "Excellent work," the man said, surveying the grim scene.

Merv groaned in fury. How could anyone call this 'excellent' in any form? Men and women were dying!

As his men set off small charges around the vault in the back, the black-garbed figure caught sight of the determined guard. He strode towards Merv, kneeling when he was within an arm's reach of the guard. He watched Merv's fingers trembling helplessly on his holster's latch.

"You're a strong one, aren't you?" the stranger said, his voice distorting strangely within the gas mask. "I think I'll let you live… a witness to the glory of what is to come." The man reached into a pocket and withdrew a syringe, checking it briefly before inserting the needle into Merv's neck. "Tell them who did this. Tell them that Prof. Lycos is about to claim ownership over Great City!"

Merv moved his lips gamely, trying to utter some sort of angry retort… but he grew weaker by the second and with the madman's words echoing in his brain, he passed out.

Chapter II
The Night Terror

The ballroom was packed with Great City's finest, all decked out in their finest splendor. Debonair Steve Thatcher stood near the punch bowl, wearing a dapper black suit that emphasized his lean physique. Young and handsome, he had received a number of appreciative glances from the various ladies in attendance, but the detective-sergeant had eyes for only woman tonight: his date for the evening, Sue McEwen.

Sue was at his side, her hair cut very stylishly and her complexion looking attractively peaches-and-cream. The daughter of Stephen's good friend and direct supervisor, Gill McEwen, Sue was one of the few people who shared in both aspects of Thatcher's life. She was a steadfast ally in his duties as a police officer… and she was also keenly aware of his nocturnal habits as the Moon Man.

"There's James Craddock," Sue whispered. Her hand felt light on Steve's arm.

Steve glanced over, watching as their host for the evening made the rounds, shaking hands and making jokes. Craddock had made his fortune by buying up broken down tenement buildings, knocking them to pieces and then rebuilding whole areas as high-scale apartments. The tactics he had used in persuading the residents of said tenements to sell their properties could only be described as excessively shady. "He looks like a million bucks," Thatcher said. "Too bad it took the blood and sweat of good people to line his pockets."

"You're still planning to go through with this?" Sue asked, accepting a cup of punch as they made their way to the front of the line.

Thatcher smiled in response. "Who? Me? I'm an officer of the law, you know."

Sue laughed softly, looking back towards Craddock as the man stepped up onto a small pedestal and gestured for the crowd to give him their attention. She felt a flutter of nervousness, but excitement as well. It was such a dangerous game that her lover played, barely avoiding the daggers of both the police and the underworld. But it was such a necessary task, for even here in Great City, there was so much suffering on the city streets. Men like Craddock lived in luxury while others starved to death only a block or two away.

"I would like to welcome all of you to my home tonight," Craddock began. "As many of you know, we'll be opening the doors on Craddock Plaza in just a few weeks. Hard to believe that the Plaza was once a filthy cesspool, isn't it?"

A round of laughter made Sue shiver in disgust. She turned to check on Steve's reaction but found that she was now standing alone. Sighing, she crossed her fingers that all was going to go according to plan.

Stephen Thatcher, unseen by any of the partygoers, had ducked out as soon as all eyes were upon Craddock. In a darkened closet where he'd earlier stashed a small leather case, he set about transforming himself from an officer of the law to an enemy of it.

From within the case, he withdrew two ebon gloves. A long black cloak followed, which he wrapped tightly about his shoulders. The final component of his disguise consisted of two silvery half-shells, hinged at the middle. These shells fit together around Steve's head, hiding his face behind an Argus glass orb. The helmet was mottled to resemble the moon, giving Thatcher's alter ego his name. A special filter pushed his breath downwards to avoid fogging the inside of the glass, but there was nothing to provide additional support to the helmet. A lucky shot could tear right through the glass and scar him for life, if not kill him instantly.

The lunar-faced vigilante lifted out a small handgun from the interior of his cloak and crept through the mansion, taking note that the cost of the furnishings here could feed a family of four for the rest of their lives. It chilled him how anyone could ignore the plight of their common man, but Craddock had certainly done that – he'd profited from it, in fact.

The Moon Man made his way to a small hallway just behind the platform upon which Craddock was standing. True to the rumors he'd heard, the Moon Man saw that Craddock had revealed a small bag filled with stacks of money. The millionaire's words burned into the hero's mind: "And so, this amount before you is only the beginning. This money comes from those investors who have wisely chosen to invest in the Craddock Plaza project! Just think how much more we'll all make once the Plaza is open for business!"

"Just like the idle rich – you have to boast about every little penny!" The Moon Man's words were punctuated by his sudden appearance from the shadows, eliciting a flurry of screams from the crowd. Two armed men – private security for Craddock – moved forward but the Moon Man dispatched each of them with well-placed shots that knocked their guns right out of their hands.

Craddock remained frozen in place, the bag full of money held in one shaking hand. "No! This is my money! This is my house!"

"That money belongs to the good citizens of Great City," the Moon Man hissed quietly. Realizing that the façade of the Moon Man carried great power, however, he shouted "I'm taking it for myself! Now fork it over!"

The Moon Man snatched the bag from Craddock, whirled about with his cloak billowing behind him. He charged from the room, leaping through a window that he'd noticed was left ajar. Outside the mansion, he found a waiting roadster, with the engine idling. A massive brute of a man, no-necked and bearing a cauliflower ear, leaned out from the driver's side window. It was Ned "Angel" Dargan, a former prize fighter who had become the Moon Man's ambassador to the poor and needy.

"Angel! Take this and go!" The Moon Man shoved the bag of money through the window, beginning to strip himself out of his uniform at the same time. Within seconds, the helmet, gloves and cloak were in the car, as well.

"What about your case, boss?"

"I'll get it later, Angel." Thatcher smoothed his hair down and stepped back. "I'll meet you back at our base. Go ahead and start passing out the cash – the orphanage on Fifth Street would be a good place to start."

Angel nodded and pressed the accelerator, roaring away in a cloud of dust. Thatcher, meanwhile, moved to join the large crowd of frightened people that were gathering on the front lawn of Craddock's expansive property. He pushed through them until he was inside, finally locating the party's host. The terrified millionaire was still standing right where the Moon Man had left him.

"Mr. Craddock! I'm with the Great City police!"

Craddock stared at him, his shock slowly replacing with anger. "Did you catch him? That damned thief made off with my money!"

"We've been after the Moon Man for ages, I'm afraid. I took off after him but he had a car waiting."

"Worthless police!" Craddock exclaimed. He shoved Thatcher aside, moving towards the exit. "I'll take care of him my own way if I have to...."

Thatcher watched him go, feeling quite satisfied. He'd gained a good bit of loot tonight, enough to help a lot of needy people... and he'd been able to stick it to a slick operator like Craddock while doing so.

"You look like the cat that ate the canary," Sue whispered, sashaying up beside him. "My dad's on his way – I called in the tip."

"Good girl," Steve replied. He put an arm around her shoulders and gave her a squeeze. "Let's go greet him, shall we?"

Chapter III
The Golden Dagger

Max Davies perilously balanced on a thin stretch of rock, while the ocean waves crashed down below. He wore the long black cloak of the Rook, which was flapping wildly in the strong winds, making it difficult for him to maintain his balance. From the direction he'd come he heard the sounds of pursuit: Nazis, at least four of them, each armed with automatic weapons. They had zealously guarded the prize which Max now clutched against his chest: an ancient manuscript describing, in detail, the treasures of the Knights Templar. Though some of the details within could have increased his wealthy immensely, Max had no interest in such. He had stolen the book from the German occultists because it held the true origins of a golden dagger that he had held in his possession for several years.

Max had a slightly olive complexion to his skin and wavy black hair, the sort that made women want to run their fingers through it. He favored well-tailored suits and wide-brimmed hats, but today his handsome features were hidden beneath a billowing cloak and a small domino-style mask that ended in a bird-like "beak" over his nose.

The Rook moved forward, trying to make it to the other side of the mountain before the Nazis caught up to him. He took his steps cautiously, aware that there would be no hope of survival if he fell the more than two hundred feet to the surf below. The jungles of Brazil were not his usual stomping grounds and they came with dangers that he was not normally faced with in Atlanta.

He had just stepped foot on the other side when a voice bellowed after him. "Thief!" the man yelled in German. Max understood him well enough, for he was fluent in almost every language on Earth.

Replying in the man's same tongue, the Rook answered, "This book doesn't belong to you either, my friend! Just be glad I didn't kill you when I had the chance!"

The scarred visage of his opponent darkened in rage. "I will hunt you down, Herr Rook! I will make sure you die – slowly and painfully!"

The Rook turned, ignoring the threats. He had heard similar things before and never paid them any heed. The scar on his left palm burned incessantly, but that was nothing new, either. He had received it as a parting "gift" from a demonic entity three months ago and its presence had made his work all the more difficult. Those with occult senses could now trace his movements, making it nearly impossible for him to sneak up on them. That had led to a bout of gunfire earlier in the evening, but he'd escaped unscathed.

At the base of the mountain, he found one more disappointment, however. Two of the Nazis had found his modified car, a pitch-black vehicle that made no sound whatsoever and which could travel several hundred miles on a single fueling.

The first of them, a broad-shouldered brute with a short, bristled haircut whirled to face him. "So! This odd car does belong to you...."

"Brilliant deduction, Mr. Holmes," the Rook taunted. He slipped the manuscript into the folds of his cloak, pulling forth two pistols of his own. "Why don't you and Fritz back away from the car?"

The second man sneered, but waited for the first to give the order to fire. The broad-shouldered man merely smiled, keeping his gun pointed at the Rook's chest. Overhead, the moon hung full in the sky and the hot, humid air seemed particularly oppressive.

"Herr Rook, we have no desire to kill you... but we will, if need be. Who do you work for? Some Zionist guild, perhaps?"

Max rolled his eyes at that, but said nothing. Instead, he took one step forward, fingers twitching on the triggers of his guns.

"Stay where you are!" the Nazi shouted.

"You're supposed to bring me in alive, aren't you?" the Rook whispered. "Is that why you haven't fired yet?"

"We have been given orders to defend ourselves if need be..." the Nazi answered. He seemed to be in no hurry to instigate combat, perhaps because he had heard how ferociously the Rook had fought his comrades earlier.

"You'd best do that, then." The Rook sprang into action, firing both pistols while simultaneously jumping to his left. While the Nazis struggled to respond in kind, his bullets ripped into their legs, sending them moaning to the ground and making their own shots go askew.

The Rook kicked their weapons away from him, feeling a strange compulsion to end their lives. Earlier in his career, he would have done just that, making sure that they did not live to trouble him another day. But an encounter with the mysterious Mr. Benson had left him with a changed outlook on that: avoid unnecessary murder and Mr. Benson would make sure that the authorities worked with the Rook, rather than against him.

Max settled into his car and sped away, leaving the two Nazis writhing in the dirt. He had memorized the path through the jungle and he knew that a plane was waiting for him in a clearing not more than three miles away. The car would fit smoothly into the cargo hold of said plane and then he'd be on his way back to his home in Atlanta. Evelyn was away filming *Return of the Queen of Atlantis*, another in a long line of bodice-ripping adventure yarns, but he was still anxious to return to the States.

Within moments, the Rook was onboard his specially built plane and was taking off into the air. After setting the controls to automatic, he pulled the manuscript from his pocket and flipped through it, ignoring everything until he found a drawing of the golden dagger.

Max ran his fingers over the words, memorizing them.

> *The mystic blade known as the Knife of Elohim is said to have been soaked in the blood of Christ on the day of his crucifixion. It has had many owners, but came into the possession of the Knights in the 11th Century, becoming one of our most potent weapons against evil. The wielder of the blade is able to pierce the hides of animals that are immune to all other weapons and is protected by the grace of our savior.*

The Rook grunted. He had traveled the world enough to gain a healthy appreciation of all religions, not just Christianity. Nevertheless, there was certainly something powerful about the weapon, leading him to believe that at least some of what he was reading was true.

Max set the manuscript aside, pulling the dagger from the sheath he wore at his waist. The golden blade glimmered in the dim lighting. Holding it seemed to lessen the pain in his left palm and Max sighed to himself, wondering what madness lay waiting for him when he did finally make it home. It seemed more and more like his life was one adventure after another. Truth be told, he sometimes enjoyed it, especially when Evelyn or McKenzie were at his side. But he was also growing older – he would turn 38 later this year, having been born at the turn of the century. How much longer could he withstand the rigors of age? Evelyn was several years younger and had begun broaching the subject of children... would it be fair to bring them into this dangerous lifestyle of his? Could he avoid putting them at risk?

Such thoughts loomed large through the rest of the flight.

Chapter IV
Craddock's Plea

Max Davies had a slightly olive complexion to his skin and wavy black hair, the sort that made women want to run their fingers through it. He favored well-tailored suits and wide-brimmed hats, but was going decidedly casual today, wearing a pair of pressed slacks and a sweater vest over a tan-colored shirt.

The clothing suited his surroundings. William McKenzie's office was not the sort that you usually associated with a police chief in a major American city, but then again William McKenzie was not your usual police chief. The youngest to hold the position in the entire country, McKenzie had an easy air about him that spoke of endless enthusiasm and a tireless dedication to his duty. Unfortunately, he was not a tidy housekeeper. Huge stacks of papers lay on every available space and a surprising number of medals and awards were stuffed under desks and beneath tables.

"The Rook is not for hire," Max said, sipping from a glass of water. It was hot in Atlanta, with the temperatures dancing around 100 degrees. As such, Max's fine clothing was plastered against his skin. Somehow, he managed to make it look good.

"I don't think Mr. Craddock would look at it that way. He contacted Mr. Benson, who in turn sent Craddock to me. And I'm bringing it to you... so it's not like you're out selling your services."

"Why doesn't he go to the local authorities? Why turn to a vigilante for help?"

"He doesn't think the police there can catch this Moon Man character. I know a guy there – Gil McEwen. He's a grade-A cop, but he's been made a fool of by the Moon Man, over and over again. Heck, one of their officers was in attendance at the party where the crook made off with Craddock's loot!"

"What kind of man shows off his cash at a party?" Max wondered.

"An arrogant S.O.B.," McKenzie admitted. "Look, all I'm asking is that you drop by and see the guy – he's staying at the Manzini Hotel."

Max stared into his water, feeling a vague sense of unease. He'd heard about the Moon Man, but only in passing. It sounded like the sort of thing that Benson himself might be interested in... but instead the mysterious figure had elected to pass the case on to another. The entire affair made him remember the events of a few months past, when Richard Benson had paid him an unexpected visit, informing him that he knew about Max's dual identity and offering a deal: Benson would smooth over the Rook's problems with law enforcement in exchange for Max's vow to avoid taking lives if possible. In addition, Benson's organization would aid the Rook in other fashions, in return for the Rook assisting them on certain cases.

Like this one, apparently.

"I'll stop by and see him," Max said, finishing off the last of the water and standing up.

"When's Evelyn due back?" McKenzie asked, rising to walk Max to the door.

"Not sure. I heard from her last evening and she said the director had called for another week's worth of filming. Apparently he didn't like the original ending and wants to rework it."

"Well, enjoy your temporary return to bachelorhood while you can," McKenzie joked. His youthful face grew serious. "Do you think we'll get caught up in that mess in Europe?"

"Hitler, you mean?" Max paused before answering. He'd clashed with enough Nazis in recent times to know their capacity for violence was extremely high. And Hitler's growing interest in the occult spelled certain trouble. "I wouldn't be at all surprised. Not at all."

The Rook crept in through a partially open window, stepping into Craddock's darkened hotel room. The millionaire was sleeping soundly, his snores echoing off the walls. Max noticed a finely made suit tossed haphazardly over the back of a chair. It was enough to make Max wince – the clothing must have cost a small fortune but Craddock seemed to treat it like an old rag.

Creeping near the bed, Max retrieved a small flashlight from his cloak and turned its burn on, shining it full force into Craddock's face. The man jumped up, blinking in alarm. "What the hell–?"

A playing card flew through the air, landing atop Craddock's sheets. It sported a white background, upon which a black bird was captured in flight. "You can call me the Rook," Max whispered, keeping his voice low. "I understand you need my help."

Craddock clutched at the playing card like a drowning man clinging to a life preserver. "Did the police chief tell you…? About that damned Moon Man?"

"I know he's a costumed criminal… and that he made off with a small fortune from your party."

"You've got that straight." Craddock raised a hand to ward off the harsh glare of the flashlight. "Could you lower that thing?"

"No," the Rook answered. He'd read up on Craddock on the way over and he knew about the man's techniques in earning his fortune. He'd follow the letter of the law in this affair, but he wouldn't seek out the man's friendship. "What does the Moon Man spend his loot on?"

"How the hell should I know?" Craddock replied testily. "I'd imagine he's living it up. Probably has six cars and a harem of women."

"Over the past few years, he's made quite a haul, stealing money from the idle rich. But he keeps coming back for more... that makes me think he's either got some very expensive habits or he's driven by something more than mere greed. A compulsion, perhaps... or the thrill of the chase."

"I could care less why he does it or what he spends the cash on. The point is it's my cash he's spending!"

The Rook abruptly turned off the flashlight, sending the room into pitch-black darkness. "I'll be in Great City by tomorrow night, Mr. Craddock, and I'll deal with your Moon Man problem... but I'm doing this only because I owe someone else a favor. From what I know of you, you're scum... and probably more than deserving of what's happened to you."

"You're gonna plug him?" Craddock asked, a dangerous sort of glee in his voice.

"I won't kill him, if that's what you mean. I don't do that anymore."

"If you turn him over to the cops in Great City, he'll be free before morning. They can't handle him!"

Craddock waited in the dark for a response, but heard none. When he finally worked up the nerve to turn on the small lamp on the nightstand next to his bed, he found that the Rook was gone.

Chapter V
Invisible Death

"I can't believe it! The nerve of him!"

Stephen Thatcher stood in the corner of his father's office, watching as his immediate supervisor, Gil McEwen, vented his frustrations to Steve's father, the chief of police. Two days had passed since Craddock had returned to the city, his return trumpeted in the newspapers as an indictment of the local police. It was well known that the millionaire had gone in search of help, having abandoned hope that the Great City police force would assist him.

"Calm down, Gil," the elder Thatcher was advising. With a stern expression, the old man was generally feared around the department. But his expression often softened when he gazed upon his son, whom he loved more than life itself. "Steve told you there was nothing that anybody could do. The Moon Man was in and out of there so fast, it wouldn't have mattered if we'd had a dozen officers on the scene!"

Gil chewed on the end of an unlit cigar. He was a thirty-year veteran of the force and widely regarded as the finest detective in Great City, but his inability to capture the Moon Man ate away at him. "He's making us all looks fools, Chief! And now we've got Craddock saying he's bringing some vigilante with him from down South! We can't let it happen!" Gil leaned forward in his seat. "Let me organize a full task force, Chief. Let Steve handle my usual duties – if I focus every bit of my attention on this case, I can catch him! I know I can!"

"We need you on other cases," the elder Thatcher cautioned. "I understand your position but I've got to look out for the entire city, not just focus on one thief – even one as notable as the Moon Man."

Gil harrumphed but didn't argue any further. He recognized the look in the chief's eyes and knew there was no hope of persuading him.

"Steve, did you find out anything related to where that money was taken?"

Steve stood up straight when his father addressed him, nodding quickly. "Sure did. Stacks of it have shown up all over town, all wrapped up in silver bands of foil. The Moon Man dispersed the money to a local orphanage and to old man Wilkinson, the one who lost his wife last fall and just had a heart attack."

Gil rubbed his chin. "I just don't get it. Why does he do it? I'm not even sure he keeps anything for himself!"

"Maybe he's doing what he thinks is right," Steve offered.

Gil considered the notion and quickly dismissed it. "Nah. There's an angle he's got. We just haven't figured out what it is yet."

Steve nodded, as if in agreement, though the man's words gnawed away at him. How would Gil react if he knew his daughter was dating the Moon Man? Would it make any difference in how Gil viewed the Moon Man's actions?

"So are we gonna get the money back from those folks?"

Gil's words brought Steve's attention back to the conversation. Without thinking, he blurted out "Why would we do that?"

"Because it's not their money," Gil replied, staring at him. "That cash belongs to Craddock."

"But he doesn't deserve it," Steve said, his voice quavering. "And those poor people that got the money need it."

"Sounds to me like you're forgetting what your job is," Gil pointed out. "We're agents of the law. We don't make those kinds of decisions. It's Craddock's money."

Steve stood his ground, wondering if he'd made a serious miscalculation in revealing where the money had ended up. "We can't take that money away from them, Gil. It's not their fault that the cash was stolen from someone else."

"Yeah, but–"

The conversation came to a halt when the office door flew open, revealing the young face of a rookie cop. "Sorry for interrupting, Chief… but you better turn on the radio!"

Steve saw a nod from his father and did so, turning on a small desktop radio near the window. The voice that came through the air was muffled, like someone was speaking through a mask of some sort.

"It's been repeating for the past five minutes," the rookie cop said. "It's on every station, too!"

"That's enough, son." The chief waved the young man out of the office, rising from his seat so that he could join his son and Gil in crowding around the radio. "I bet it's related to that strange robbery-murder that took place at the bank, Gil.

We've been waiting for the mastermind behind that to make an appearance ever since that guard told us what happened"

"Maybe this Dr. Lycos is working with the Moon Man," Gil wondered aloud, drawing a smile from Steve. *At least this has turned the conversation away from the money and those poor souls who've gotten it,* he mused. Steve's grin disappeared as soon as the madman's voice on the radio began to grow clearer.

"I repeat," Lycos was saying, "if the leaders of this city want to avoid a catastrophe of the highest order, they will give in to my demands. My name is Prof. Lycos and I have grown tired of my brilliance helping to line the pockets of my employers… from now on, I'll use my creations to benefit my own existence! What happened at the bank was nothing more than a test run and I'd imagine that the sole survivor of that attack has made it quite clear that my men and I are deadly serious about getting what we want. Within the hour, details on the amount of money we expect and where we want it delivered will be made clear to the authorities. In the meantime, prepare yourselves for another example of my power!"

"What the heck does that mean?" Gil wondered.

Steve moved over to his father's desk, plucking up a sealed envelope that had arrived from the coroner's office just prior the beginning of the Moon Man discussion. "Dad? Can I open this?"

"Might as well. Maybe the coroner's report will give us a clue about what that madman's up to."

Steve pulled out a small packet of papers, scanning through them quickly. "That gas that Lycos used… when it gets into the lungs of the victim, it begins to solidify into larger and larger chunks of salt and rock. The poor souls are suffocated from the inside out!"

"What a horrible way to go," Gil murmured, shaking his head.

"Oh lord… he wouldn't dare!"

Steve looked up from the paper, glancing over at his father, who had just spoken up. "What is it?"

Steve's father pointed out the window with a trembling finger. "Sound the alarm! Tell everybody who'll listen to get inside and shut all the windows!"

Steve moved to look outside, the blood freezing in his veins. A zeppelin was on the horizon, partially obscuring the full moon that hung in the sky. From the belly of the great airship protruded a nozzle of some kind… and Steve felt certain that it was spraying invisible death down upon the city below.

Chapter VI
The Rook in Flight

Max Davies had been in Great City for less than 48 hours, but in that time he had been reminded of both the best and worst about big city life. There was an electricity to the air that spoke of endless opportunity... but there was also a coldness to the place that permeated the place. He had checked in to a fine hotel, making sure to pick one that afforded him easy access to and from the city streets below. After getting settled in, he had begun making frequent visits to the local library, scanning through the archives for all stories related to the Moon Man. It was while doing so that he'd come across the peculiar murders at the bank several days before. The whole affair had piqued his interest but it had not deterred him from his primary goal: that being the careful study of the master criminal who had plagued this metropolis for so very long.

He was returning from a visit to the library when he'd heard the screams: panicked and sharp, full of terror. Max was standing near a newsstand at the time and he rushed over immediately, pushing his way through a small crowd of citizens. The group was huddled around a radio, listening intently. "What's going on?" he asked, shivering a bit from a cold wind that was blowing.

"Some nutcase says he's gonna show off his power," a stout fellow to his left said. "Says he's the one who killed those folks at the bank!"

"Did he say how?"

"I bet it has to do with that thing!" the man replied, pointing upwards. A large airship was passing overhead in the distance, some sort of strange nozzle pointing downwards from the ship's underbelly. "And I'm gonna get the heck outta here!"

Max ignored the crowd's dispersing. A few car horns blared as frightened citizens ran through the streets, seeking shelter. Max had read enough of the news to realize that some sort of invisible, odorless gas had killed those poor people in the bank. He stepped into an alleyway, retrieving a small collapsible breathing apparatus from a hidden compartment in his overcoat. The breath mask served a dual purpose, hiding his identity in addition to purifying the air.

The Rook ascended up a nearby fire escape ladder, reaching the roof just in time to see the great airship approaching. Max narrowed his eyes and made out a few gas masked figures through the windows of the zeppelin. He glanced around, eager to do something – anything – to prevent what must be occurring, but for long moments there seemed to be nothing he could do. And then he reached into the pocket of his coat, pulling forth a small device that looked like black matchbook. A small red dial on the center of the device was soon depressed and the Rook stood stock still, waiting....

Over the screams below, he heard the approaching engines of his personal airplane. He had flown into the city, parking the unusual craft at an airfield outside the heart of the metropolis. The original had been lost over Germany during an adventure involving the Rosicrucians, but he'd spared no expense in building a second craft – one that would answer his summons, homing in on the signal given off by the strange device he carried on his person at all times.

The ebony colored plane flew low over the rooftops, slowing as it neared its master. The Rook timed his movements just so, leaping from the building and landing nimbly on the wing of the craft. The door slid open as he approached and he threw himself in before the winds knocked him askew. Once inside, he pulled off his breathing apparatus and made for the cockpit. The plane was well armed, carrying enough armaments to frighten a horde of fighter craft... one lone airship would pose not threat against it – but how to destroy it without drenching the city below in the strange gas?

The Rook's plane quickly overtook the slower moving airship, a spray of well-placed bullets striking the nozzle that protruded from the ship's underbelly. The nozzle bent first one way, then the next, before finally shattering into several pieces.

Onboard the airship, the men who served Prof. Lycos stared in surprise. They hadn't expected to face such resistance – the master's orders had seemed simple enough: spray the gas over the heart of the city and then flee before the authorities could mobilize a response. Unfortunately, Lycos had not planned on the Rook!

The Rook flew his plane in a controlled manner, directing just enough gunfire to herd the airship towards the ocean. When he felt certain that they were far enough away from the city that the threat to life was minimized, he opened fire again, strafing the ship enough that it quickly began to lose altitude. He did this as carefully as possible, well aware that the combustible gases onboard the zeppelin could explode at any time, killing the men onboard. He relaxed a bit as several parachutes sprang into view, as the cowards within the ship opted for the better part of valor.

The Rook picked up the radio transmitter in the cockpit and directed it towards the local police band. "I count four men in the water, about half a mile outside the city. They won't be hard to find – not with that zeppelin of theirs beginning to burn. If I were you, I'd move quickly – assuming you want to save all of them."

The gravely voice of Gil McEwen answered back. "Who in the blue blazes is this?"

"Men call me the Rook," Max intoned, using some of the techniques he'd learned from Evelyn to deepen his voice melodramatically. She'd convinced him that the need for theatrics was present in his work – and it certainly did make things more fun for him. "I've come to deal with the Moon Man problem you gents have been having... but it looks like I'll have more than just that to keep me busy. I'm sure we'll talk again soon, officer."

Before Gil could respond, the Rook silenced his radio. He turned his plane back towards the city, knowing that he'd have to fly with his lights dimmed to avoid being tracked. He'd come to Great City with only goal in mind – that being the capture of the Moon Man – but as he'd told the police officer, it was becoming abundantly clear that there was another, more imminent threat to be dealt with....

Chapter VII
Without the Masks

"**D**amn it!" Gil chewed with renewed vigor on his unlit cigar, pacing up and down the sterile hallways of the Great City Hospital.

Steve stood nearby, arms crossed over his chest. He looked dapper in his police uniform, but he was also bone weary and it showed. After the attack that Lycos had launched, nearly forty people had been hospitalized – with nearly half that many dying within the first half hour. Given how deadly this gas appeared to be, it was daunting to think what the madman could do if his demands weren't met. "We'll catch him, Gil. You know we will."

"And how many more will die before we do, eh?" the older man wondered aloud. He ran a hand through his thinning hair and turned a thankful gaze upon Steve. "Go on home, will ya? You don't have to stay. Or at least go back to the station and wait for that madman's instructions to arrive."

"I'm not going anywhere," Steve answered firmly. "I... love her, too."

Gil nodded, swallowing hard. "You're gonna make a great son-in-law someday."

I doubt you'd say that if you knew about the Moon Man, Steve mused. *But I appreciate the sentiment regardless.*

Both men looked up as a doctor emerged from behind a set of swinging doors. "Gentlemen," he said, nodding at them both. "Ms. McEwen received only a light dosage of the gas – she's luckier than most I've seen tonight."

"How bad is it?" Gil asked. Steve placed a comforting hand on the man's shoulder. Sue meant everything to her father and the normally tough-as-nails cop had nearly fallen to pieces when he'd received the call from the hospital. Steve had barely been any better, truth be told.

"She's going to be okay, but I'd like to keep her at the hospital for another 24 hours. The damage wasn't severe but she still has some difficulty breathing."

"Thanks, doc." Gil quickly shook the man's hand. "Can we see her?"

"Yes... but please keep it brief. She needs her rest."

Steve started in after his partner, but hesitated when another figure emerged from a nearby stairwell. Steve recognized him at once, having spotted his face on society pages. Max Davies, a wealthy socialite who'd moved to Atlanta some years back... his marriage to Evelyn Gould had caught many people's attention. "Gil, you go on inside. You should have a moment alone with her."

"I'll give you two lovebirds one in return," Gil promised.

When the police detective was gone, Steve moved over to Mr. Davies, who was chatting with the same doctor who had treated Sue. To Steve's surprise, Max appeared to be flashing a badge of some kind and his questions were not the ones to be expected from a socialite. "Can you get me copies of the tests you've conducted tonight? I'll need them as soon as possible."

"Sir," the doctor was saying, shaking his head. "There are ethical concerns here. These patients are trusting me not to just turn over their medical records to anyone who asks."

"Cross out their names, then. I just need to know the toxicology results and any pertinent details about the victims – age, physical condition, etc."

"I'll see what I can do," the doctor replied, moving away from him.

Max frowned, knowing that even if the doctor decided to ignore his request, the information would end up in his hands regardless – only the manner in which he gained it might change. If necessary, the Rook would take what he needed, for the good of mankind.

"Mr. Davies," Steve said, moving up beside Max. "I didn't realize you were an amateur sleuth."

"Do I know you, Mr....?"

"Stephen Thatcher."

Max shook the officer's hand, feeling a tingling at the base of his skull. The mental powers he possessed were annoyingly inconsistent, but something about Mr. Thatcher seemed to set them off. "Son of the police chief, I take it?"

"Sure am. So what brings you to Great City?"

Max shrugged, glancing around at the men and women hurrying by. "I'm here visiting friends, actually. When I heard about the awful crimes that had occurred, I grew curious and decided to stop by the hospital."

"Where you happened to flash some sort of identification before asking for privileged medical information?" Steve pressed, keeping his smile in place.

If Max felt uncomfortable, he didn't let it show. "Amateur sleuth... like you said."

"What's the name of your friend? I might know him," Steve continued.

"I doubt it." Max nodded again. "Sorry to run, Mr. Thatcher, but I'm going to be late for an appointment. Nice to meet you."

"Same here – but if you don't mind, leave the detective work to the professionals."

Max laughed good-naturedly, walking briskly towards the stairs. Steve watched him go, but something gnawed away at him. This whole business with Mr. Davies was incredibly suspicious... and suddenly things seemed to fall into place. Davies had fled to the South under suspicions of being the vigilante known as the Rook. Curiously, despite the fact that both Davies and the Rook were subsequently active in the same city once more, no arrests had ever been made – in fact, word had been sent out a few months back that Davies was 100% cleared of suspicion and was not to be troubled any further. But now Davies was in Great City, just as the Rook was? It didn't take a master detective to piece this one together.

Steve cast a glance at the door to Sue's room. He'd spend a few minutes with her, but then he needed to change clothing. The Moon Man was going to pay Mr. Davies a visit… and find out what the heck was really going on.

Chapter VIII
The Madman's Rant

Prof. Lycos paced back and forth, his anger seething forth. "The Rook! What's he doing here?"

A fellow dressed in black watched him with concern, hoping that his master's wrath was not about to be turned in his direction. He was named Smitty and he'd served with Lycos longer than anyone else, having known the professor when he'd been a chemist working the right side of the fence. "Don't know for sure, boss… but word on the street is that he's not here for you at all. He's after the Moon Man."

Lycos stopped immediately, his breath sounding quite loud through the gas mask he wore. Smitty knew that a chemical accident had badly scarred Lycos' features and some in the gang wondered if it hadn't unbalanced his mind, as well. Lycos wore the mask 24 hours a day, even when there was no risk of being exposed to the gas they'd all dubbed the Gasping Death. It was said that Lycos had a terrible fear of people seeing his face – and had killed everyone who had. "Interesting. Perhaps they'll keep each other so occupied that we'll be able to proceed without further interference."

"Uh, boss," Smitty said, hesitating before bringing up what would be a thorny subject. "The cops… they recovered our guys from the blimp. And they got some of the Gasping Death solution, too – not much, 'cause the guys had emptied most of it before the Rook shot 'em down, but they do have some of it now."

Lycos waved a hand dismissively. "The brutes they employ won't be able to crack my formula. The Gasping Death is my life's work – no, we have no concerns there. But as for our men… they may talk in hopes of getting lenient sentences. Something will have to be done about that."

Smitty watched in confusion as his employer moved to a closet and retrieved a small radio transmitter. The hidden base that they called home had been paid for with dirty money and the authorities wouldn't be able to trace Lycos to it… but he'd had the same fears about their boys talking to the cops. The question was what did Lycos think he could do about it?

"All of you enjoyed that feast I paid for after the bank heist, didn't you?" Lycos asked, flipping a dial and activating the transmitter. An eerie hum filled the air.

"Sure we did, boss. It was the biggest meal some of us had ever eaten."

"Implanted within the food were small capsules that can rest in the lining of the stomach for up to four years." Lycos looked over at Smitty. "If any of the boys get out of line… this transmitter will cause the capsule to break apart, releasing highly concentrated does of the Gasping Death into their bloodstream."

Smitty felt a shiver of revulsion go down his spine. He pictured those poor souls right now, their bodies seizing up in terrible agony. There would be no hope for them – not with the stuff already inside them. He placed a hand on his own belly as he thought about the full ramifications of the professor's words. "You could kill me too, couldn't you?" he asked.

"Of course… but I won't need to do that, will I?" Lycos asked teasingly. "Because you're going to be loyal to the end, aren't you?"

"Of course I will, boss. To the end."

Lycos nodded, finally turning off the transmitter. It only needed to be run briefly – once the order was receiving by the capsule in their bellies, things would proceed along their own course. "I have a package I want delivered to the police chief. I won't be as nice from now on – this Rook has made me angry!"

Smitty moved to do as his master wanted – now that he knew just how far gone Lycos was, there was no alternative.

Chapter IX
Evelyn Returns

Max sat in bed, eyes tightly closed. There was a pounding in the back of his skull, a familiar sort of agony that had haunted him since his childhood. The act of seeing his father gunned down had set in motion a series of events that would eventually lead to the creation of the Rook. Foremost amongst these events was that Max's father, Warren Davies, remained behind on Earth as a ghost. Warren haunted his son, helping to awaken the boy's latent mental abilities in the hopes that he would grow into the sort of man who would take revenge on the types of criminals who had slain him. Through vivid, sometimes painful visions, Max's father was able to give his son clues to the future… warnings of evil tidings that would threaten innocents.

Those visions were more painful than usual now. They seemed to cause a terrible ache in the demon-induced scar on Max's left palm, making it burn horribly.

At the moment, however, Max merely gritted his teeth and rode out the vision, carefully sorting through its contents in hopes of discovering what direction the Rook should take.

Max saw himself standing in the middle of a burning building, expensive tapestries going up in flames. The Moon Man was there, his features hidden behind an odd helmet shaped of Argus glass, painted to resemble the craggy terrain of the moon. The third man there was obviously Prof. Lycos, for he wore a long overcoat and a gas mask, matching the descriptions given by witnesses to the bank heist. Max could tell that he himself was injured, for blood flowed freely from a wound on his left side… but far more painful was the intense throbbing in his palm. The scar given him by Nyarlathotep felt like it was about to split open….

Max gasped as the vision passed, leaving him covered in sweat and his heart hammering. In recent times, he'd come to some sort of relationship with his deceased father – in fact, he'd thought once or twice that they might actually become friends. But when he sent these damned visions it eradicated all the good will that Max felt for the man. Each and every one of them came directly from the realm beyond life, channeled from Max's father directly into his son's psyche.

A soft rapping at his hotel room door made him jump, but he was soon on his feet, pistol in hand. "Who's there?" he asked, raising his voice so that it could be heard clearly through the walls.

"Open the door and find out," a familiar voice answered and it filled him with pleasure to hear it.

"Evelyn," he exclaimed, pulling open the door so quickly that he forgot that he still held the pistol in his grip. He followed her surprised gaze and tossed it away, pulling her to him. She looked ravishing, her auburn-tinted hair full of curls and her eyes sparkling. "How on earth did you find me?"

"I heard about the Rook on the radio," she explained, kissing his cheek and breezing into the room, several small bags in her arms. "And since filming ended a bit early, I took the train to Great City. And here I am, ready to help."

Max grinned, setting his gun down on the nightstand. Ever since she'd discovered his dual identity, Evelyn had served as his makeshift sidekick – or "partner," to use the term she preferred. In truth, she'd come a long way in that regard and had actually saved his life on several occasions. "I actually have a dual purpose at the moment: I'm supposed to tracking down the Moon Man, but there's also the matter of this Prof. Lycos."

"All the more reason to have a partner about," Evelyn said. She put her hands on her hips and regarded him. "You look simply awful."

"Why thank you, dear," he deadpanned. "I had a vision. I think this Lycos fellow is more dangerous than I would have first thought. His Gasping Death gas has the entire city in an uproar and I can't blame them. It's a horribly gruesome way to die."

Evelyn nodded, absorbing his words before speaking. It was one of the things he loved most about her – the way she analyzed every situation before acting. "Then I'd say deal with Lycos first. He is a sadist and a murderer. The Moon Man's a simple thief."

"My thinking as well. In fact, I…."

Max's words trailed off as both husband and wife heard a small thumping sound against his hotel room window.

"What was that?" Evelyn asked, watching as her husband moved to open the curtains.

"I have no idea… but it sounded odd, didn't it?"

Max pulled the curtains apart and blinked in surprise. What he saw seemed patently absurd at first, but a rapid realization hit him that this was no dream or joke. Balanced perilously on the small ledge outside the window was the Moon

Man… and he held the muzzle of a gun tight against the glass, pointed directly at Max's head.

"Mr. Davies," the domed figure said, his voice sounding oddly distorted by the strange mask. "May I come in?"

"I don't see where you're leaving me any choice," Max replied, unlatching the window and swinging it open. "If you're looking to steal from me, you're out of luck. I'm traveling light."

The Moon Man paused when he realized that Davies wasn't alone… but there was no turning back now, not with Sue lying ill in the hospital and that maniac Lycos still on the loose. "Actually," he began, dropping to his feet on the carpeted floor. "I wanted to discuss the Rook."

Chapter X.
Clash of Heroes

It was Evelyn who acted first, surprising both men with her actions. She sprang forward, throwing her left leg up in a deadly arc. Her foot struck the Moon Man squarely on the side of his helmet, knocking him off-balance and causing his aim to drift.

Max moved to take advantage, grabbing hold of the vigilante's wrist and wrestling with him for control of the pistol. He didn't harbor any doubts about whether or not the Moon Man knew of his dual identity – it was quite obvious from his presence that he knew Max and the Rook were one and the same – so he threw caution to the wind and yelled "Evelyn! My gun!"

Max's wife was already there, pulling the specially modified weapon up into her grip. She pointed it at the struggling men but held off on firing for fear of hitting her lover.

"Mr. Davies," the Moon Man hissed, his voice sounding oddly distorted by the helmet. "Don't do this."

"You're the one barging into another man's apartment," Max pointed out.

The Moon Man suddenly relaxed his grip, allowing Max to momentarily take control of the gun. Using boxing techniques taught him by Angel, the Moon Man belted his opponent hard in the chin. Max flew backwards, the gun landing on the floor, where it slid under the bed.

Max wiped at his bloodied lower lip with the back of a hand before retaliating. Unlike the Moon Man, Max had traveled the world, training under many of the greatest fighters known to man. He parried another attack from the Moon Man, feinted to his left, and then kicked the vigilante's legs out from under him.

The Moon Man, however, was not so easily foiled. He rolled out of the way of a finishing blow, managing to drive the back of his elbow into Max's side. "I don't want to hurt you, Davies. Honestly. I'm not the man you think I am! "

"Really? And what kind of man *are* you exactly? "

The Moon Man backed away, gasping. Evelyn had a clean shot now, but something held her back. She wanted to give this helmeted figure a chance to explain himself. "The kind who risks his life on a daily basis, Mr. Davies. The kind of man who takes the ill-gotten gains from those who profit off the suffering of others and makes sure that those monies end up in the hands of the needy. "

"You're wanted for murder, remember?" Max retorted.

The Moon Man sighed, raising his hands in submission. "I'm innocent… but that's going to haunt me for the rest of my days. Look… sometimes you have to go outside the law to see justice done. You have done it often enough, haven't you? Why would you even try to bring me in?"

"It's… a favor to a friend." Max relaxed his stance, shaking his head as he did so. "You're right, though. My actions as the Rook aren't much different than yours. I wonder if Benson knows that. Maybe he wanted me to come here to learn some lesson about myself."

"Honey," Evelyn whispered. "You're doing it again."

"Doing what?"

"That thing where you think out loud and disturb people."

"Sorry." Max rubbed his chin thoughtfully. "So… let's start over. What did you come here for?"

The Moon Man knelt, reaching under the bed to retrieve his pistol. He put it away carefully, aware that Evelyn was still watching him, her own gun held at the ready. "I can't afford to waste time worrying about you hunting me down… not when Lycos is out there killing people. I need you to either get out of Great City and leave me be or work together with me to bring in this killer!"

"Do it," Evelyn urged. "There's no point in the two of you working at odds with one another when you have so much in common."

Max nodded, offering a hand to the Moon Man. "I'm game for it. The Rook's at your side, Moon Man."

The Moon Man hesitated before reaching up to remove his Argus glass helmet. When his handsome and slightly disheveled features came into view, he grinned. "Call me Stephen."

Chapter XI
New Allies

Ned "Angel" Dargan sat in the dingy top room of the tenement flat that the Moon Man used as a base of operations, impatiently wondering where his employer was. He'd received the call less than an hour ago, telling him to meet at their usual location – but there had been sign of the Moon Man in the time since.

Angel looked out the window, noticing the clouds that obscured the lunar surface above. He truly believed in the work that the Moon Man did but he also knew it was only a matter of time before the long arm of the law finally snaked its grip around them both. What would happen to poor Mr. Thatcher? His career would be ruined... it was one thing for a palooka like Angel to go to the Big House, but it'd be a shame to have such a thing happen to the Moon Man.

A tell-tale squeak from below made Angel's ears perk up. The downtrodden building was perfectly suited for the needs of the Robin Hood of Crime – and several of the floorboards below had carefully arranged to provide ample warning of someone entering the establishment and making for the room upstairs. Angel moved to stand next to the door, his slab-like fists closed. There were multiple footsteps ascending the stairs and Angel knew that only and the Moon Man knew of the place's location.

When the door creaked open, Angel sprang into action. The figure who had emerged first was wearing a long coat and some sort of odd mask that ended in a bird-like point over his nose. "Say yer prayers, pal!" Angel warned, drawing back a balled fist.

The stranger was quick, however, leaning back to use Angel's bulk against him. The former prizefighter tumbled over, landing hard on his back.

"Hold it!" a familiar voice yelled from the doorway and Angel peered up to see the eerily garbed Moon Man entering. "It's my fault, Angel! I should have come in first. These folks are on our side!"

Angel accepted the Moon Man's help back up to his feet, gazing suspiciously at the masked figure and the stunning beauty that had also entered the room. "Who's the dame?" he asked, finding her somewhat familiar in appearance.

"Evelyn Gould," Steve whispered. "And the gentleman is the Rook!"

"The Rook!" Angel parroted. "But, boss, isn't he on your trail?"

"We've made our peace," the Moon Man replied. "For the good of the city, we're going to unite in our attempts to track down Lycos."

"You don't live here, do you?" Evelyn asked, looking at the ramshackle surroundings.

"No. This is just a safe house for Angel and I to meet," the Moon Man replied. He felt strangely embarrassed about the place, which he'd never been before. "Angel, have you heard anything on the newswire or the police band?"

Angel shrugged, looking somewhat bashfully at Evelyn. "I've seen your pictures, miss. You looked especially nice in that one about Atlantis and—"

"Angel..." the Moon Man prompted.

"Sorry, boss. No, I ain't heard nothin' except for the police telling everybody to be on alert. And they say they're running a search on this Lycos character."

"I've beat them to it," Max said. "On the way over I contacted some friends of mine in a group called the Nova Alliance. One of them – a nice chap named Lamont – gave me the full rundown on Lycos."

"How did you manage to contact them?" the Moon Man asked. "Short-wave radio?"

"A specially modified version," the Rook explained. He produced a small boxy apparatus with a pair of rabbit-ear antenna on top. "Allows everyone on the same wavelength to stay in touch."

"Well, don't keep us in suspense!" Angel exclaimed. "What did you find out?"

"The professor's first name is Travis. Apparently, he used to work for Schlessinger Chemicals, a large firm based out of Maryland – they've recently become the source of a government investigation into their dealings with certain European nations. Part of the concerns the Feds have is that Schlessinger has apparently been working on chemical weaponry. One of the higher-ups on their projects was Prof. Lycos. Two years ago, Lycos was involved in a terrible explosion – resulted in the deaths of nearly twenty people and over a $1000 in damages. Lycos was hospitalized for quite some time and the treating physicians described his mental condition as worsening daily. Schlessinger didn't want any scandals involving one of their top scientists being institutionalized so they paid his way out onto the streets... from there, things get a bit fuzzier, but it seems that Lycos continued his work on his chemical weapon. He performed a few hits for the mob while testing its properties and eventually collected a criminal gang of his own."

"Seems like small potatoes to hold up Great City," the Moon Man offered. "He could make a lot more going overseas to visit the Axis."

"He's insane, remember?" Evelyn reminded them. "So we're headed off to the airfield then?"

"I think that's the wisest course of action," Max agreed. "Do you need to check in with the station?" he asked Steve.

"I'll give them a brief call and then I'll check on Sue. After I do that, I'm ready to go."

Angel leaned over to the Moon Man, whispering "What airfield is he talking about?"

"There had to be a place nearby where that zeppelin of the professor's could have been housed. The old abandoned airfield is the only answer. There's even a house on the property!"

"How long before dawn?" Evelyn asked.

Angel checked his pocket watch, smiling at her shyly. "Three hours or so, Miss."

"Let's not waste any more time, then." Evelyn stood up, her eyes moving from the Moon Man to her dramatically garbed husband. "What a pair the two of you make!"

The Moon Man nodded to the Rook. "It's going to be an honor," he said.

"Same here," Max responded.

Together, the four heroes moved out of the building. Lurking in their near future was a confrontation with a lunatic and none of them took this lightly but there was an undeniable bounce in their steps as they descended the stairs. It was all too rare that men and women of a heroic bent met others of similar nature... but today was one of those days.

Chapter XII
The Dark Man

Lycos sat down on the small cot in his private quarters, anger flaring through him. He'd thought for certain his plan would work – how could it not? Unlike many other cities, there were no costumed vigilantes in this area to interfere with his scheme: nowhere to be found where the likes of the Spider, the Shadow, G-8 and his Battle Aces or the arrogant Doc Savage. No, in Great City, there was only the Moon Man... another criminal like Lycos himself.

But then had come the Rook, flying north from his Atlanta home. Why had the man come here? Had one of the men in Lycos' gang tipped off the vigilante? Was it Smitty?

"Paranoia runs deep in you, doesn't it?"

Lycos jerked his head up, his hands going to his face. His mask was still there, thankfully. He took it off only rarely and never in front of strangers. But who had spoken? The voice belonged to no one he knew. "Who's there?" he asked into the darkness.

A figure emerged, barely discernible in the gloom. He wore a dark suit and had a dark cast to his skin, like that of an Egyptian. His hair came to a small widow's peak on his forehead and eyes that seemed as old as time stared out from under a thick brow. "I am called by many names, Professor. But the one I favor most frequently is Nyarlathotep."

"Your name... sounds oddly familiar to me."

"Have you wandered alone on a moonlit street in the dead of winter, when all around feels cold and dead? The wind blows softly, rustling the multicolored leaves at your feet and you could almost swear that the rats lurking just beyond your vision are talking, gibbering... that is my name they speak. Your ears hear it, though your brain denies it."

Lycos swallowed hard. "How did you get past my men?"

"Only those who choose to see me may do so." Nyarlathotep moved forward, kneeling before the professor's cot. "An enemy of mine – the Rook – comes for you tonight."

"He knows where I am?" Lycos asked, alarmed.

"He comes with the Moon Man at his side," the stranger continued, ignoring the question. "I can help you prepare for him. I can help you… in many ways. But you have to give me something in return."

"What?"

"Nothing that you'll need, I assure you." Nyarlathotep reached for the professor's hand, clutching with his own. Lycos shivered at the touch, for it was as cold as the grave. "All I require… is your soul."

Lycos stared into the ancient eyes, seeing doorways to places and times undreamt of. Whatever war was going on between the masters that this stranger served and those who directed the Rook was far greater than any concerns that Lycos might have had… but the war had come to Lycos nonetheless.   "After I kill the Rook," Lycos muttered, so entranced by the man's gaze that he gave no thought at all to the fact that the Moon Man – a criminal by all accounts – was traveling with the vigilante. "What happens then?"

"You use the powers I'm going to give you to do whatever you please," Nyarlathotep replied. "Do as thou wilt," he chuckled. "Do you want it, Travis? Do you want what I have to offer?"

"Yes," Lycos replied. "Give me the power to take what I want."

Nyarlathotep smiled, channeling a wild sort of magic into the scientist. The pain was intense and caused Lycos to howl like a wounded animal… "Welcome to servitude, Prof. Lycos," Nyarlathotep whispered.

Chapter XIII
Words of Strength and Loss

The setting was the same as it had been the last few times Max had visited his father: that of a snow-covered mountain in the deepest reaches of Tibet. It was here that the series of events that had culminated in the opening of Lucifer's Cage had begun… and for some reason it had come to symbolize the slowly thawing relationship between father and son.

Warren Davies sat outside the small temple that dominated the mountaintop, dressed in the same clothes he'd worn the night he'd died. Like his son, Warren was an intensely handsome man with dark wavy hair and a penetrating gaze. He stared out into the field of white, watching silently as his son approached. Though this place was merely an astral projection, he noted with interest that his son was dressed not as Max Davies, but rather as the nocturnal avenger known as the Rook.

"Son," Warren said. "To what do I owe the pleasure?"

"I need help."

"Of course you do. It's not like you stop by for small talk, is it?"

The Rook frowned at his father's words, feeling the sting of truth in them. "Why should I treat you with kindness? You pushed me into being something that I might not have been otherwise."

"Don't all fathers do that? Besides, you've turned out well. If you hadn't been the Rook, you never would have found Evelyn."

"I want to talk about the last vision you sent me."

Warren gestured for his son to sit in the snow. "Take a load off."

Max hesitated but then relented, sitting down heavily a few feet from the ghostly apparition. "My hand hurt like hell in the vision. Why? There's nothing supernatural about this Lycos...."

"There *was* nothing supernatural about Lycos," his father corrected him. "I've seen things... vague and hazy, as usual... that indicate that the Dark Man is working against you."

A chill ran down Max's spine. Nyarlathotep... dark messenger of the chaos gods who lurked just beyond the psyche of modern man. He had been the power behind a madman named Darkholme some years back and then had then played a role in the Lucifer's Cage affair, though it had been behind the scenes. He had taken a more direct involvement in the so-called Kingdom of Blood adventure, going so far as to "mark" the Rook so that all his agents would sense the hero's approach. "Why does he think I'm so important?"

"It's just the way things work. You're aware of him. You've interfered with his plan... that makes you a threat. He doesn't like mortals who cross his paths and don't run away screaming. That makes him feel weak... and it threatens his place in the hierarchy around him. His masters aren't very forgiving of failure."

"Do you have any suggestions about how to deal with him?"

The elder Davies paused before responding. When he finally did speak, his voice had an odd tone to it that Max had never heard before. "Focus on your love for Evelyn. In the end, it's love that keeps the whole world spinning 'round."

"Are you all right?" Max asked, concerned despite his usual anger towards his father.

"You won't be able to come here again... at least not to see me."

"Why not?"

"Because my time is nearly up... I was able to keep my spirit tethered to you for a very long period but nothing is forever." Warren Davies reached out and put a hand on his son's shoulder. "It's time for the Rook – and Max Davies – to stand on his own two feet."

"The visions...."

"Will continue, I'm sorry to say. All I've done is opened your mind to something that's far greater than my power. You're attuned to a radio wave of sorts – one that's not audible to most people. But some are able to tap into it and use it as a warning system or sorts. That's what you have now. My last gift to you, I suppose."

Max found himself unable to speak for a moment. For so long he'd harbored ill will towards his father for having turned him into a killing machine... but now he was faced with the fact that he was about to lose his father for a second time. He was surprised by how much it hurt. "There must be some way to save you...."

"There's nothing to save," Warren replied with a laugh. "I'm not going off to the inferno, you know, though I don't blame you if that's what you were expecting. What comes next isn't going to be so bad… but it does mean that you and I won't be able to talk for awhile."

"I… really don't know what to say."

Warren's normally stern expression melted into a mask of compassion. "I am sorry for the pain that you had to suffer through. But I really think it's worth it when you think of all the lives you've saved. My death seemed so meaningless but it's not that way at all… not as long as you're alive and well."

"I love you," Max blurted out. He felt embarrassed to say it, but for a moment it was like the little child who'd watched his father die was back again.

"I love you, too." Warren took his hand away and stared out into the horizon. "I think this will be the last time you face Nyarlathotep, son. I can tell you that much. Win or lose, it's going to end."

"But I can't kill something like him… can I? He's virtually a God."

"*That is not dead which can eternal lie- for o'er strange eons even death may die….*"

"You're talking crazy," Max replied.

"It's an old saying – it applies to the masters Nyarlathotep serves, but it might apply here as well. Nyarlathotep inhabits a physical form… one that can be destroyed. It would be a long, long time before it could reform. He wouldn't return until long after your lifetime was over."

"When do you have to leave?" Max asked, returning to the previous subject.

"That's up to you. When you go away… I will, too."

Max remained where he was, silent. Taking a deep breath, he said "Well, I guess we should have ourselves a long talk then, shouldn't we?"

Warren nodded, his eyes growing moist. "I think we should. I really, really do."

Chapter XIV
The Proposal

Sue opened her eyes, feeling a great weight in her chest. Every breath hurt like the dickens but it was still better than how it had felt just a few hours before. Through the gloom of her hospital room, she could make out a familiar shape seated nearby, watching her closely. "Steve?" she asked, her voice reduced to nothing more than a whisper.

"It's me, honey." Steve moved his seat closer so that he could take Sue's hand in his. "I talked to your dad a few minutes ago… he's worried sick about you."

"Have you caught that Lycos person yet?"

"No," he laughed. "I can't believe you're more concerned with that than with your father's worry."

"Daddy's a grown man and he's got more experience handling stress than you or I will hopefully ever have." Her beautiful blue eyes fixed on his. "So you haven't caught him?"

"No, but I'm working on it. We're about to take a trip out to the madman's base. Hopefully things will go smoothly once we're there."

"Angel's going with you?"

"I'm going with the Rook and his wife."

"The Rook?"

"A vigilante from down South. He's here to capture the Moon Man, but I've convinced him that there are bigger fish to be fried."

"What about after Lycos is captured? Will he turn on you then?"

"I think I can trust him. He's a lot like me… and seeing him with his wife made me realize something."

Sue felt her heart speed along like a locomotive. Something in Steve's voice made her feel weak in the knees. "Yes?"

"Let's not wait any longer… as soon as I'm done with this, let's get married!"

"Oh, Steve!" Sue leaned forward in her bed and embraced her beloved. "Nothing in this world would make me happier!"

"Good… tomorrow we'll tell your father that we're going to set a date." The happy couple kissed before Steve pulled away. "I have to go."

"Be careful," she whispered. The weight in her chest seemed to have lifted, leaving her feeling like she was floating through space.

Steve nodded briskly, moving out into the hallway before she could see the tears of happiness in his eyes. Once he'd made it downstairs and on to the street, he saw that Angel was waiting with the roadster.

"What did she say, boss?" Angel asked, wearing a knowing grin.

"You're talking to a soon to be married man, Angel. No more waiting around for us."

"I knew it!" the big man exclaimed. He pulled a shocked Steve into a tight embrace before stepping back in embarrassment. "I mean… congratulations, boss."

"Thanks, Angel. You're a good friend." Steve ran a hand through his hair and lowered his voice. "That's why I want you as my best man at the wedding."

The shock that registered on Angel's face was almost comical. "But… people will ask questions! Like how a top of the line cop like you knows a palooka like me!"

"Let them ask the questions. I'll come up with the answers." Steve put a hand on Angel's shoulder. "Will you do it for me?"

"Of course I will. Be an honor."

"Good. Then let's go stop this Lycos, shall we?"

Chapter XV
Lair of Evil

Smitty tried to avoid the professor's gaze as much as possible. Though the man's gas mask hid most of his features, the blazing eyes of Lycos could be seen clearly enough. They now pulsed with a madness unlike any that Smitty had seen before. "Boss? If those guys are comin', shouldn't we be doing something? Like… running away? Or at least getting the Gasping Death ready to use on them?"

Lycos stood in the front room of the house, watching the airfield from the window. "There's no need for such preparations. We're ready now."

"But…."

Lycos raised his left hand, gesturing dramatically. A cloud of thick gray smoke momentarily appeared in his palm, swirling like a miniature hurricane. "Do you know what this is?"

"No," Smitty replied, a cold chill running down the length of his spine.

"It's the Gasping Death. I made it. I carry it inside me now and I can project it outwards whenever I want."

"How are you able to do that stuff?" Smitty asked, hoping that it would prove to be some new invention of the professor's. Somehow he knew that wouldn't be the case… but the thought of magic, for that's what it appeared to be, was almost too much for the crook's fragile mind to bear.

"I'm not the same man I was before," Lycos said. "I have new friends now. Powerful friends. And they've promised me even more power if I kill the man who's traveling with the Moon Man. So we're not going to run away, Smitty. We're going to wait for the Rook to show himself and then we're going to kill him."

"So this isn't about the money anymore?"

The professor laughed coldly. "No. It's not about the money anymore." He looked over at Smitty, his eyes narrowing to dark points behind his mask. "Is that a problem?"

"Of course not, boss. Not at all."

Lycos whipped his head around, sniffing at the air. "They're here."

"But I didn't hear anything…"

"That's because there's nothing to hear, simpleton!" Lycos strode towards the interior of the house. "Keep them busy, Smitty. If you get lucky and manage to kill one of them, there'll be a bonus for you!"

Smitty watched his master retreat from the scene, swallowing hard to choke down the fear that now gripped him. He couldn't betray the professor – not if he wanted to live – but he harbored doubts about his ability to hold off the Moon Man and the Rook. He drew a small automatic from the interior of his jacket and checked the number of bullets it held. *I shoulda listened to my momma,* he mused, *and became a furniture mover like Uncle Sal.*

"**A**mazing vehicle," Steve said as he stepped out of the Rook's specially modified roadster. "It purrs like a kitten!"

"Makes it easy to sneak up on my enemies," the Rook agreed. "If you like, I'll do some work on your own car and give it the same abilities. You'll be able to get a hundred miles to a gallon, too."

"Incredible," the Moon Man murmured. He was glad that his face was hidden behind the Argus glass because he was feeling woefully out of his depth. The Rook was a master of several disciplines… *Reign in the low self-esteem,* he reminded himself. *You're a highly decorated police officer and you're marrying the most beautiful girl in Great City. You have plenty to be proud of.*

The Moon Man put up a hand to stop Angel in his tracks. "I want you to stay with the car," the Moon Man said. He'd held off on giving his friends this last order because he'd known what the reaction was going to be. Before Angel could bluster out a response, Steve leaned closer and whispered, "If something happens to me, I want you to look out for Sue."

Angel hesitated, warring between his natural desire to take part in the conflict and his loyalty to Steve. Finally, he relented, muttering under his breath. He moved to stand on the other side of the vehicle, trying in vain to look like he wasn't disappointed.

Evelyn and Max were a few feet away, looking over the debris-strewn airfield. Evelyn reached up to make sure that her own mask was still in place. "When we get a chance, love, I need to speak to you about something."

"What is it?"

"Now's not the time." Evelyn came him a soft smile that made Max's heart skip a beat. "Trust me. It's nothing terrible."

The Rook accepted her words at face value. He did trust her… with all his heart. "Too bad McKenzie's not here," he said, changing the subject. "He'd love this."

Evelyn laughed, thinking about their enthusiastic friend back home. "Next time, we'll make sure he comes along."

The Moon Man's approach made the young lovers pause. Though the Argus Glass, the vigilante said "I think we should get a move on."

The Rook murmured an agreement, leading his wife and his new friend through the shadows. A house, boarded up and showing no signs of recent use, lay a short distance away. The trio had reached it in no time, splitting up so that the Rook ascended the front steps while his partners each went to a separate side of the house to check for a means inside. To Max's surprise, the front door swung open at his approach. Keeping his voice low, he barked "Forget about sneaking around back! The door's open!"

The Moon Man peered around the side of the house. "A trap?" he hissed.

"No doubt," Max answered. "But if they've worked this hard to set something up, we shouldn't keep them waiting." As soon as the others were at his side, the Rook entered the building, prepared for the worst.

Chapter XVI
The Devil's Snare

"Look out!" the Moon Man yelled as the trio stepped into the foyer. The Rook looked around quickly, spotting a gunman peering around the corner of the next room. The fellow fired his revolver at Evelyn, but the nimble actress threw herself to the side as soon as the Moon Man had spoken. The gun blast narrowly missed her, tearing a chunk out of the front door instead.

The Rook sprang into action. He jumped for their attacker, knocking the man to the floor and sending his pistol flying away. The Rook backhanded the gunman harshly, eliciting a cry of pain from the man. "Where's Lycos?" the Rook demanded.

"Upstairs," Smitty coughed. "Please… I thought we were just in it for the cash! But he's changed and… I don't want any part of this anymore!"

The Moon Man stepped forward, holding out a pair of police issue handcuffs. "I'll truss him up," he offered. "You two go on ahead and I'll catch up."

Evelyn followed her husband up the stairs, glancing around in confusion. "What do you think that meant? 'He's changed.'"

"I talked to my father," Max answered. "He said that Lycos had become a servant of Nyarlathotep. He also told me I wouldn't be seeing him again."

"What? My god, Max, I'm so sorry."

"Don't be," Max whispered, but the words lacked conviction. He was sorry, too.

Sounds of movement up ahead made them both pause and the Rook gestured for her to arm her own pistol. Like his, it was modified so that it could unleash a steady torrent of bullets without need of reloading.

From inside one of the bedrooms a voice rang out. Its tone was taunting and full of scorn. "Mr. Davies. That is you, isn't it? You've become quite the nuisance as of late. My employer says you've taken to sticking your nose into situations that do not concern you… and I quite agree. Great City was going to be mine – and then you had to take a vacation!"

The Rook paused outside the door and then spun inside, scanning quickly for his opponent. He directed his gun at the professor, who stood calmly in the center of the room. He wore a brown trench coat and a gas mask that hid his face.

Tendrils of gas moved about the professor's legs and arms, coiling about his limbs like trained snakes.

The room contained only a small cot and one open window, but the place smelled like a tomb. Something about the place Max's hand ache terribly.

"You shouldn't have listened to Nyarlathotep, Lycos." Max glanced at Evelyn, who moved to stand near him. "You'll never be anything to him except a tool, one to be used and discarded at his whim!"

"That's a chance I'll have to take, Mr. Davies. You see, not all of us are lucky enough to have a private fortune, a beautiful wife and heavenly powers. Some of us have lost things… opportunities, our appearance, even our soul! All Nyarlathotep did was give me the power that should have been mine to begin with!" To prove his point, the madman pointed both hands at his enemies. The Gasping Death solution that roiled about him was like a living thing and it responded to his command. The gas rocketed through the air, wrapping around both the Rook and Evelyn's heads. They wore small breathing devices that were pushed high into their nostrils but the demonic gas seemed to push and pull at the plugs, hoping to gain access to their victims' lungs.

Evelyn tried to ignore the cloud enveloping her. She squinted and made out the slim form of Lycos, walking towards them with obvious glee. She kicked her leg high, catching the villain under the chin with the heel of her foot. The blow caught him off-guards and he tumbled backwards, his head smashing against the wall. The living gas broke off its attack in confusion, no longer having the professor's consciousness directing it.

The Rook moved forward, trying to capitalize on his wife's success. He grabbed hold of the professor's gas mask, hoping to pull him to the floor, but the aged leather straps gave way and the mask tumbled free in the hero's hand.

The Moon Man entered just as Lycos' face came into view. The professor's face was misshapen and almost inhuman. His nose had been pushed to the side so that the left nostril appeared to have melted into the skin of his face. The bottom of his chin had partially sloughed away, leaving white to shine through. The man's eyes were the worst, though: they appeared to be popping out of their sockets, each fleshy orb looked heavily bloodshot and crazed.

"Good lord," the Moon Man gasped.

His words caught the professor's attention, for the villain suddenly threw his hands up over his face and staggered back. "Stop looking at me!" Lycos screeched. Evelyn tried to grab hold of the flailing arms, but Lycos knocked her hands away. He lost his footing and careened towards the open window. Before any of the heroes could reach him, the professor had tumbled out into space. He screamed as he flew through the air, landing hard in the grass below. From the way his neck tilted dangerously to one side, the Rook knew that one thing was certain: Professor Lycos and the Gasping Death were threats no more.

Chapter XVII
Final Battle!

"**G**reat City's a nice place, but I wouldn't want to live here." Evelyn squeezed her husband's hand as they sat together in the back of the First United Church of God. Stephen Thatcher looked handsome and proper in his tuxedo, standing at the front of the church. Angel was there, serving as his best man, but Gill McEwen was the one who caught Evelyn's eye. The father of the bride looked proud as could be, even as he handed off his daughter's hand to his future son-in-law.

"I agree. I'm looking to getting back," Max murmured. "Heard from McKenzie. Says he wants me to look into a new mystery back in Atlanta."

"Wonderful," Evelyn said, cracking a grin.

"You know… you never told me what it was you wanted to talk about before we fought Lycos."

"Oh…" Evelyn paused, wondering if now would be the right time to bring it up. She elected to do so, keeping in mind how busy they both were. Who knew when they'd have the opportunity to really talk things through? As everyone in the church watched the long-awaited wedding, she leaned close to her husband and said, "Well, you and I are going to be pare—"

Max stood up, his face a mask of fury. "Evelyn. Wait here."

"But…."

Max moved towards the rear of the church, stepping out into the late afternoon light. He hated to run out on Evelyn when she was obviously telling him something important but he'd been expecting something like this… his father had said a final battle was coming with Nyarlathotep and yet the ancient killer hadn't been present during the confrontation with Lycos.

But here he was now, having walked through the back of the church before leaving again, making sure that Max had seen him.

Nyarlathotep was crossing the street and Max followed, keeping pace even when the Dark Man entered an alley and began ascending a fire escape. When Max joined the villain on the rooftop facing the church, he yelled "Is this going to be the end? Because I'm sick and tired of chasing you and your pawns across the globe!"

Nyarlathotep smiled coldly. "Yes. This is an ending… of a sort. You see, there are cycles to all things. For the past few years, the barriers between the worlds of life and death have been thinning... I tried to take advantage of this so that my masters might rise again. But now I see that there is something at work here... something empowering the champions of humanity. There are too many of you now, too many fighting against the encroachment of darkness."

"So you're just giving up?"

"Our agents will always be present, Mr. Davies." The swarthy-faced man smiled coldly, revealing a set of perfectly white teeth. "Rest assured you will have plenty to keep you busy. But as for myself... no, the time has come for me to rest."

Just like my father, Max thought. *Some of the spiritual powers are going into hibernation... but for how long?*

"You will live a long time, my friend. My gift to you will make sure of that." Nyarlathotep gestured towards the Rook's hand. "You will outlive everyone you love... and you will see the rise of a darkness that you will scarcely comprehend."

"Sounds like a lot of talk to me." The Rook reached into his suit jacket and retrieved his golden dagger. It gleamed in the afternoon sun. "I assume we're going to fight?"

"Oh, yes." Nyarlathotep laughed heartily. "One last tussle between us... before I go to sleep. And when I awaken, I'll hunt down your heirs and kill them, one by one. I curse you and your line, Mr. Davies. You shall know only madness and despair."

The Rook didn't bother replying. He moved forward, slashing and cutting with the blade, while his opponent parried with his claws. Blood ran freely from both combatants, as each moved so quickly that they appeared to each other as blurs.

When Nyarlathotep tried to rip open the Rook's stomach, the vigilante spun out of the way and struck home with his golden dagger. The blade dug deep into the villain's neck, sending a red gush of fluid into the air. Nyarlathotep put a hand over the wound, trying to staunch the bleeding, but to no avail. He stumbled backwards a few steps, trying to speak, but his words were lost in the burbling of fluid.

The Rook paused before performing the final stroke. Was there truth to the words of this monster? Would his family really be cursed from here on? *Doesn't matter,* he thought to himself. *I can't worry about what might come down the line. All I can concentrate on is doing the right thing when I can.*

A burst of clarity came to him, then... and he wondered if his father had felt the same way, when he'd made the decision to transform Max into what would eventually become the Rook. *Don't worry about the future... Worry about what's right and wrong – right now.*

Carrying those thoughts in his head, the Rook struck again and again, each blow of his blade leaving behind more wet red flesh in the body of Nyarlathotep. When the messenger of the chaos gods finally collapsed, the Rook crouched over him, panting hard. The demon stared up into the Rook's eyes and his lips, stained red with his life's blood, mouthed words that seemed to sear themselves straight into the Rook's brain. Though they seemed to make little sense to him, they would never be forgotten: *When the good is swallowed by the dark, there the Rook shall plant his Mark!"*

A sudden hissing sound made the Rook fall back from the corpse. Heat was rising from the dead man's heart and before Max's frightened eyes, the clothing covering the skin there blackened and burned away. Pushing up from beneath the flesh was a lump of metal, one shaped like the Rook silhouette that Max used on his trademark playing cards. Max reached out tentatively, plucking it up with careful fingers. It was small enough to be set atop a ring, making it an excellent stamp or brand. An idea ran through Max's head then… a way of harshly punishing criminals without killing them as he once had. And it fit very well with whatever nonsense Nyarlathotep had said at the very end…. *Plenty of time to think about that,* he mused. He rose to a standing position, casting one last glance at the entity before him.

"Whenever you come back," Max whispered, "I'll be waiting for you."

That evening Max and Evelyn sat side-by-side in a private train car, heading back towards Atlanta. Saying goodbye to the Moon Man and his new bride had been somewhat bittersweet, but Max felt certain that Great City was being left in good hands.

Evelyn sat staring out the window, her lips drawn tight.

"Something bothering you?" Max asked, wincing as he moved his left shoulder. Nyarlathotep had scratched him badly there and the wound was seemingly prone to infection.

"You didn't even bother asking me to finish what I'd started telling you back at the church."

"Oh." Max leaned back in his seat, waiting for Evelyn to turn and face him. When she didn't, he asked softly "What were you going to tell me?"

"I'm pregnant."

Max didn't speak for a moment, lost as he was in the full meaning of her words. When at last he found his voice, he said "I'm going to spoil that child rotten."

Evelyn turned then, her eyes alight.

The Rook's Nest was about to get a bit more crowded.

THE END

ABOMINATIONS

Chapter I
Unholy Alliance

Atlanta - April 30, 1939

"Quite a speech that Chancellor Hitler gave at the Reichstag, eh?"

The dark skinned fellow in the tightly wrapped Egyptian garb said nothing. He continued sitting in the back of his taxi, watching with amusement as the men and women of Atlanta moved through the streets.

The driver glanced back at his passenger, wondering if the fellow was mute or just plain rude. It didn't really matter to Tommy Lancaster, though. He'd had all types in his cab and had learned to carry a conversation all by himself. "I tell you, he's trouble, that one. Renouncing that pact like that – what was it called?"

"The Anglo-German Naval Pact of 1935," the passenger said, his voice sounding deep and weary.

Tommy blinked in surprise but carried right on. "That's right! The Naval Pact. Anyway, that fella's big trouble, mark my words."

"Stop here," the passenger said, indicating with a languid hand an alleyway located between two abandoned buildings. The impact of the Depression could still be seen throughout the nation and Atlanta was no exception, with many small businessmen having been driven out of business. In their place, a shady underworld of black market dealers had arisen. This particular part of the city was home to quite a few of them, including Boss Thorne, the meanest man in town.

"Uh, I'm not sure you really wanna be here," Tommy said, pulling the car up to the curb. "This is a bad neighborhood and you seem like... well, a real out of towner, if you know what I mean."

"I appreciate your concern." The man reached into the depths of his robes and retrieved several small coins, which he pressed into Tommy's hand. "Your payment shall be life everlasting."

Tommy blinked in surprise, casting his eyes down to the strange objects he now held. They didn't look like any money he'd ever seen before. They were a dusky brown in color and bore the carved likeness of a jackal. "I need American money, pal. This stuff won't fly."

Tommy's passenger said nothing, merely closing his eyes and smiling softly. A strange scent caught Tommy's attention – it reminded him of burning paper. Old, dry paper from books that were no longer loved or taken care of. Before he could comment on it specks of something like ash flew past his eyes and he suddenly screwed. It was his hand and arm that he smelled, as the skin turned as brittle as dried parchment. Bits of it were breaking off from the rest of his body, swirling in the wind.

Within seconds, there was nothing left of Tommy save for desiccated flesh clinging tightly to bone. The cabbie still stirred, propelled by some inhuman mockery of life. It pushed against the door and shambled out into the street, moving around the vehicle to open its master's door. The Egyptian stepped from the car, sparing not even a glance at the poor soul who now followed at his heels.

Together, the two men entered the alleyway, stopping only when the Egyptian saw a figure emerge from the shadows. The man was of Oriental origins, attractive and well-groomed. He wore a brown suit, white shirt and dark tie. "Mr. Ibis?" he asked in flawless English.

The Egyptian nodded. "I had hoped to be met by your master."

"You will meet him soon enough, Mr. Ibis. But I have been sent to make sure that you have brought the items that were promised."

Ibis gestured to the creature that stood behind him, stirring slightly. "You see evidence of my power. Is that proof enough?"

"Forgive me, but it is not."

Ibis narrowed his eyes, feeling a flush of anger welling up in his heart. He tried to keep his voice calm as he retrieved a small wooden box from the insides of his robes. "The ear of the Abomination," he said. He opened the box to reveal a yellowed hunk of meat. "I also have with me the creature's lungs and its tongue."

"My master has the heart," the Oriental replied, his eyes fixed on the ear. "That leaves only the hands and the brain, does it not?"

"You never introduced yourself," Ibis said, closing the box and putting it back into the dark mass of robes that he wore. "Usually your people are more polite that this."

With a deep bow, the Oriental answered "So sorry. I am Mr. Li."

Ibis gestured to the thing at his side and the creature moved forward with surprising speed. It clutched at Li's throat, lifting him off the ground and pushing him hard against the wall.

"When we reach your master's lair," Ibis whispered, "you will impress upon him the fact that I do not appreciate having my word questioned. If he wishes to deal with the Sons of Anubis, he shall treat us as equals. Is that understood?"

Li fought to form his words around the rigid grip of the monster. "I... understand," he gasped. "And I am sure that my master meant no disrespect!"

Ibis accepted the words, gesturing for his pet to release Li. The Oriental fell to his knees coughing and clutching at his throat. "Then take me to the Warlike Manchu."

Chapter II
Mark of the Rook

The smell of sizzling flesh hit the Rook's nostrils but he kept up the pressure, digging his glowing signet ring into the mook's forehead. The petty criminal howled in agony, thrashing like a fish out of water. "When the good is swallowed by the dark, there the Rook shall plant his Mark!"

Evelyn stood a few feet away, putting the finishing touches on the hogtieing she'd done on the rest of the crooks. Each of them bore the same raven-silhouette brand on their foreheads. The whole thing made Evelyn's stomach churn in disgust.

When the Rook finished with his victim, he tossed the crook aside and took a deep breath. These men had run a white slavery ring for months, trading the flesh of young women for money and opium from the Far East. Max had worked closely with McKenzie to track down the thugs but the final bust had included only Evelyn – McKenzie was away on other business and Max's wife had insisted on coming along. Though he loved having Evelyn at his side, he knew what was coming and was dreading it.

Sure enough, Evelyn wasted no time in asking the inevitable question. "So how long have you been doing this?"

"Doing what?" the Rook asked, pulling a black glove back into place. The glowing signet ring disappeared from sight.

"Torturing people. Burning them like they were animals."

"It's better than a bullet to the brain, isn't it?"

"Not much."

The Rook looked at his wife, noticing that she was definitely beginning to show signs of pregnancy. "You shouldn't come out with me anymore. We have to think about the baby."

"Don't change the subject," she replied. "Besides, I'm not going to be bedridden for some time yet, I hope."

"We don't want you getting bruised up before the awards show, either," Max pointed out. He began searching the sleazy apartment for more evidence, stacking everything he could find on the kitchen table. He'd call McKenzie and let the cops sort out the details.

"The awards show isn't for another week… and you're doing it again. Changing the subject. When McKenzie told me you were doing this, I didn't believe him. But it's true."

"Is that why he begged off coming tonight? So you and I could talk?"

"Yes."

"The stone came from the battle in Great City. It burns any flesh it touches… except mine. I don't really understand it."

"It comes from that evil being… and you wear it like a ring. That's… insane," Evelyn commented.

"I always believed that the only way to make sure a criminal wouldn't hurt anyone ever again was to end their life. Benson made me think otherwise – and if I want to continue taking advantage of Benson's contacts and the police, I have to keep to that. But I want the criminals we stop to remember us – and for everyone else to know what kind of person they are."

"Something's… not right with you." Evelyn flinched a bit as Max approached her, reaching out to her face. "You still haven't told me what Nyarlathotep said to you before his avatar died."

"He said I'd outlive you."

"Is that all?" she asked, staring into his eyes.

"Yes," he lied. "That's all." Max pulled her to him, letting one hand drop between their bodies to rest on her stomach. "I think this is the right thing to do."

"The branding or the baby?" she asked.

"Both."

Evelyn sighed, not responding for a moment or two. She hugged him back and finally disengaged from him. "I'm not going to argue with you about it, but I don't think it's right. And one thing definitely has to change."

"What's that?" the Rook asked with concern.

Her answer made him laugh aloud. "That stupid saying of yours when you do the branding. Very silly."

Chapter III
The Man with the Dead Face

Benson was a man of striking appearance. Not particularly tall or wide, but possessed of a rugged strength that spoke of many physical pursuits. It was Benson's face that most captivated those who met him, however. It was as white and dead as a mask from the grave. Pale gray eyes stared out from under rigid brows, flashing with an internal fire.

Max Davies had met Benson several times before but familiarity did nothing to deter the sensation that filled the Rook's heart: he was in the presence of someone who had lost everything and been reborn in the flames of despair. Benson had lost his wife and daughter to the criminal element and the shock had changed him, physically and emotionally. He had formed an organization devoted to tracking down criminals of all types and he had become a patron of sorts to the Rook, offering him protection from the law in exchange for Max's vow of non-lethal crimefighting.

"What can I do for you, Mr. Benson?" Max asked, pouring them each a glass of water. It was a typically humid Georgia night and both men were already sweating. "It's not often you make the trip down to Atlanta."

"I brought information… and a few questions."

"Let's start with the latter then, shall we?" Max sat down across from Benson. The two men were seated in the study of Max's home, a restored Civil War era plantation house. As Max took a sip of his water, he reached up with his free hand, allowing the fingers to run through the dark curls of his hair. With a faintly olive complexion, Max had a Mediterranean look to him that appealed to most women. "What do you need to know?"

"Is it true you've begun branding the criminals you face?"

"Yes. Does that cause a problem in our relationship?"

"No. Just something I like to keep informed on. Planning on doing anything else different?"

"No," Max answered, feeling annoyed.

"Good. Then we'll move on. Have you ever heard of the Warlike Manchu?"

"Rumors, here and there. They say he was a member of the Imperial family backed by the losing side in the Boxer Rebellion. Now he's some sort of kingpin for the underworld."

"That's putting it mildly. He's a master criminal whose real name is unknown. He goes by any number of identities but the Warlike Manchu is the translation for his most frequently used title. He controls the majority of the gangs in the United States and Europe right now – his fingers are deeply involved in everything from assassination to drug running. He's a master of every known language, an expert in finance and has trained with the finest killers on the planet."

"You make him sound like the devil incarnate."

Benson leaned closer, his eyes burning brighter. "Imagine a tall, almost feline figure, Max… high-shouldered with a close-shaven skull and magnetic green eyes. Give him all the cruel cunning you can imagine and a cruel smile, hidden beneath a long thin moustache. That's the Warlike Manchu. He's the most dangerous person you're likely to ever meet."

"I take it that he's here in Atlanta," Max said. "Or else you wouldn't be here. True?"

"Yes. But I don't believe he's alone. A man named Ibis was spotted recently… he's a priest of Egyptian origins. A murderer, whose fanatical followers claim he's old enough to have lived through the time of the Pharaohs."

Max stood up, pacing across the room. The conversation was making his palm ache, in the way that the supernatural always did. "What could bring them together? What common interest could they have?"

"I'm not certain," Benson admitted, his steely gaze following the other man closely. "But I'm confident you could find out."

Max nodded quickly, already formulating plans for how the Rook could launch his investigation. "I'll call McKenzie and get started." He paused before the window, looking outside. Nettie, the old woman who kept house for him, was retrieving the last of the day's wash from the line. She was a good woman, though of a somewhat testy bent from time to time. "Nyarlathotep cursed me, Benson. He marked me, both physically and spiritually. Ever since I've been heading down some dark paths... and I can't seem to stop. How do you keep yourself from going over the edge? The things you've seen... the people you've lost... how do you make sure you don't become as evil as the men and women you hunt down?"

"I don't sit around and whine about my situation," Benson replied. When Max turned in surprise, Benson locked eyes with him. "Do what you must to soothe your conscience, Max... but never forget that you're putting criminals away for life. You're protecting the innocent. Never forget that."

Stunned by the power in the man's voice and eyes, Max could do little more than nod. "I... won't. I promise."

Chapter IV
Hands of the Abomination

McKenzie stared at the mummified hands in mounting disgust. They smelled like they'd been pickled at some point in the recent past and they gave him the honest to god creeps. He'd called the Davies house earlier in the night, wanting to show these things off to Max. It had turned out that the Rook was in some sort of meeting but Nettie had promised to pass on his request for a midnight get-together as soon as Max was free.

"Working late, Chief?"

McKenzie looked up from his desk and nodded at one of his subordinates. "Perils of being the boss," he said with a laugh. "Go on out on patrol. I'll watch things here at the station."

"Whatever you say," the man agreed.

McKenzie watched him go, running a hand under his hat and through his hair. The youngest police chief in the nation, he had earned the respect of his men through his fearlessness and dedication to his profession. It certainly hadn't been for his skill in housekeeping, however, as one glance at the messy office would attest.

He sat down behind his desk, wondering what was keeping Max. Working with the Rook had given McKenzie some real frights but it had also allowed him to see things that a normal man would never conceive of. The whole affair with the Kingdom of Blood still woke him up on some nights... but whether it was from terror or excitement was unclear even to him.

Movement outside the window brought a smile to his handsome face. Young and fit, there were many in the city who thought he could have been a movie star if things had gone differently. Enough people had said it to prompt McKenzie to think about asking Evelyn her thoughts on the matter. As he rose to move to the window, he said aloud "'Bout time you showed up. I was beginning to wonder if I was being stood up tonight."

As the policeman pulled the curtain to the side, however, he received one of the biggest shocks of his life. On the other side of the window was not the mysterious vigilante known as the Rook but rather a group of four men dressed in black clothing. Their faces were obscured by cloth masks that covered their mouths and chins but McKenzie could see from their eyes that they were of Asian descent.

McKenzie barely had time to back away before one of the men slammed a small baton of some sorts through the window, sending shards of glass flying. The sound was terribly loud in the quiet police house but McKenzie was the only officer still on duty.

The four men – ninja, McKenzie thought they were called, though he was far from an expert on such things – climbed through the window with incredible speed and grace. Each of them produced small curved blades and looked about the office, their eyes coming to a halt on the bizarre hands that lay upon the desk. McKenzie swore under his breath, wishing that Max had gotten here faster.

McKenzie drew his service revolver but was far too slow against the trained assassin. The first of them knocked the officer's hand aside with the flat edge of his blade and a second ran forward, leaping into the air to deliver a kick straight to McKenzie's head. The blow knocked him onto his back, scattering a number of papers.

The one who had struck him first then knelt over him, putting the edge of his blade to McKenzie's throat. In heavily accented English, the man whispered "Prepare to die, Imperialistic dog."

"Wait!" another hissed. McKenzie turned his head as far as he dared and noticed that this ninja had picked up the hands and placed them into a small box. "Someone approaches!"

One of the ninja ran to the window and looked out, nodding. "It is the Rook. How did you know?"

"His car is made to be silent," the ninja explained, "but the master thought to have me place small sensing devices all around the area before we approached. When his car approached, he ran over one of them."

"Bully for you," McKenzie hissed. He struck out while the ninja were distracted, knocking away the one who had been perched upon him. The officer scrambled to his feet quickly but not before one of the other ninja had speared him through the side with his sword. Pain flared throughout McKenzie's body and he cried out as the world began to swim around him.

As the police chief sagged to his knees, the ninja hurriedly abandoned the office, fleeing through the window once more. They had vanished into the stillness of the night long before the Rook reached the station. He took immediate notice of the broken window and the flurry of footprints outside in the damp soil.

With his pistols in hand, the Rook sprang through the window, landing in a crouch. When he saw that McKenzie was alone and that the man was badly wounded, he holstered his gun and rushed to his friend's aid. "McKenzie!" he exclaimed, checking to see that the wound, while deep, would not be a fatal one. "What happened?"

McKenzie coughed as Max lifted his head and cradled it in his arms. "Wanted to show you something that was picked up from a small-time crook… think he was going to sell it to someone on the black market. But those ninja decided they wanted it first."

"I'll get you some medical attention," the Rook said. "And then you're going to tell me everything you know about those… what were they again?"

"Hands," McKenzie said with a groan. "Only they weren't with the rest of the body anymore, if you catch my drift."

The Rook merely nodded, turning over the facts in his brain. Ninja… so soon after Benson had warned him about an Asian warlord loose in Atlanta? The connection was stunningly obvious. *You picked the wrong town to come into, Mr. Warlike Manchu….*

Chapter V
Council of Evil!

Ibis ran his hands over the girl's supple flesh, admiring the curves of her nubile young body. She was freshly dead, having been pulled from a car wreck less than two hours ago, and still had some of the appearance of life. "She will do very nicely," he purred, turning her head to the side so that he might view the wound that had killed her. From all appearances, she had been thrown forward and smashed her skull against the windshield. The injury did little to mar her features, which marked her as having Egyptian ancestry… exactly the kind of girl that Ibis had specifically requested.

Mr. Li watched all of this with hidden distaste. He wore a finely tailored suit that emphasized his fit nature and his hair was smoothed back from his prominent forehead. "If you are capable of making slaves out of people as easily as you did your cab driver, why do you still require the use of corpses?"

Ibis glanced up, having almost forgotten the little man was present. They were in the quarters set aside for Ibis, a set of rooms located in the heart of the Warlike Manchu's headquarters. The furnishings were spare with only the minimum of furniture, but Ibis had made to quite well. The girl was spread out over the dining table, a long wooden rectangle that had creaked slightly under her weight. "I desire more than mere soldiers, Mr. Li. I desire companionship as well."

This time, Li could not hide his horror. "You mean to bed this… corpse?"

"Do not judge the things you cannot comprehend," Ibis responded. He marched towards Li, sending the other man scrambling away. "Get out of quarters! Now! Leave me alone with my bride-to-be!"

"You speak harshly to your betters, Mr. Ibis."

Ibis stiffened in surprise. He turned to see the Warlike Manchu standing behind him, on the other side of the table. How he had entered was beyond a mystery but equally surprising was the fact that Manchu was speaking to him in a dialect that few living men outside of Ibis could understand. Ibis let his eyes roam over the man's lithe physique and startling green and gold robes, upon which the image of an Oriental dragon was rampant. "I did not realize," Ibis replied, continuing to speak in the secret language of the Pharaohs, "that your servants were considered my superiors."

The Warlike Manchu reached a gaunt hand to stroke at the long moustache he wore. "Mr. Li has distinguished himself over years of service. I will not have him threatened again."

Ibis considered making an angry retort but he held his tongue. Though he could summon his mummified followers with a mental command, they would take precious seconds to enter the room. By then, he knew, the master criminal before him could strike with deadly skill. "I will attempt to restrain my anger in the future." Changing the subject, Ibis asked "Have your men recovered the hands?"

"Yes," the Warlike Manchu answered, reaching out to squeeze the dead woman's leg. His touch left deep imprints in the flesh. "They narrowly avoided a confrontation with the Rook. He is a deadly foe and should be met only when we have no other alternative."

"You are afraid of him," Ibis countered, pleased to see that the Warlike Manchu was capable of human faults.

"I am wisely cautious," the Warlike Manchu said. "We are on unfamiliar ground here, testing an enemy who knows how to handle himself. We should pursue the remaining component – the brain of the Abomination – with great haste."

"My servants are ready for the task," Ibis swore.

"Do not lose yourself in illicit pleasures," the Warlike Manchu warned, casting one last glance at the corpse. He strode past Ibis, gesturing for Li to follow suit. When the two men were outside the room, the Warlike Manchu whispered in Mandarin. "It is time that I paid a visit to the Rook."

Li blinked in surprise. "You are going t confront him directly, Master? That is not like you!"

"Have I not told you?" the Warlike Manchu said with a knowing smile. "I have met this man before... during his long travels in the Orient. He was younger then, filled with rage about the murder of his father. He sought to learn from the aged masters, he became an adept in all forms of martial arts and meditation."

Li shook his head. "Then you know him well?"

"Of course. I was his Sensei."

Chapter VI
An Evil History

"**A** package just arrived," Evelyn said, setting a heavy envelope down on the kitchen table in front of Max. She was dressed in a very pleasant floral print skirt and blouse, her auburn hair falling in gentle curls around her shoulders. "And I'm off to see McKenzie at the hospital. I don't suppose you'll coming with me?"

Max looked down at the rumpled pajamas he was still wearing at half past ten and shook his head. "I called in special favors to get this delivered so quickly. I owe it to McKenzie to find out what's going on."

"Why not just find the kid who was trying to sell the hands? He must know what's going on."

"Can't. He was found facedown in a puddle of mud around six this morning. By me."

Evelyn watched as Max tore open the envelope and withdrew a small leather-bound pamphlet. "So what is it?"

"An associate of mine – Felix Cole – handles rare books. Binds them himself when necessary. I called Leopold last night to see if he'd heard of anything like this… hands and such being traded on the black market… and he told me that Cole might know something. Turns out he does. There's been several instances of body parts being stolen or even killed for in recent months. Turns out they're all parts of the same being."

"You make it sound like it's not human."

"I don't think it was."

"Well, I'll leave you to it then." She leaned forward and kissed him on the cheek. "Don't run off to fight demons without me."

Max nodded, already focusing on the book. There was a note attached – from Leopold – asking when Max was going to return to regularly attending Nova Alliance meetings. Max set the note aside. As much as he enjoyed the company of Leopold Grace, Clark Savage, Lamont Cranston and all the rest, he had no time for them at present. *Of course, you're still using them whenever it's convenient,* he reminded himself. *You should really take a weekend and introduce Evelyn to your friends.*

Max smiled. His inner voice was beginning to sound a lot like his father.

The pages of the book were old but in reasonably good condition, the handwritten script on their pages flowing legibly:

In the final years of the Pharaoh's reign, the advisor known as Ibis came to full power. His command over the dark arts became the stuff of legend but nothing he accomplished – not the reviving of the dead nor the enslavement of the living – equaled the summoning of the Abomination. An entity from the stygian depths, the Abomination was the embodiment of all that was evil and chaotic in the world. The Abomination was too powerful to control, however, and he became a force unto himself. He raped or murdered all he encountered, using forces beyond human comprehension. Ibis attempted to restore his control over the creature but succeeded only in driving the entity into hiding. From the shadows the Abomination lurked for many years, becoming known by many names all over the world: the Bogeyman, the Walker of the Dead, the Chaos Lord. In the year 1724 A.D., the Abomination was at last trapped by a great sorcerer and his spirit was taken to the World of Shadows, which lurks just beyond the range of human understanding. There he became the most powerful warrior in a great army of demons but in time he encountered a human who had traveled to the World of Shadows. Eobard Grace did defeat the Abomination, using a magical sword known sometimes as Excalibur. Grace carved the monster into bits and had the body parts scattered far and wide, but in time they came to all reside on Earth once more. Should they be brought together, there is a spell that may be used to recreate the monster – and, it is said, that he will be weak enough for a strong-willed man or woman to finally bind him forever to their spirit.

Max closed the small book and set it aside, his mind whirring. He wondered if Leopold knew about the connection between the Abomination and his father Eobard… but he quickly surmised that his friend was probably all too aware, given that Felix Cole had married into the family as well. *Such a small world we live in,* he mused.

"Mr. Davies," Nettie said, making Max jump in surprise. The maid was so thin that her brown skin seemed to barely stretch across her bones but she was an amazingly strong-willed individual. "Sorry to bother you so, but there's a man here and he… well, he seems to be quite an odd sort of fella."

Max stood up immediately. Nettie had seen quite a bit since becoming part of his household and anything that she dubbed 'odd' was worrisome. "I'll get dressed and be right out. Is he in the parlor?"

"I don't think you should bother with the dressin' part," she said, rubbing her hands together. "He ain't in the mood for waitin'."

"Very well," Max said, though he wondered at what could have moved her to say such a thing. Nettie was never one to have the Master or Mistress of the house appear less than perfect. She usually took it as a personal slight.

Max allowed the old woman to lead him out of the kitchen and down the hall to the parlor. When he stepped inside, after smoothing down the front of his pajamas as best he could, he stopped in place immediately. The man who stood with his back to the fireplace was a vision from Max's past… from a time when Max had traveled the globe in the hopes of finding a way to avenge his dead father. The Rook had not yet been born – not truly – but the painful visions had already begun. The Asian man before him was tall and lean, like a powerful cat waiting to spring into motion. He wore a robe of green and yellow, his somewhat sallow skin set off by the darkness of his hair and moustache.

"Sensei?" Max asked aloud, gesturing for Nettie to leave the room. She did so, thought her hesitation was palpable. "How did you find me? What are you doing here?"

"So many questions," the Warlike Manchu replied with a smile. "Your inquisitive nature has always impressed me. A man should never be ashamed to admit that he is curious for that is how he may gain knowledge of the world around him."

Max hesitated for only a moment, stunned by the sudden arrival of a man he had thought gone forever. The painful summer he had spent under the Sensei's tutelage had been amongst the hardest days of his life. He had suffered physical and mental torment that seemed close to breaking him. But in the end he had mastered the arts he had sought to learn and left a more whole and wiser man. "You're him, aren't you? The one that Benson warned me about. That's the only possible explanation for you being here right now."

"Again, you reveal yourself to be a most challenging opponent," the Warlike Manchu said with the briefest nod of his head. "I wish to give you one last sign of respect. You were the only Westerner to ever survive my tutelage."

"What are you planning to do with the Abomination?" Max asked, moving closer to the man whom he now recognized as the foe he was.

"Merely fulfill my destiny. I will use him to conquer the world."

"I'll stop you."

"No," the Warlike Manchu said, "You will not. But I will give you this gift: the final component of the Abomination left for us to gain will be arriving in Atlanta this evening. It will come by train from Tennessee. Onboard will be a man named Kenneth Harvick. He believes he is going to sell the brain to us… but we have no intention of paying for it. The train will be boarded before it reaches Atlanta and Harvick will be killed, allowing us to steal the brain."

Max blinked in surprise. "Why are you telling me this? You have to realize you've given me plenty of time to stop you. The Nashville train won't even reach Atlanta until nearly ten o'clock."

"I tell you this because I want to give you one opportunity to succeed. If you accomplish your task, I will be most saddened… but respectful… when I kill you later. If you fail, then you have lost all honor and I will kill you with glee."

"You're insane."

"I am practical."

Max started to lunge for the Warlike Manchu but a wave of nausea hit him and he staggered, his back coming to rest against the wall.

The Warlike Manchu remained where he was, watching as the Rook slowly slid to the floor. "I released an airborne toxin upon entering your home. I am, of course, quite immune to it. You will awaken with little time to spare this evening. Look for the place where we will most likely board the train and attempt to perform your usual heroics. This should prove most amusing, I would think."

Max coughed, rolling over onto his stomach so that he could crawl towards the hall. He reached it with great effort, seeing that Nettie was lying face down halfway towards the kitchen. "I'll stop you," he whispered, as the Warlike Manchu stepped over him and exited the house.

Chapter VII
Terror Train!

Ben Gallagher had worked on the railroad for over twenty years and he loved his job. A slightly pot-bellied, genial fellow, Ben strolled from one end of the passenger car to the other, taking tickets and ensuring that everyone had a pleasant stay while on board. He liked to think he was good at the job but tonight he'd met his match when it came to dealing with surly passengers.

Kenneth Harvick was the source of Ben Gallagher's confusion. The thin-faced little man had demanded to have a car all to himself, despite the fact that his ticket allowed for other passengers to ride with him. Ben had done his best to placate the man but to no avail. In the end, Harvick had returned to his cabin, clutching a small bag to his chest. Ben had offered to help put the bag into the overhead compartment but Harvick's snarling refusal had left him flabbergasted.

It takes all kinds, Ben mused. *And given the European accent that Mr. Harvick has, I can't blame him for being a little tense. Things are going so rough in that part of the world… those damned Nazis are going to—*

An unusual feeling crept over Ben's spine and he stopped in place as he made his rounds. The dining car was usually empty at this time of night but there was a group of four men standing together at the rear of the hall, near the door that connected to the adjacent car. Ben usually had a good memory for things like faces and clothing, but he couldn't recall anyone onboard dressed like these fellows. Each of them wore hooded robes that were a dark gray in color, with gauzed-covered hands protruding from under the sleeves.

"Excuse me, fellows," Ben said, moving forward. This trip had already been an odd one and he had the feeling it was only going to become more so. "But I'm going to have to ask to see your tickets."

The nearest of the men turned with a hiss that sounded like a cornered cat. His face was heavily lined and sunken-featured, as if all the water had been drained from it. Up close, Ben could smell the stench of the grave from him. "Prepare to meet your gods," the man whispered, reaching out a hand to clutch at Ben's neck.

The Rook piloted his helicopter low over the moving train, unstrapping himself so that he could move towards the open door. A small mechanized device would serve as the autopilot in his absence, with orders to keep pace with the train. Anything more sophisticated – such as evading an enemy – would be beyond the device's capabilities, but the Rook hoped that it wouldn't be necessary.

Max seethed inwardly, still furious that he had been bested so easily by his old teacher. Both he and Nettie had been found by Josh within a few moments of falling unconscious but nothing could rouse them from their drug-induced slumber until nature took its course. By then, Evelyn was beside herself with worry and the Warlike Manchu had worked for hours on his nocturnal plans.

The Rook pulled his cloak tight against his body as he leaned out of the moving helicopter. He was flying as low as he dared but it would still be a risky move… girding his loins, he threw himself from the helicopter, coiling himself into a tight ball for acceleration before throwing his arms and legs open wide for impact. He landed in a roll, coming to a stop perilously close to the edge of the car's top. He held on for dear life and finally released his grip when he felt comfortable enough to attempt movement. He slid across the surface of the train until he came to a spot where he could swing down and land on the narrow walkway between cars.

The Rook slowly opened the door, peering inside. He was in one of the passenger cars but saw no one in the hall. All the doors leading the passengers' rooms were closed and the porters were obviously off taking care of other business so the Rook slipped inside and moved stealthily down the passage, checking door numbers as he went. A careful examination of train records – courtesy of a bedridden McKenzie – had allowed Max to figure out that the man he sought was staying in berth 17-B. Max silently thanked the gods that he'd ended up on the right car by chance. Given how long he'd been delayed in taking action, he was fearful that the Warlike Manchu had sped up his own timetable and already made off with the Abomination's brain.

When he came to the right room, Max was disturbed to see that the door gave indications of having experienced a forced entry. The area around the handle was cracked, despite being built of steel. The Rook drew one of his specially modified pistols and pushed the door open gently. He felt secure going into any kind of battle with the gun in his hand for it could reel off several dozen shots without need for reloading and each of the bullets was encased in pure silver.

Inside the car, Max came face-to-face with four creatures from out of a nightmare: shriveled husks of men cloaked in gray garments that left them looking like Egyptian mummies with exposed faces. They stood over the crumpled form of Kenneth Harvick, one of them pawing a small box that the Rook knew contained the final component of the Warlike Manchu's awful plan.

To Max's surprise, the one holding the box was capable of speech. The few animated undead that the Rook had encountered during his career had been able only to grunt or moan unintelligibly. "So, Atlanta's resident mystery man has shown his masked face," the zombie whispered harshly. The thing gestured to the other three. "Kill him."

The Rook didn't wait for them to respond. He discharged his pistol, death shooting from the barrel of the gun like lightning. The bullet struck home, embedding itself deep between the eyes of the zombie. A small gush of a blackish-red fluid jetted from the wound and then the creature went down to the floor, flopping like a fish on dry land.

One of the others struck during this time, flailing out his stiff limbs until one of them slammed into the side of Max's head. The vigilante saw stars for a moment but regained his footing enough to dodge a second blow. He fired again, point-blank, into the monster's midsection and a chunk of flesh and gore rocketed outwards as the bullet passed through the body. Max drew his golden dagger and stabbed it into the thing's neck. As the third reanimated creature shambled forward, the Rook jumped into the air, nimbly vaulting over his attacker. He landed just behind the creature and stabbed back with his blade. The knife, potent against all things magical, cut right through the flesh and bone.

The Rook then turned to the last of his foes, the obvious leader of the group. The creature was backed up against the far wall, the box containing the brain clutched tightly in its grip. "Give it up," Max warned, sheathing his knife and pointing the gun at his foe. "If there's any way to help you in your current condition, I'll try to do it."

Outside in the hallway, a commotion had sprung up as men and women responded to the sounds of gunfire. Several of the braver men peered inside and then backed away quickly as they saw the multiple bodies on the floor.

"There's no need to 'help' me, Rook," the monster replied. "I am more than fine. In fact, my armies of servants are going to help me finally gain the power I deserve! This shell you observe now is but the merest expression of my abilities!"

Max blinked at the thing's words for they implied that this creature was being spoken through, that he was being used as a mouthpiece for some more malevolent force. Keeping in mind what Benson had told him, he jumped to the logical conclusion and voiced his thoughts. "You're Ibis, aren't you? The one who works for the Warlike Manchu?"

"I don't work for that buffoon! I am my own master!"

"Odd. That's not the way he described it."

The animated monster snarled, tossing aside the box so that it bounced off the seating unit. He lunged for the Rook and the two men went to the ground, landing atop one of the sprawled corpses. The Rook was surprised by the thing's strength but he managed to get the barrel of his gun under the creature's chin. He fired the weapon, causing the back of the thing's head to explode outwards.

Max moved slightly so that his glowing signet ring could press against what remained of the monster's skull. He hissed out the words that had become his recent mantra: "When the good is swallowed by the dark, there the Rook shall plant his Mark!"

After the deed was done and the Rook began pushing the body off of himself, he heard a harsh voice from the doorway. "Drop your weapon and put your hands in the air!" someone commanded.

Max saw one of the porters was brandishing a small pistol, holding it in a shaking hand. The Rook stood slowly, snatching up the box in a fluid movement. He rushed the door, sending the porter scrambling back in surprise and fright. "Sorry, friend – but I have someplace I have to be!" he yelled after himself. He ran down the hall, not fearful of being shot as he fled – the porter would never dare discharge the weapon with so many passengers on the scene. One or two of the men looked like they were ready to slow the Rook's progress but a steely-eyed gaze from the vigilante caused all to reconsider that course of action.

The Rook made it back outside, crawling to the roof of the train car. Once there, he pulled out a small radio transmitter that ordered the helicopter to land nearby. He would have to jump from the train and make his way to it but there was no other way to return to his escape vehicle.

Before he could do so, a stinging pain in his neck made him slap a hand up to the source of the discomfort. His fingers came away with a small feathered dart, one that had been embedded in his neck. "Not again," he murmured, even as dizziness threatened to overtake him. He swayed on the moving rooftop before falling over onto his back, the box lying beside him.

Mr. Li crept forward, a blow gun in his hand. He knelt and retrieved the box, a smile on his handsome face. Into a small, almost invisible communications device he whispered "I have him, my master. Both the Rook and the Abomination are ours!"

Chapter VIII
Truth and Consequences

McKenzie sat propped up in bed, his handsome face broken into a heart stopping grin. The pretty young nurse who was tending to him during his hospital stare blushed under his gaze, picking up his dinner tray. "You certainly have quite an appetite, Chief."

McKenzie chuckled. "You have no idea… Macy, is it?"

"Yes, sir," she said, reaching up to push a lock of blonde hair behind an ear. She was about to offer up a suggestion that they go out for a soda after his release – which was far from her usual behavior around men – when a soft knock came from the doorway, making Macy jump.

Evelyn stood there, looking gorgeous in a green blouse and tan slacks. Her auburn hair was pulled back from her shoulders, revealing the slender length of her neck. She wore a bemused expression on her lips. "Sorry. Am I interrupting anything?"

The nurse shook her head in embarrassment, sliding past Evelyn. "Of course not, Miss. I was just heading out." She cast one last longing glance at McKenzie, who winked at her.

"You're robbing the cradle, aren't you?" Evelyn chided, moving closer to the bed. "She can't be more than nineteen, if she's a day."

"She says she's twenty three – she *is* a nurse, you know."

"You can get your nursing degree fast these days. There's a shortage because of all the unease overseas." Evelyn shrugged, moving away from the subject. "How are you feeling?"

"Great. Doc says I'll be released in the morning. How about you? Feeling the baby kick yet?"

Evelyn put a hand on her stomach. "I feel a few flutters… but I'm not sure if it's kicking or just nerves."

"Where's Max?"

"He didn't come home last night," Evelyn said, trying hard not to show her concern. She failed miserably, though, and McKenzie surprised her by reaching and taking her hand.

"He'll be fine," he said soothingly.

"I'm worried about him," she admitted. "Not just this mission… the whole thing with wearing that ring. Using it to brand people like they were cattle… and that weird thing he says when he does it! Where in the heck did *that* come from?"

"Something happened to him when he fought whats-his-name," McKenzie agreed. "But he's still the same guy you fell in love with. He's a good one."

Evelyn smiled. "What did either he or I do to deserve a friend like you?"

"I'm a real ray of sunshine, aren't I?" he agreed, laughing aloud. "Listen, if he hasn't come back by the time I'm out of here tomorrow, I'll help you look for him."

Evelyn pursed her lips. "I hope I won't have to take you up on that."

Chapter IX
Tortured!

The Rook woke slowly, his head throbbing painfully. Without fully opening his eyes, he took stock of his current situation, feeling the tight bonds that suspended him spread-eagled off the floor. His weapons were gone, even the ones that were normally hidden on his person, and his pistols lay on a table on the far side of the room. A mild buzzing in the back of his brain told him that he'd been injected with some sort of drug meant to slow his thinking process, inhibiting his mental abilities.

The room was a large one but held little in the way of furnishings. A large Oriental rug hung on one wall, depicting a rampant dragon, while on the floor lay a yellow-and-gold mosaic. Two tables, one on either side of Max's body, held various implements of torture: pliers, knives, pokers and a burning brazier full of hot coals.

The smell of expensive cologne hit his nostrils as a thin, handsome Asian entered the room. He wore a finely-cut suit and had his hair slicked back from his prominent forehead. The stranger stopped just in front of the Rook and bowed low. "There is no need for such dramatics, Mr. Davies. I am quite aware that you are awake. I am Mr. Li."

Max opened his eyes but did not return the greeting. He watched as Li moved to the closest of the tables, stirring the coals. When the Rook finally did speak, his words were cold and clipped. "Where's Manchu? Tell him I want to see him."

"My master will be along shortly," Li replied. "In the meantime, he wishes me to test your limits of endurance. He says you were his greatest pupil." Li looked up at Max then, a hint of malice in his expression. "I had always hoped that I would be the bearer of that particular honor."

Max strained to activate the mental powers that had served him so well in the past but the drugs in his system were still too potent. Resigning himself to the fact that his freedom would have to come through other means, he locked eyes with his would-be tormentor and said "I know he can be very compelling… it's easy to fall under that man's spell. But he doesn't care about you. In the end, he'll discard you just like he has every other person in his life."

"Perhaps," Li agreed, using a pair of tongs to lift up a piece of hot coal. He moved towards Max, using one hand to tear away the hero's shirt. When Max's bare chest had been revealed, Li paused to study his prey's skin for a moment. Max's body was covered in scars, mementos from a score of harrowing battles, but there was no hiding the rippling muscles and healthy tone of his body. Li seemed appreciative, licking his lips in anticipation. "You and I are quite different, Mr. Davies." Li brought the hot coal close to Max's right nipple, making the Rook instinctively angle his body in an attempt to avoid the contact. "Whereas you are a physical man, reacting first with your fists and then with your mind… I am a being who covets intelligence above all else. Though I am trained in the arts of combat, it is never my first inclination… but if you were to find yourself suddenly free to move there is no doubt in my mind that you would waste no time in striking me down. You enjoy inflicting pain, do you not?"

"No. I don't." Max gritted his teeth as Li shoved the coal against his flesh. The sizzling sound melded together with the scent of burning flesh, making his already buzzing head even worse.

"Ah, says the man who brands his victims like cattle," Li laughed softly. "Pardon me for not believing you." Li repeated the application of the coal twice more, leaving horrible burns along Max's chest. Then he set the tongs aside and picked up a small knife. The sight of it made the clouds of pain part slightly in the Rook's brain. His golden dagger had been amongst the weapons he'd had on his person… it was across the room now, piled with the pistols and capsules that Li had removed from his person. According to the things he'd learned, the dagger was the sacred Knife of Elohim, a weapon that was reputed to have been soaked in the blood of Christ. This gave the blade special properties against evil and also protected it wielder under the grace of God.

Max stared at the tip of the blade, noting that it protruded slightly from its place in the pile. Though his own mental abilities were still weakened, he reached out now, calling upon whatever higher powers had enchanted the weapon. *I need your assistance,* he thought. *If ever I needed you, now is the time.*

To his surprise, he thought he heard a reply – and it was far from a heavenly voice that spoke to him. Instead, it sounded very, very old and its words were unknown to him. They were spoken with a wet kind of lisp and the melodious quality of the speaking sounded almost like a chant: *Quilos angelus c'thughu, Quilos angelus c'thughu amonna chi*. The nonsense words repeated again and again and Max suddenly knew, with dire certainty, that they were words of entreaty from a dark power. Fearing that it had something to do with the horrible curse put upon him by Nyarlathotep, Max tried to silence the voice but found himself unable. In clear English, the voice suddenly spat out: *Cursed you are, cursed to wander the earth 'til all you love is dead, cursed never to know peace, cursed to combat the Great Work in all its forms!*

Max screamed out then and the terror in his voice made Li draw back in surprise. The Asian had been about to pierce Max's belly with his dagger but it was an attack that would never come... for the golden dagger suddenly flew through the air of its own accord, slicing deep into the back of the torturer's neck. Before Max's eyes, the blade pushed through the bone and skin until it carved its way through to the other side of Li's throat. The man gurgled something in alarm, reaching up to touch the blade in sudden realization of impending death... and then he fell forward, his body twitching madly.

The Rook swallowed hard, his body suddenly his own to control again. The bonds that held him fell away easily and he dropped to his knees for a moment, regaining his breath. Then he was on his feet, stepping over the dying Asian and gathering up his weapons. His wounds were ignored in the face of sudden freedom but several thoughts kept nagging at him: was his fate as doomed as it seemed to be? And where was the Warlike Manchu?

Slipping his birdlike mask in place, the Rook hurried from the room, golden dagger in hand.

Chapter X
Rise of the Monster

Ibis stood with his honor guard of undead, watching as the Manchu's men finished placing the body parts in their assigned places on the laboratory table. At the Egyptian's side was his new "bride," her once beautiful skin now a dead-looking blue and pock-marked by a spiders-web network of raised veins. "Do you feel the anticipation in the air, my beloved?" he asked.

The undead girl smiled, her lips stretching wide in a mockery of happiness.

The Warlike Manchu moved past the lovers, his delicate sense of smell recognizing the tell-tale traces of lovemaking in the air. Ibis had already worked out his vile sexual fantasies, which only lowered him further in the Manchu's eyes. Lust was one of the primary distractions that all men faced. The truly strong were able to put their physical desires to the side and focus on something much purer: the accumulation of power. "I think it is time to begin," the Manchu said, his voice tightly controlled. Though the majority of his concentration was on the

Abomination and the dangers thereof, a part of his mind was in another room, with Max Davies. Seeing his former pupil again had incited a strong flurry of emotions within him. He held no love for the man but he knew that the Rook – for all his faults – was as close to the perfect as he would likely ever face. A part of the Warlike Manchu craved the challenge, the pitting of wits and physical strengths, that would result from any prolonged confrontation with the Rook. *I wonder how long it will be before he escapes from Mr. Li?*

Ibis moved to stand at the side of the Abomination's table, gesturing for everyone to leave the room save for himself and the Warlike Manchu. The Egyptian pulled out a small corked vial and opened it swiftly, dumping it contents – sand from the steps of great Cheops – onto the Abomination's body parts.   "C'thul   poi noni makop," he whispered, the words spoken so softly that only someone with hearing as enhanced as the Manchu's could have heard them. Ibis closed his eyes as he spoke, letting his fingers run over the table, subtly tracing the outline of a monstrous body, one that would house these organs within its confines. With lips pulling back from yellowed teeth, Ibis allowed his voice to rise in volume and tone. "Uxal ti awanni! Iztabin arkis voltoom!" With this last pronouncement, Ibis threw his hands up high and the air seemed to become charged with electrical energy. The lights in the room dimmed and then went out completely, leaving them in absolute darkness.

"Did the spell succeed?" the Warlike Manchu asked, a hand coming up to stroke his long moustache. He felt no fear at the sudden turn of events but a peculiar sense of unease was beginning to build within him. "Has the Abomination been reborn?"

The sounds of heavy footfalls coming closer made the Warlike Manchu take a step back. Harsh, labored breathing reached his ears and a voice that seemed to echo from the depths of some stygian hell answered his query. "I am here," the Abomination rumbled, his breath smelling like burning brimstone. "Who dares summon me?"

"I dare," Ibis answered. As the Warlike Manchu's eyes adjusted to the gloom, he made out the Egyptian scrambling forward in the darkness, a look of almost orgasmic joy on his face. Ibis had tried and failed to contain the monster's power once before and the Warlike Manchu knew that Ibis had too much pride to allow an opportunity like this to slip away again. "You should remember me... I am your once and future master!"

The lights abruptly returned to life again, sparking as they did so. The Abomination was now revealed in all his unholy glory and even the Warlike Manchu had to admit that he was a daunting creature to behold. Over eight feet fall and covered in reddish-gold scales, the monster's head bore a dark visage and a wide mouth, one brimming with sharp teeth. Atop his skull were two small but dangerous looking horns and at the base of his back stretched out a long reptilian tail. The Abomination was completely nude and of formidable musculature.

While the Manchu was admiring the creature, the Abomination was turning the full weight of his gaze upon Ibis. "I remember you well, sorcerer. The little fool whose reach exceeds his grasp."

Ibis stopped in place, fury glowing in his ancient eyes. "How dare you! I brought you forth! I command you!"

The Abomination sneered in mocking disbelief. "I *am* weakened in spirit, sorcerer, but it will take more than the likes of you to rule over me. I come forth to serve the one whose will is the strongest. And in this room, I fail to see how that could possibly be you!"

Ibis raised a bony finger and pointed it at the Abomination, his voice rising as he began to recite more of his spells. The Warlike Manchu moved forward, gliding across the floor like a silent wraith. He understood the Abomination's words very well – the creature was announcing that he would serve the only true being of power in this room. Given that Ibis was never anything more than a useful tool to be discarded when necessary, the Warlike Manchu realized that the time had come to rid himself of the troublesome Egyptian.

Ibis whirled about just in time to find the Warlike Manchu descending upon him. The Oriental mastermind delivered a powerful backhanded chop to the Egyptian's neck, sending the older man to the floor. Before the sorcerer could respond, the Manchu drove the heel of his foot against the man's neck, pinning him to the floor.

"No," Ibis wheezed, struggling in vain to push the Manchu's foot off his windpipe. "I... we... were partners!"

"We were never partners," the Warlike Manchu responded. "In the end, there can only be one who bears the title of Master!" The Manchu stomped downwards, crushing the man's windpipe beneath his heel. Blood swelled up and out of the Egyptian's lips as his eyes bugged outwards. After a moment of frenzied thrashing, the sorcerer lay still and quiet.

In the hallway outside, the sounds of reanimated corpses suddenly collapsing to the floor could be heard. Without their dread creator to empower them, they were nothing more than fodder for worms.

"It pleases me to see him brought low," the Abomination said, a mirthless smile on his horrid face. He towered over the Warlike Manchu, studying him. "I must rest. It will be many days before my power is at its peak."

"You will have to rest later," the Warlike Manchu answered. "You have power enough to deal with my enemies and begin the process of consolidating my rule."

The Abomination stirred but nodded, bound by the will of his new master. "As you command," he replied, sealing a relationship that could doom the world.

Chapter XI
Hero vs. the Beast!

The Rook still felt awful but he was much more secure now that he was back in his long cloak and mask. The golden dagger was sheathed at his waist while one of his specially modified pistols was clutched tightly in one gloved hand. The Warlike Manchu's lair was alive with activity as the man's Oriental followers scurried about to check on the lights, which had flickered off and then returned moments before. The Rook noticed that many rotting corpses – like those which had confronted him on the train – were now lying still on the floor, where some of the Warlike Manchu's servants were making ready to remove them.

Stealthily, Max crept down the clean white halls, keeping his back to the wall. Several times he was forced to duck hurriedly into empty rooms to avoid detection by the staff members who were patrolling the base. At length, he began to hear the voice of the Warlike Manchu. Though he could not yet fully make out the words, it sounded as if the Manchu was speaking to a subordinate, detailing various names and locations.

A low, rumbling voice answered him and this time the Rook could make out the specifics very easily. "You wish me to kill all these men for you?"

The Warlike Manchu seemed to answer in the affirmative and the Rook felt a painful burning sensation emanate from the ring of power that he wore. The Abomination was here… and the evil stench of the beast now reached Max's nostrils, making him wince.

The heroic vigilante burst into the room, gun barrels blazing out hot death. The bullets struck home on the Abomination, sending the demon staggering back in surprise. Max took only a second to digest the awful visage of the creature before continuing his attack. The Warlike Manchu sprang into action, dodging another volley of bullets and fleeing towards the door. Max made a move to stop him but felt strong arms suddenly grip him. The Abomination had recovered quickly and Max realized that his guns would do him no good against a beast such as this.

The monster began to squeeze, using inhuman strength to immediately break Max's arm. He fought to avoid black out, aware that the Manchu was escaping but having no alternative but to focus his attentions on the Abomination. Max called upon the mental powers he possessed, knowing they were still dulled from the drugs. He projected outwards with as much psychically charged energy as he could and the Abomination let out a howl of surprised pain, loosening his hold on the Rook. As Max fell free, he reached into his cloak with his good hand, retrieving the golden dagger. It glowed brightly in the presence of the Abomination and the beast stared at it with undisguised hatred.

"Agent of Order, are you?" the Abomination sneered. "But one tainted by Chaos. Such an odd little man you are."

The Rook's broken arm was cradled against his body and Max knew that he was one more injury away from being helpless. Acting with as much speed as he could, the Rook ignored the monster's taunts and instead feinted to his left. The Abomination lunged in that directions, leaving the Rook's true target undefended. Max kicked the monster hard on the right side and as the creature fell back he jumped high and brought the golden dagger down hard atop the Abomination's skull. As first the blade embedded itself in skin and bomb and Max found himself dangling in the air, holding on for dear life to the handle of his dagger.

As the Abomination bared his teeth, a cloud of smoke began to emerge from the monster's mouth. The Rook realized with unearthly clarity that the creature was about to breathe flame on him, burning him to a crisp. With strength born of desperation, he began twisting the dagger, its magical energies ripping chunks of flesh from the demon. The combination of a weapon bathed in the blood of Christ and a demon born of Hell was astonishing to behold. As the Rook pulled the dagger free and landed hard on his back, red and black energy began to pour from the wound, making the lights dim once more and the ground to shake. Max heard the Abomination's wail of frustration just before the creature exploded, chunks of his flesh splattering on the walls. The building began to crash in upon them, pieces of the roof tumbling to the floor. Max barely avoided being crushed by one as he scrambled to safety.

In the hallways, men and women ran about in confused horror. Without the Manchu to direct them, no one seemed certain about what steps to take.

The Rook ran forward, not stopping to look back. His mystic senses strained to their fullest, he followed his hunch about the quickest way out and eventually burst out into the morning air. Behind him, the lair of the Warlike Manchu finished its awful cave-in, destroying all those left inside and burying for all time the remains of the Abomination.

Max fell to his knees, coughing. His entire body ached and he was close to passing out… but the realization that someone was watching him made him look up in alarm.

The Warlike Manchu, the man who had once tutored Max in the ways of violence, stepped into view. Now that Max was outside he recognized the wooded area as being on the outskirts of Atlanta, far from the prying eyes of the city folk. There was no one nearby who could help Max now… and he knew that there was little chance that he would be able to defend himself in his current state. Even at full strength, it would be a difficult battle but now….

"You impress me," the Warlike Manchu whispered. "You managed to disrupt years of planning in just a few moments… it's astonishing just how deadly you could be if you truly applied yourself." He held out a hand. "Will you join with me? Become my true heir in all things."

"Go to Hell," the Rook wheezed, blackness beginning to creep in around the edges of his vision.

The Manchu studied him for a moment and then shook his head. "I was wrong, Mr. Davies. You are too weak to ever become a true heir to me. You place too great an emphasis on others when you should be concerned with your own acquisition of power." The villain leaned close. "But you, amongst all those I have trained, are still the best. I give your life to you... but when next we meet, you shall receive no mercy."

The Rook fell forward into the grass, the Manchu's words echoing in his head. He managed to project one final thought straight into his former master's brain, however:

Come back to Atlanta and threaten me or my wife or my baby – and I'll kill you.

The Warlike Manchu blinked at the vehemence of the telepathic wording and then laughed aloud. "Good luck with your child, Mr. Davies. I can only hope that they will not be as much of a disappointment to you as you were to me."

With a quick turn, the Warlike Manchu disappeared into the woods, leaving behind the unconscious form of the Rook.

Chapter XII
Heirs to the Power

Max held his baby boy in his arms, marveling at how small the hands and nose were. He was perched on the side of his wife's hospital bed, letting her get some much needed sleep. Jamison Davies was only twenty-four hours old but he'd already won his parents' hearts.

"Figured I'd find you here."

Max looked up, surprised that he hadn't heard McKenzie enter. He smiled softly at his friend, gesturing for him to be quiet.

McKenzie lowered his voice, coming over to brush his fingertips over the baby's cheek. The police chief was handsome and crisp in his uniform but Max could see worry lines around his eyes. "Hate to interrupt at a time like this," he began, whispering so as to not disturb Evelyn. "But there's been another murder."

Max sighed, leaning forward to kiss Jamison on the forehead. The baby let out a little grunt and twisted in the blanket. "I'm taking time off. I told you that."

McKenzie nodded, shifting his weight from foot to foot. "I've been keeping my eyes out for any sign of the Manchu but he hasn't popped up in months... until now."

Max blinked in surprise. He set the baby down in its crib and turned back to his friend. "Neither of the previous murders seemed to have any link to the Manchu."

"Both of 'em were athletic types," McKenzie said. "Both died in strange ways, with bruises and cuts all over 'em. Some of them looked pretty old, like they'd been abused over the course of weeks or months."

Max pursed his lips, a cold place forming in his heart. "And the new one?"

"Same deal. We found him in a gym down on the west side of town. But there was a note on him." McKenzie reached into a pocket and pulled out a folded piece of yellow-colored paper.

The Rook took it, already slipping into the mode of thought that usually accompanied the donning of his mask. The clear, precise script was definitely that of the Warlike Manchu. It read:

I hope that this note reaches you, my former pupil. The past few months have been frustrating ones for me. Your interference in my plans led me to the decision to rededicate myself to finding a true heir. Three men auditioned and failed, each never passing their increasingly more difficult tests. But now I have found one for whom I have very high hopes... I think I shall have his final test be the slaughtering of you and your entire family.

The Rook was reading over the note for a second time when Evelyn asked, "Something wrong?"

Max looked at his beautiful wife, who looked pale and tired in her hospital gown. "Not at all," he lied. "It's nothing I can't handle." Moving over to squeeze her hand, he said "McKenzie and I have to step out for a minute."

"It's not Rook business is it?" she asked, eyes staring into his.

Max kept a straight face, wondering if she should just tell her the truth: that his career as the Rook was going to put her and their children at continual risk. Choosing the path that would eventually come to haunt him, he said "Nothing like that, honey. You sleep for awhile, okay?"

Evelyn watched Max step out with McKenzie, noting the way that the police officer kept his eyes averted from hers. "Be careful, Max. Please."

Moments later, a familiar figure appeared on the rooftops of the city. Clad in black, his features hidden beneath a domino mask, the Rook took flight.

THE END

THE BLACK MASS

They called it the Black Mass Barrier. No one really knew where the name came from or what it truly meant… but the media seemed to agree that it fit. The Barrier was a cloud of darkness that enveloped the Earth, casting it into eternal twilight and giving the daylight skies an odd pink cast. Even worse were the changes you couldn't see right away: the spreading of magic, subtle and dangerous, into every corner of humanity. Creatures from myth appeared in full bloom, walking side by side with the citizens of the world. 2006 was the dawn of a new age, one that had become almost commonplace only a few years later… when heroes were reawakened.

London, England. 2009.

Ian Morris sat in the back of the club, nursing his second pint of the evening. He wanted to keep his head clear and alert, but it was hard not to drink a bit when you were surrounded by creatures out of myth. A topless girl with pointed ears and Elfin features was dancing in a cage not too far away from Ian's table, her gyrations greatly exciting a group of goblins seated beneath her. They chattered away loudly, occasionally tossing their drinks up into the air. Each drop that landed on the girl's body sent her into a frenzy, grinding to the heavy industrial music that filled the air.

Ian couldn't help but wonder if he'd stumbled into a dream.

He'd been in London's East End when the Black Mass Barrier had gone up. He'd felt a chill in his bones and the hair on the back of his neck had stood on end. Even as he stared up into the pink-tinged sky, he'd known that his entire world had just been turned upside down.

He didn't sleep for 46 hours following the Barrier's emergence. Like most everyone else in the world, he'd been taken by surprise. Who could have foreseen a magical cloud blanketing the Earth, raising the dead by the thousands and infusing everyday life with the stuff of fairy tales? *Sure as hell wasn't me,* he mused.

Since then, his condition had stabilized a bit, but he was still diagnosed as Hyperactive. He was typically awake 23 hours out of the day, constantly filled with energy. Perhaps it was the Barrier, perhaps not. He didn't really care, for being awake that often had certainly helped his career. He was a documentarian, having won numerous awards for his films on British radio dramas of the Fifties; the plight of the homeless in London; and the rise in mystic-related hate crimes since the rise of the Barrier.

"Heya, pal. You buyin' the drinks?"

Ian wrinkled his nose before he even saw who had spoken. The smell was awful, like rotting meat left out in the sun. He glanced up into the putrid features of a brown-skinned man named Tommy. He was one of London's newest residents – the undead. "Sit down and start talking," Ian said, covering his nose with one hand. "I'm paying you plenty without giving you any drinks."

"That's not very nice," Tommy replied. He was dressed in a ratty t-shirt whose faded image of Kylie Minogue was barely recognizable. His jeans were several sizes too large for him, cinched tightly with a frayed leather belt. A cap was pulled over his forehead, hiding everything above his yellowed eyes.

Tommy's appearance was in stark contrast to the handsome Morris, who wore a casual, open-necked button-up shirt, blazer and slacks. He was a handsome, vibrant man with dark hair and a penetrating gaze. The living dead seemed to sense the difference in their natures, slouching back in his seat. "And here I thought we were going to be pals – I mean, since I'm so valuable to your research and all."

"You're not that valuable – there are dozens more just like you out there. I have my pick." Ian leaned forward, passing over several shiny DVDs. "Hardcore stuff here, Tommy. Just like you wanted."

The corpse lifted the discs and stared at them hungrily, almost as if he could view the information through sheer force of will. "They good lookin' birds?"

Ian sipped his drink in distaste. The Barrier had given rise to a number of new black market enterprises, not the least of which was mystically-oriented pornography. It was stunning how far human depravity could go... These particular DVDs featured the popular "Sex with the Dead" series, in which living women allowed themselves to be degraded by the dead. Ian had only watched a few minutes of one scene before he'd come to the conclusion that this was not his cup of tea. "I think you'll be pleased." He reached into his jacket and removed a small digital camera. "Let me see the brand."

Tommy sighed, but did as he was asked. He removed his cap, revealing a deep mark burned into his forehead. It was a curious shape, looking a bit like the head of a raven.

Ian stared as if transfixed. He snapped off several pictures, asking "How did it feel?"

"How did it *feel?*" Tommy asked, laughing. "It hurt like hell... but it was more than just pain. It was like I was being judged or somethin'." He played with the discs in his hand, caressing them absentmindedly. "And that voice of his. God...."

"Tell me what he said," Ian prompted, though he knew very well what the man had said. He'd heard these words before, dating back to the days of Ian's childhood, when this vigilante was merely a fictional hero on the radio and in pulp novels. But he was real... had always been real... and now he was out in the public eye in a way that he'd never been before. Acting desperate, like a man on the edge....

Tommy's voice sounded far away, as if his mind was replaying the events of his death all too clearly. "*When the good is swallowed by the dark, there the Rook shall plant his Mark!*"

Ian grinned. He loved those words.

Later that night, Ian entered his flat and tossed his jacket carelessly over a chair. He'd gotten some good material from Tommy – the audio might not be too clear at the moment, but Sally at the Beeb might be able to filter out the background noise. At this rate, Ian's documentary on the Rook would be finished within the week—

He stopped dead in his tracks, halfway to his refrigerator. He'd meant to pour himself a glass of unicorn milk (the stuff was majorly addicting, in a good way), but the sight of a silhouetted figure seated at the table had brought him short. Ian thought about the large walking stick in the living room – it could deliver a good, sound crack to the head of a burglar... and Ian himself was the athletic type, burning off his excess energy through boxing, tae kwon do, and swimming. "Who's there?"

The voice that replied sounded raspy, like someone who had spent too long with a cigarette between their lips. "You should know, Mr. Morris. You've spent enough time and energy trying to find me."

A chill went down Ian's spine... for that voice was so familiar to him. It had tantalized him on old recordings for so very long. "The Rook," he whispered, scarcely believing that this moment in time was actually occurring. He thought about turning on the recorder in his pocket, but thought better of it. This man was known for not enjoying celebrity, after all. "You know about the documentary I'm doing?"

"I'd have to blind, deaf and dumb not to know. You're sloppy. That kind of thing could get you killed."

"Are you threatening me?"

The Rook rose from his chair, moving to join Ian at the refrigerator. He reached out and pulled open the door, partially illuminating the two of them. The Rook was shorter than Ian, but stockier. He had the look of a middleweight boxer about him and an air of danger. Pistols were strapped across his chest and his face was hidden behind a peculiar bird-like mask. "You were getting yourself a drink, Mr. Morris?"

"I prefer you'd call me Ian... and I'll pass now. Thanks."

"Suit yourself." The Rook closed the door and the room was once more dark and foreboding. "Why have you been seeking me? Answer quickly."

Ian swallowed, sensing that his answer was somehow important. *Is he going to kill me or just destroy my videos and recordings? Or both?* "When I was a kid, you were my idol. I used to dream about you swooping in at the academy and bashing little Nigel Rushford's head in. He was a bully... Even when I got older, I always remained a fan." He pointed into the living room, where a *The Rook vs. the Six-*

Fingered Demoness poster hung on the wall. "I always wondered why you became darker as the years progressed, adopting the whole branding thing and the special saying...."

"There was a part of me that wanted to really punish criminals," the Rook murmured. "I never enjoyed doing it. Made me feel dirty... but it marked them for life. If I couldn't kill the bastards, then at least I could make sure they never forgot that they were spared by the Rook. I'd prefer that people didn't dwell on that part of my career... but for that I blame that one on the bastards who fictionalized my adventures." The Rook laughed softly. "Evelyn used to say it was cruel... but she never pushed the issue. She'd seen the horrors those people were capable of. If Benson hadn't talked me into stopping the killing, I would have kept doing it. That's the only way to really make the world safe – make sure the bad people can't keep coming back. Not that death stops some of them, mind you."

Ian thought he heard a hint of madness in his hero's voice, but he ignored it. His heart was still pounding in his chest and he found himself eyeing the pistols that the Rook wore. Were they the famous 'specially modified' weapons that hardly ever ran out of bullets? He hoped so... "When I heard that you were active again, I started snooping around... discovered how you used to pass on some of your exploits to your friends for use in the novels and serials, like you were just saying."

"And?"

"And I think people need to remember that there are heroes out there. People who do the dirty work that the cops wouldn't dare touch. The whole world's gone crazy and they need to know that there are men and women out there who've been fighting these kinds of horrors for years!"

The Rook grunted and then coughed. The cough became deeper and more frightening, wracking his entire body. Ian started to reach out to him, but stopped himself. The vigilante straightened up again, but there was something different about him now. Something more vulnerable. "I'm dying, Morris. But the world still needs a night watchman... and I don't have time to sire another heir." The Rook paused before speaking again. "I had a son and a daughter. Both did their time in the mask, Morris. Both ended up in a grave, along with every other friend I've ever had. That's why I came back here... to where our honeymoon took place. Good memories... not that the visions didn't come here, too. Ended up becoming the Rook again... will be the Rook until I die, I suppose. I used to blame my father for that. Stupid. It was bigger than him, bigger than me." The Rook looked away, as if staring at something that only he could see. "Evelyn and my father are both waiting for me... on that mountain in Tibet. It's been too long since I saw them."

Ian hesitated, not sure where this was going. Hope began to flare in his heart. "You want to give me a last interview?"

The Rook's laugh was cold as ice. "I'm giving you something better than that. It's in your bedroom. Trust in the mask." He moved past Ian, heading towards the door.

Ian's hand shot out and gripped the Rook's arm, but the vigilante whirled about, chopping at the unwanted touch. Ian cried out and yanked away.

Rubbing his injured hand, Ian said "Why did you do that? I was just going to ask you to stay!"

"I don't like being touched." He leaned close and Ian found himself unable to look away. The odd bird-like beak that adorned the man's domino mask was inches from his nose and Ian flinched in the face of the vigilante's gaze. "I'm about 43 minutes away from dying. I think you're a damned idiot who has too much time on his hands, but the helmet thinks you have potential, so here we are. So get your ass into the bedroom and try it on."

Ian didn't make a move to stop him this time. The Rook disappeared with a dramatic flourish of his long coat, leaving Ian Morris standing in his kitchen feeling disconnected from reality. He looked about, noticing that the vigilante had helped himself to a plate of fish while he waited. Ian wondered at the Rook's words...about dying in 43 minutes. How could he know the exact instant he would die....?

"The bedroom," he whispered. He nearly ran to that area of the flat, flipping on the light switch as soon as he'd entered. There on the bed was a uniform of some kind, super lightweight body armor from the looks of it. It was purple and black, looking like a more modern version of the classic Rook attire. Resting next to the uniform was the helmet that the Rook had mentioned... a form-fitting device that bore a bird motif. Unlike the Rook's mask, this one was a full face version. "Try it on, he said." Ian moved over slowly, lifting the helmet in his hands. The eye lenses gleamed at him.

"Try it on."

✳ C O N T A C T ✳

Ian rolled over onto his back, his breath coming in quick heaves. At his side, Fiona Grace lay with a contented smile on her face. They were both nude, the covers sticking to their sweating forms. Outside, the waves lapped up on the shores of a beach.

He turned his head to face hers and was rewarded with a stunning megawatt smile. "You are so gorgeous," he whispered.

Fiona rolled onto her side and placed her head on his arm. "I love you, too... It's amazing how quickly we've become inseparable, isn't it?"

Ian nodded. "Seems like just yesterday I was visiting the Nova Alliance for the first time, learning that I wasn't the only one carrying on a legacy. You were dating that contractor... what was his name?"

"John." Fiona sat up a bit, looking at him. Her eyes twinkled and her long blonde hair fell about her shoulders invitingly. "Are you going to stay in bed with me tonight?"

"Probably not," he said. "You know I'll be awake again in an hour... and lying here staring at the ceiling isn't very exciting."

"Okay." She kissed him on the nose. "Go work out, then. I'll be here when you get back."

Before Ian could respond, a tremendous explosion rocked them both. The wall in front of their bed shattered inwards, showering them in dust and bits of stone.

The two moved quickly, each rolling out of bed and falling into battle mode. Fiona reached under the bed and drew a gleaming sword, one that was lined with mystic runes. Ian, meanwhile, made a lunge for a helmet which rested on the nightstand. A well aimed bullet knocked it out of his grip, however, and caused him to cry out. Ian glanced towards the sizeable hole that had appeared in their bedroom wall, his heart skipping a beat as he saw the figure standing there.

"No, no! Don't want to go and hide that pretty face away, do we, sweet Rook? I mean, I went to all the trouble of watching your predecessor's face go all blue and pulpy when he died... I'd hate to miss the chance to do the same with you!"

Ian stared up into the face of pure evil. Dark skinned and flame-eyed, the being known as Nyarlathotep was a horror to behold....

End Contact — Future Probability 68.4%

Ian yanked the helmet off his head, tossing it across the room. It landed in a crash, knocking over a pile of videotapes. "What the hell was *that*?!" he screamed. It had felt so real... the feel of that woman's flesh against his all the way to the sense of mounting terror when that Suture thing had come to him...

"Nyarlathotep. How did I know his name? And what in the hell is the Nova Alliance?"

He sat down on the bed, waiting for his pulse to slow back down. The uniform seemed to beckon to him, like a new lover. He felt an urge to try it on... He knew it would fit him perfectly.

Forcing himself to be calm, Ian thought back to the things he'd seen. Fiona Grace... he was familiar with her, if only from the television. Descended from Eobard Grace, a man who had made the trip over to the World of Shadows again and again, Fiona was the most recognizable woman on Earth these days. It was from the World of Shadows that the power behind the Black Mass Barrier had come. Fiona had appeared on CNN numerous times, trying to explain how it had happened, how the so-called Wheel of Flesh had been turned just right, plunging Earth and the Shadows into some sort of merged situation. Some folks blamed Fiona for all the current problems that faced the world, but most recognized her for what she was: a flawed but heroic woman, one who struggled hard to save as many lives as possible.

On somewhat shaky legs, Ian retrieved the helmet. One way or another, it was the key to all this. The Rook had said it was the reason he'd come here... that it had led him to Ian. He stared into the lenses for a long moment, making his decision.

He was ready this time.

* Contact *

Ian Morris stared at a younger version of himself. The eight-year old Ian was seated on his bed back home, earphones turned up so loud that they vibrated from the noise. His Walkman CD player was lying in his lap, blaring out the sounds of a Rook adventure entitled *The Return of Prof. Lycos*. It was one of his favorites and Ian still had a remastered version of it sitting in his car, even today.

Downstairs, his parents were fighting again. Ian remembered this day very well, for it was the day his father had walked out on them. Over twenty years later and he'd never come back....

"You're weaker than I thought. This is how you react to emotional heartbreak? You lose yourself in fantasy."

Ian turned to see the Rook standing behind him. The young version of Ian didn't seem to notice either his older self or his masked hero. "What the hell's going on here, Rook? Why am I seeing something from the past?"

"Because it's one of your formative memories." The Rook moved through the room, stopping now and again to pick up some piece of Ian's past. "You're the one who shapes Looking Glass, not the other way around. Remember that."

"The Looking Glass....?"

"The lenses of the Rook mask. They're shards of a mystic orb. I took them from a bastard who was hypnotizing young women into lives of prostitution."

"*The Case of the Stolen Maidenhead.* I remember that one... the mystic was an Oriental mastermind named Lu Chang."

The Rook grunted. "Yes. I've had it in my possession since 1953, but it took years for it to really regain its power after it was shattered. It eventually led me to you."

"For what? I don't understand –"

"Listen, Morris. I'm dead. But I can't leave the night undefended... According to the helmet, you're the perfect candidate. Driven. Athletic. Tireless."

"You want me to be the new Rook..." Ian whispered, feeling a surge go through him. How many times had he dreamed of this, as a kid? Of course, he'd never imagined it would in a world filled with wizards and the undead, but none of that mattered in the end. He was talking to the Rook...!

"You don't have to use that name, if you don't want. I'm dead, remember? You can be something else for all I care. Something more suited to this god-forsaken age of MTV, cell phones and pixies."

Ian shook his head in confusion. "Look, I work out, but I'm not ready to take on psychopaths and mob lords!"

"You have the basic tools. Everything else will come later." The Rook gestured to Ian's body, indicating the uniform that had appeared upon him. "The suit will enhance your natural abilities and the helmet will give you brief flashes of what your opponent is intending to do. It'll help you avoid their attacks." The Rook drew his guns so quickly that Ian barely had time to register the sudden move.

Ian jumped backwards, doing a handstand that twisted in midair. The bullets seemed to pass by in super slow-motion and Ian was able to land in a crouch before any of them struck the wall behind him. To his surprise, they blew huge holes in the plaster, but the younger Morris just kept listening to his compact disc.

Ian felt the helmet guiding him as he pointed his right hand at the Rook, who was rolling to his left, still firing. Ian fired several bullets from a device housed in his gauntlet, striking the Rook on the side. The Rook cried out, falling to the floor in a bloody heap.

Ian paused, blinking in horror and surprise. "Why are you acting like you're hurt? You're not even really here. It's all some sort of... holodeck scenario, right?"

The Rook coughed – it was a wet, painful sound. "Bloody Star Trek. No one can go a day without comparing something to it. Rotted the collective mind of the planet." He looked up, seeming to shimmer and grow dim. "My time's up, Morris. Try to make something of yourself."

"Wait!" Ian called, reaching out for the other man. It was no use, however, for the Rook was gone.

✳ E ɴ ᴅ C ᴏ ɴ ᴛ ᴀ ᴄ ᴛ ✳

The new Rook took to the streets over the next few weeks. He began with small excursions, breaking up some of the drug rings that he'd come into contact with during his research. Gradually, he became more confident and with that confidence came greater and greater risks.

Ian had scanned the papers for any sign of the Rook's death, but there was never any mention of it – not that he truly expected there to be. He wasn't sure how the original Rook could possibly still be alive anyway – he had to be over a hundred – but Ian had no doubt that the man who had visited him was the same one who had originated the Rook identity.

Out of respect for the elder hero, Ian had abandoned the film project, much to the chagrin of his financiers.

Finally, on the eve of the Black Mass Barrier's anniversary, Ian decided to take a major step.

Moving stealthily through the darkened streets of London, Ian followed the woman of his dreams. She'd figured prominently in a number of visions that the helmet had shown him, with a 97.1% probability that she'd offer him membership in the Nova Alliance. He didn't really care about that... but sharing her bed was definitely something that intrigued him. It had been a long, long time since he'd been with a woman in any capacity... there were few who could keep pace with his current schedule and even before the Barrier, he'd felt like a man adrift... seeking purpose. But now he had that in spades.

Fiona Grace walked from the restaurant to a nearby alleyway, moving with purpose. None of the night's denizens approached her, though a few who recognized her waved in pleasure. Though there were many who blamed her for the rise of the Barrier, she was a popular figure with most, for her beauty and courage were well regarded. As such, she was quite surprised to see a costumed man waiting for her in the alley. She immediately reached for the small dagger strapped to her left leg, drawing it forth quickly. "Who are you?"

"A friend. You can call me the Rook."

The woman who carried on the legacy of Eobard Grace didn't look impressed. "I'm in a bit of a hurry, so if you could explain what it is you wanted...?"

Ian smiled, despite himself. He knew the taste of her lips and remembered where she liked to be touched... *Patience. No need for her to know all your secrets. She probably likes a bit of mystery anyway.* "Well Fiona, I was wondering if you would be interested in a new member of your organization – the Nova Alliance."

Fiona moved closer to him, noticing the way he smiled at her. It should have been creepy, the way this chap just assumed he could be so familiar with her. In fact, though, he seemed to radiate something that appealed to her.

"A fan of the original, I take it? Well, you seem to know an awful lot about me and I know absolutely nothing about you, aside from your affection for old vigilantes. Before I take you into the heart of the Alliance, don't you think I deserve to know more about you?"

The Rook reached up and removed his helmet, his smile never wavering. "My name's Ian. And I'd love to tell you a bit about me... Over coffee perhaps?"

Fiona laughed. "Cheeky devil, aren't you? Okay." She reached out and took his hand. "Nice to meet you, Ian. I get the feeling you and I might have quite the time together."

He surprised her by kissing her hand. "You have no idea," he laughed.

THE END

About the Author

BARRY REESE is regarded as one of the leaders in the Modern Pulp Revival. His first novel, *Conquerors of Shadow: The Adventures of Eobard Grace*, introduced readers to the World of Shadows and was hailed as a return to classic pulp adventure. The best-selling *Rook* series has spanned five installments so far, with more on the way. He also served as editor and contributor to *Thrilling Adventures*, an anthology of pulp-inspired tales by modern writers. When he's not writing novels, he's done work for Marvel Comics, Khepera Publishing and West End Games. Barry has a Master's Degree in Library and Information Science and works as a Library Director in middle Georgia. He is married to artist Cari Reese and together they have a son named Julian. More details about his work can be found at http://www.aric-dacia.com.

About the Artists

WILLIAM CARNEY

A professional graphic artist for almost twenty years (and a fantasy illustrator almost from the cradle), Bill Carney has recently seen the first publication of his pulp artwork in Wild Cat Books' *Lost Sanctum No. 3* and *The Adventures of The Scarlet Shroud*, the first collection of short stories chronicling the exploits of the 1930's-era pulp hero Alexander Holt—co-created with younger brother, Chris.

A lifelong fan of comic book and science fiction art, he credits his inspiration to the master Frank Frazetta, Jack "The King' Kirby, Bernie Wrightson, Virgil Finlay, Mark Schultz, and many others too numerous to mention. Thank you all for the ride.

He is currently hard at work on the next Scarlet Shroud adventure, *Dagon's Disciples,* coming soon from Wild Cat Books.

STORN A. COOK

My mother is an artist. So, I was surrounded by the environment and tools of the trade from the beginning. I left the humble hills of Ithaca, NY at 17 to pursue art at New York University. Alas, it was a poor fit. I spent two frustrating years at New York University. The art program was geared to Fine Art and Performance Art than to Illustration.

Many years later, I attended the much more commercial & illustrative minded Columbus College of Art & Design. Three and 1/2 years later, I walked out with a degree in Applied Arts. But CCAD was much more than a piece of paper. It really gave me the tools to pursue my career.

I've worked in the role playing game field for a decade. My client list is available on my website. But I'm also branching out into doing novel covers, children's books and whatever else could find use for my skills. My website is www.StornArt.com.

Pulp Lives!!

A WILD CAT BOOKS PUBLICATION

WILD CAT BOOKS

The Adventures of
THE SCARLET SHROUD
by
Chris and William Carney

Ron Hanna and Wild Cat Books presents

A PULP HERO FOR THE 21ST CENTURY

The Adventures of
THE SCARLET SHROUD
by
CHRIS AND WILLIAM CARNEY